The Windelton

By D. A. Adamson

1

Dedication

To Jenny Lewis
Without whom this book would never have been written

Acknowledgements

My thanks go to Dennis Hamley for his wise editing, counsel and ability to see the funny side of The Windelton Absurdities. Carole Hastings for her early comments and my dedicated test readers: Michael Astrop, Marcus Green, Lynsey Morris, Bridget Stewart, Sue Swales and Sarah Adamson.

To Mathew Bottomley for the cover design and Natalie Dalkiran for her invaluable assistance in the promotion, formatting and collation of this book.

- Table of Contents -

Prologue

PART 1
1. Climate
2. The Money's Mine, All Mine!
3. Pastimes
4. The Inverhapless Fishing Hotel
5. Trout
6. A Bit Rich
7. A Short History Lesson
8. Nearly an Injustice

PART 2
9. Café Society
10. A Bedtime Story
11. Lost on the Golf Course
12. The Vulgarity of Commerce
13. Bogeyman
14. The Chameleon
15. Magnetic North
16. The Best Laid Plans
17. Making a Play
18. A Festival of Drama Begins
19. Hangover Caller
20 A Robbery, No Violence
21 Uncle and Nephew
22 The Call of the Argentine
23 Delayed Departure

PART 3
24. Disco Maniacs
25. Getting Away From It All
26. A Night Time Stroll
27. Inspector Payne
28. Half Vision
29. Fading Daylight Robbery
30. Party Over
31 Changed Lives

Epilogue

- Prologue -

As he banged the telephone back on the cradle Harry Webster knew he had been dumped on. He was furious; his professional standing had been compromised. As editor of the Windelton Bugle *he* decided what appeared on the pages of the newspaper, not the damned publisher!

Harry had just been told to pull the front page story; a story that he had spent days carefully researching and writing. Now it was splashed across every national newspaper and had even been mentioned on the BBC. Harry studied the press statement he had received from the Murchison's Bank press office. It was a masterpiece of understatement:

"The Directors of Murchison's Bank regrets to announce the immediate retirement of Gerald Astle, Manager of their Windelton branch office, owing to sudden illness. Mr. Astle, a long serving member of the Bank, has managed the Windelton branch for the last eight years and has helped maintain Murchison's position as one of the leading banks in the North Riding. His forceful presence will be missed and the Directors send their sympathies to his wife, Daphne, at this difficult and worrying time."

'Difficult and worrying time?' thought Harry, difficult time be damned. It was the heist of the decade and he was expected to whitewash the story just because the Bugle's publisher was in hock to the bank. Editorial truth was always a casualty of ownership in the newspaper world; particularly if your publisher owed Murchison's Bank over a hundred thousand pounds for recently installed web presses!

His publisher's 'phone call had been unequivocal: until the police or the bank made an official statement he had to run the story as supplied by the bank's press office. If it had been twenty years ago Harry would have resigned in protest but old age, pragmatism and a pension to protect had dulled his once fine principles.

Although it was only a little after nine thirty in the morning, Harry opened the top right hand draw of his roll top desk and brought out a quarter bottle of Bell's whisky. Carefully checking that neither his junior reporter nor sub editor cum secretary were watching, he poured himself a generous measure of the amber liquid.

"Bugger it! So much for freedom of speech," he muttered to himself raising his coronation tea mug in a gesture of a toast. Fortified from a hefty draught from his treasured drinking receptacle featuring Queen Elizabeth's faded features upside-down, Harry set about burying the text deep inside his newspaper. He slotted the short statement between *'Old Mold's Gardening Tips'* and *'Nurse Johnston's Guide to Healthier Living'* that this week featured the benefits of regular cigarette smoking on frayed nerves.

Harry knew the bank's press statement was a cover-up of the truth and so would most Bugle readers.

~

Laurence Payne, the wizened deputy manager of Murchison's Bank, Windelton, tottered out from the rear of the black Wolseley police car. He was accompanied by a tall, urbane man wearing a grey pin stripe suit. At the same time two detectives both sporting cheap trilby hats alighted from the front seats. PC Robson from Windelton police station had just arrived and was busy leaning his bicycle against a drainpipe next to the bank's side-door staff entrance. The two detectives perfunctorily acknowledged their uniformed colleague's presence with a bored glance in his direction and a near imperceptible nod of heads. The detectives were not happy about having to turn out from Mill Garth station in Leeds at seven-thirty on a Sunday morning. Their air of subdued irritation was no match for Laurence Payne's nervous agitation or the suppressed anger of Alexander Haymarket, Payne's very senior colleague from the bank's regional office. Haymarket had a dreadful feeling that what they were going to uncover was going to be bad, very bad, and the badness was somehow going to trickle down as far as him.

Payne's trembling hands fumbled with the two door keys, a lit cigarette dangled from his lips dropping ash down his blue suit and making his eyes water. Haymarket sighed impatiently as the two detectives looked on with an air of bemused impertinence. PC Robson stood with his back to the bank's outer wall in the narrow side street; he was nearly at attention as he stared down grimly at his highly polished steel-capped boots wondering what the hell was going on. His instructions from his sergeant had been brief, "Be at the bank at eight-twenty-five sharp, the plain clothes boys are paying us a visit."

"But it's a Sunday chief, what's up?" he asked.

'Dunno, just *be* there!' the sergeant had replied tersely.

The two stern faced bankers accompanied by the detectives disappeared inside the bank.

As soon as the safe door opened Payne gasped. To an untrained eye nothing looked out of order. The bags of coin and pristine blocks of wrapped new notes were all neatly stacked up and undisturbed. What Payne had immediately noticed was the missing used ten shilling, one pound and five pound notes. Haymarket saw it too.

"How much do you reckon Payne?" asked Haymarket?

"Fifty or sixty, I'll check the ledger," said Payne, his voice cracking with emotion. Payne pulled a large book from inside the safe that held the closing balances from the last day of business. He licked his right thumb and forefinger and deftly flicked over the pages to Saturday's entry, running his finger down he did a quick mental calculation of the used notes. "It looks like over sixty-three."

"Sixty-three pounds?" said the shorter of the two detectives in a 'Am I wasting my time?' sort of voice.

"Sixty-three *thousand* pounds!" said Haymarket very quietly as if talking to a recalcitrant child.

"Blimey!" said the taller detective.

8

PC Robson, who was standing outside on the cobbled street guarding the door against some potential but unknown enemy, was wondering when he could stand down and get back to the station for a decent mug of tea.

PART 1

- Chapter 1 -

Climate

Windelton was aptly named for it described the town's meteorological misfortune.

Whatever the season, searching winds blew in the high street. In summer they gusted up the curved hill; in winter, they headed icily downhill and under the door of the Nags Head pub.

The often tempestuous weather was a natural course of events to Windelton locals and whilst it astonished visitors, it was considered as natural as an outbreak of TB or polio to the residents. Hot or cold, the breezy climate insinuated its way into every household. On sultry August nights, Windeltonians (as they were collectively known), were thankful for such cooling zephyrs. Windelton winds sidled their way off heather-sided Pennine peaks gathering momentum as they flushed down dale. As the valley bottom narrowed the wind gathered pace, passing over the water treatment works where it sucked up a faecal tang, before finally expiring over the town's innocent inhabitants.

Windelton's climatic vagaries were the least of the town's setbacks. History recorded myriad pestilences, famines and economic hardships inflicted on this small, northern outpost. Over the centuries many footprints had been stamped into the character of the town and its kinsmen: marauding Vikings, cruel Norman Kings and border reivers had looted, pillaged, torched and exploited the populace for their own ends. The detritus from these architects of Windelton could be witnessed in place and street names: 'Cut Throat Lane', 'Hangman's Cross' and the ancient public house, 'Arrow 'n Eye' - still a torch bearer of jovial violence; their darts team being much feared in the surrounding district for their accuracy on and off the dart board.

On an early, Saturday morning in April, Ian Henderson was hurrying to work. It was that depressing should-be-spring-by-now time when wind and rain prevail and summer is still a teasing distance away.

11

He was late; he always was.

Cumbersome keys weighed heavily in the pocket of his grey worsted Burtons Director suit. The awkward metal shapes pressed against his left thigh stretching the pocket lining and disfiguring his blue gabardine mackintosh. His blackened Oxford shoes struck the pavement with a military resonance, the footfall only faltering as the hill's gradient steepened. He passed the greengrocer who had set out his produce for the morning's trade. A pathetic collection of locally grown vegetables edged their way onto the pavement with the purpose of tempting open the meagre purses of Windelton's shoppers. Passing the church hall he could hear the angelic voices of the Reverend Max Headcase's Boys' Choir. They were rehearsing what sounded like an unholy chorus in preparation for some event. He caught the words: *'Hatred our Right, Vengeance our Duty'*, and then, cresting the hill, Ian spied Murchison's Bank. The belligerent wind was playfully battering the fascia sign as it swung in its wrought iron frame like a showboat at a fairground; white light spilled from the frosted window onto the wet pavement indicating that his arrival was overdue.

Oh sod! He thought, the deputy manager had beaten him to it. He was meant to be there first to open up the office.

His pace quickened from strenuous walk, to trot, to final dash up the cobbled side alley to the staff entrance door. While he fumbled cold keys Ian tried to regain some composure. Perspiration had built up in his acrylic shirt and his waistcoat was damp, permeating the fabric of the heavy wool suit. He breathed deeply to regain his equilibrium. Ian forced one key into the mortise lock, the other into the Yale, and as the heavy door eased open the smell of wood polish, typewriter ribbon and burning cigarette smoke filled his nostrils.

"You're late; it's two and a half minutes past eight!"

Miserable old bastard, thought Ian. Should Laurence Payne ever opt for an alternative career, the role of ace detective would be high on the list of possibilities. You could guarantee 'Inspector Payne' would root out some misdemeanour in

12

seconds, never off the case when it came to finding fault in others. There was a thick haze of blue smoke; the other cigarette smoker must be Seedman, the second clerk.

Seedman was posh and thick. His wealthy father was a bank customer so Payne never ticked him off in case it got back to his old man and messed up Payne's own career prospects. It was well known the only way that Simon Seedman had ever got a job in the bank was on account of his father's massive business borrowings. Ian slipped off his dripping mackintosh and hung it on a brass peg with his name inscribed in gold lettering beneath the coat hook: 'Ian Henderson, Senior Clerk'.

"Good morning Mr. Payne," he called cheerfully. A bronchial croak, signifying decades of unstinting loyalty to sixty Senior Service un-tipped cigarettes a day, returned his greeting. Before entering the banking hall Ian wiped his rain spattered shoes on the back of his trousers, straightened his burgundy tie with the Murchison 'M' motif in dull yellow and ran a hot palm over his darkly cropped hair. Moving out from the coat lobby into the banking hall, he lifted the mahogany split counter top that gave access to staff. Walking behind the counter he ran his hands over the polished counter surface, the wood pleasingly solid to his touch, just like the institution that was Murchison's Bank. Not a speck of dust to be seen. It was here, that when the bank was open to the public, his fellow clerks sat on high stools and dangled their feet, dangerously close to the metal kick-alarm plates that summoned PC Robson on his bicycle when an armed robbery was in full swing.

Another Murchison's Bank morning of mindless drudgery had begun. It was only relieved by the thought that today was a Saturday, a half day, and in four and half hours Ian would be slipping down a pint of Bainbridge's best bitter in the Nags Head. While in the pub he would place a modest bet on the horses before heading for the golf club to indulge in his second favourite past time. The first being making love to his attractive wife and tonight, being a Saturday, was golf shoes night and another reason to be cheerful!

13

- Chapter 2 -

The Money's Mine, All Mine!

Gerald Astle was a cautious man. It was his job to be cautious, he was the manager of Murchison's Bank, Windelton. A post with status, one that demanded respect. He regarded his customers' money to be his own, and once in his care he didn't like lending it to anyone else. Astle believed that customers should consider themselves lucky that they had a manager of his integrity, calibre and taste to sequestrate their funds.

Each working morning he set off from his house on Lime Tree Road at nine minutes past eight and drove his black Morris Cowley at a steady 20 mph to the town centre bank. He passed identical semi-detached houses to his own. They were built in the 1930s by a customer of the bank; solid, uninspiring properties with bow-window frontages and pebble dash facades. Lime Tree Road was a typical Windelton thoroughfare of respectable, middle-class Britain, the haunt of white collar, golf-playing bores. Astle was completely at home.

Astle moved to Windelton on his appointment as manager. It had been a disappointing promotion, not the city branch he had hoped for. It represented a minor increase in grade, nearly an insult, but as it turned out, the move was timely. Previously, Astle had managed a small business branch in the West Riding. Coming to Windelton had meant a change in the type of bank customer. In Murchison's parlance, Windelton was a 'country branch'. This was code for impoverished farmers and the odd landowner. That was eight years ago. He felt his banking talents had been overlooked, now only retirement beckoned.

The spluttering Morris reached the road junction where the United Reform Church and the Boys' Brigade Hall faced one another. To the right was eastward to the coast, left Windelton high street. Astle wrestled with the car's enormous steering wheel, his heavy black coat pinioned his shoulders restricting arm movements and he struggled to make the ninety degree manoeuvre onto the high street. As the trundling vehicle turned, the nearside rear wheel mounted the pavement with an angry grunt of rubber on kerbstone, narrowly missing the broom of Jake, the local road sweeper.

Astle never consulted his car's rear-view mirror, always look forward was his mantra, and so he failed to observe Jake's two fingered salute or hear his expletives as Astle's Morris bumped and skidded its way over the empty cigarette packets and discarded fish and chip papers that littered the pavement.

Four hundred yards down the High Street the black car turned into a narrow passage way that led to the tiny car park reserved for the Windelton bank manager. The dingy rear of the premises belied its imposing mock gothic frontage. Astle cursed the bank's chief architect for not providing more space to park his car as he struggled to negotiate the vehicle into its parking position. It had never entered Astle's unimaginative mind that when the building was erected in 1852 there was ample room to stable a horse and trap that his predecessors had once used with customary ease.

Astle did not receive a salary of nearly two thousand pounds a year to have thoughts on matters of history. The bank did not foster the notion of free expression. The thinking had already been done for him. Each procedure worked out and conveniently placed inside a book of rules which were to be followed to the letter. Every eventuality of banking catered for, from personal behaviour to establishing an overdraft facility. These rules, slaved over by anonymous drones in far-away London, had been honed from decades of banking practice. To Astle they were the stone tablets of his life, a set of codes not to be broken; a pact that if honoured would reward him modestly with a pension until he parted this earth.

It was not surprising that Astle enjoyed a formidable reputation as being overbearing and pompous. The few acquaintances he possessed tolerated his company rather than welcomed it. Astle, who in his mind's eye, was richer and therefore by his standards superior to almost everyone else, found his customers to be interfering and tedious. He was incapable of finding the spirit within him to warm to any of them. It would have surprised his customers to know that underneath Astle's bluff, blustering exterior there was a painfully shy man who would have liked to be popular. He was lonely in his work and his marriage was an empty vessel. His only pleasure was to take out his grievances on everyone else. Well, nearly everyone, as Gerald Astle nurtured a very private secret.

~

The noise of the rumbling tyres and distinctive phut phut of the Morris as it entered the narrow cobbled street was the alarm call for the bank's staff. The imminent presence of Astle permeated the psyche of those waiting inside. Tensions rose, sphincters clenched, foreheads creased and sweat glands pumped into action, and involuntary outbreaks of wind were induced, particularly amongst the more elderly members of staff. An unexpected odour was always the harbinger of some drama at the bank and there was always an odious whiff in the air when it was time to open the big safe that nestled in the bank's vaults.

The bank safe opening team were assembled in the cellar ready for action. They resembled a terrified platoon of First World War soldiers waiting for the whistle to go over the top. Forming a semi-circular group around two sturdy, metal-wheeled, wooden trolleys, they waited perspiring, silently listening for the sound of the cellar door opening. In front of them was a metal cage that stretched the length of the underground room's rear wall. Sitting behind the bars was an enormous grey safe. Standing seven foot high and four feet in width, it sported an impressive silver faced combination lock.

Peter Firth, the branch accountant, held the key to the cage door. Mr. Payne desperately clutched a slip of paper with one half of that day's safe opening combination; the other was held by the approaching Mr Astle. Two junior clerks stood alongside each trolley; Ian Henderson's task was to supervise the trolley loading. When each cart was filled they would hold around half a ton of coinage.

To this would be added the packets of new and used bank notes that would be transported upstairs to fill the three tills in the banking hall.

One of Ian's duties was to ensure that the tills were checked before the bank doors opened at ten o'clock and that they balanced again at closing time. If a till didn't balance then the teller had to stay until it did. This could mean on occasions having to phone up customers to check whether the bank had given them too much money. This was a fool-hardy exercise as nobody ever admitted to receiving more money than they should. It was a ludicrous notion to think that any Windelton inhabitant was likely to return a free hand-out from the over-charging scoundrels at Murchison's Bank! Even the Reverend Max Headcase, the bizarre vicar of Windelton parish church, would never let his conscience get the better of him if a windfall came his way. Special funds courtesy of Murchison's Bank found its way into a mysteriously titled, 'Parish Drink Restoration Fund,' which the Reverend Max was the sole beneficiary.

When a till balanced incorrectly a telephone call was made to regional office to inform them of the counter clerk's misdemeanour. A strip search would ensue of the miscreant before leaving the bank premises to ensure nothing had been pocketed. Personnel records were marked up at head office in copper plate script in the vellum-bound 'Murchison's Medical Pharmacopoeia'. When a till enjoyed an unexpected surplus the same rigorous scrutiny did not apply. There was general back slapping as the bank employees disappeared as fast as possible into the nearest pub.

Meanwhile, in the dimly lit cellar Simon Seedman had extinguished his cigarette and was running his long artistic fingers over an acne-pocked face; the third finger of his left hand paused on a troublesome volcanic spot on his chin. He considered coaxing the pustule gently, easing the hard mound before finally finishing it off with an eye-wateringly, violent squeeze. However, before Seedman could embark on his festering, muldoon-mining mission his was interrupted by a paroxysm of coughing from little Ernie Trott, the junior clerk.

17

Ernie was feeling particularly on edge this morning. The damp underground chill, coupled with the dreadful memory of his mother interrupting him whilst engaged in the final stages of a lengthy masturbation session was still haunting him. Ernie had been so absorbed that he failed to hear his mother's footsteps on the stairs and the friendly call of: "Tea, Ernie dear, time for work!" She barged into the bedroom, the scalding brew gripped in her asbestos hands, to find her youngest son standing naked, throbbing penis in hand, staring at a photograph propped up on his music stand. The focus of Ernie's rapturous desire was a photograph of a statuesque bare-breasted Ethiopian lady that he had torn out of one of his father's National Geographic magazines.

"You've no time for violin practise now; you'll be late for Mr. Astle at the bank," remarked Mrs Trott, oblivious to her son's twitching erection and red sweating face. She plonked the steaming cup of tea down on his bedside table, "And get some clothes on or you'll catch your death," she added helpfully.

This combination of a myopic mother finding him at full throttle, an attack of pre-Astle 'will he shout at me or just kick me as normal' nerves, combined with a predisposition to asthma, had brought on one of Ernie's coughing fits.

"Get him his puffer!" shouted a terrified Payne. His concern not for the health of young Trott but in case Astle should appear and find his safe opening team incapable of performing their daily ritual to perfection. By now Ernie was doubled up on the cold stone-flagged floor, gasping for breath between bouts of incontrollable coughing. He was well on the way to expiring had not an alert Peter Firth, stepped in to render life-saving assistance.

Firth fumbled out Ernie's puffer from his jacket pocket and stuck it into his mouth. Ernie pressed the pump and quickly responded to the cocktail of gases from the whirring inhaler. Payne's relief was palpable. As Ernie regained some form of equilibrium he was propped up against the side of one of the trolleys to aid his recovery.

Laurence Payne still harboured the ambition of becoming a branch manager before he retired. However, unbeknown to him, his chances of elevation had been destroyed many years before. His error was failing to spot a sartorially dressed clerk from systematic theft. A till balancing ruse was funding his expensive tailoring bills. Once discovered, the tearful clerk offered to return the clothes and repay his debt to the Bank but he was summarily dismissed and along with it went Payne's chances of promotion.

On entering the bank Astle always went directly to his private office, the only one with a lockable frosted glass door. He hung up his black three-quarter length coat with the astrakhan collar in a mahogany wardrobe. He broke wind gently at first and then more loudly as his confidence grew and any unpleasant 'accident' seemed unlikely. Astle's wife, Daphne, a distant, mild-mannered woman, could be very scathing about the condition of his underwear on wash days. It was one of the few occasions in their uneventful life together that made her animated.

Astle threw back his shoulders to make himself larger than he already was, adjusted his Van Hewson starched white collar and finally checked his pocket watch before returning it with a satisfying, weighty pat to his ample waist coat. He vacated his inner sanctum at precisely eight twenty-eight. He quietly pulled the heavy wooden door to and it returned noiselessly on well-oiled brass hinges behind him. He then strode purposefully the length of the counter to the far end of the building where he opened the cellar door and proceeded down nineteen steps. He arrived, as always, at precisely eight-thirty to greet his team of petrified bank servants.

"Good morning Payne"

"Good morning Mr. Astle"

"Good morning Firth"

"Good morning Mr. Astle"

"Good morning Seedman"

"Good morning Mr. Astle"

"Good morning Henderson"

"Good morning Mr. Astle"

"Good morning Trott"

"Erghhaa", a half cough, half gurgle of phlegmy response emitted from Ernie Trott's throat who was now back on his feet but still far from his best.

"He's feeling a bit under the weather," Payne cut in with a half-hearted defence of his junior clerk.

"Looks more half-dead to me! He hasn't been sucking sixpences again has he?" enquired Astle with about as much interest in his welfare as he would show a customer with an income below a thousand a year.

The 'good morning' protocol was based on seniority: deputy manager, branch accountant and so on. Ian was always spoken to after Seedman, a deliberate snub as Seedman was only the second clerk and Ian his senior. Seedman would then grin slyly at Ian and throw a simpering glance of adoration towards Astle.

"Ready Firth?"

"Ready Mr. Astle."

"Proceed."

A massive iron key, blackened with age and hewn from ore produced by sweating Welsh labourers at the Merthyr Tydfil blast furnaces a century ago, was placed in the lock. It turned with oiled smoothness and the gate swung inward. Peter Firth stood aside to allow Astle to enter the caged citadel. Payne followed behind with quick short steps, his trembling hands clutching a piece of paper on which was written Saturday's seven digit combination. The others were banished outside awaiting the signal to enter; this would be given by Payne once the main safe was open. Payne delivered this in the form of a discreet bronchial exhalation that masqueraded as a command. Astle was already turning the dials of his combination with deft certainty. He had an excellent memory for numbers and spent a few minutes every Sunday evening memorising the following six days' combinations sent by head office to his home. Once committed to memory he never forgot and promptly destroyed them after reading. It infuriated Astle that Payne couldn't perform the same simple task - another clear signal to him that Payne was totally unsuitable material for the role of a branch manager.

Laurence Payne's unsteady hands were now in a state of near epilepsy. He glanced with shame at each of his numbers and then uncertainly moved the dial seven times. Eventually he stood back in relief and issued the lung clearing command, "arghhh... IN".

Peter Firth entered and pulled the safe's steel 'L' shaped handle moving it quickly from its locked twelve o'clock position through one hundred and eighty degrees. This released six locking bars of crafted Sheffield precision steel with a reassuring 'chunk'. Pulling on the handle, a half ton of metal door opened revealing shelves of new and used bank notes of various denominations. In the safe's lower shelving were bags containing halfpennies, pennies, threepences, sixpences, shillings, two shillings and half-crowns that lay heavily heaped in bloated canvas bags.

The door now wide open, Astle stood surveying his wealth like a medieval robber baron, a half-smile playing on his lips, his breath quickened at the sight of all *his* money. He resisted a terrible urge to throw himself on top of all the cash, rip open the bundles of notes and shower himself in their erotic, crispy newness. After a good twenty seconds of silent worship of all that he possessed, Astle reluctantly stood aside to allow Ian and the two clerks to enter. It was a squeeze. Astle, Payne and Firth stood with their backs jammed against the rows of deed and security boxes containing the secrets, heirlooms and assorted precious belongings of Windelton customers that lined the vault walls like an Italian mausoleum. The metal wheeled trolleys were manoeuvred into position at the safe entrance; the clumsy T shaped pulling bars resembling a cricket pitch roller clanked noisily in their bearings.

The loading commenced, the first trolley with notes, the amounts being called out by Seedman and noted in a ledger by Ian, followed by a wheezing Trott who lugged the heavy coin bags out from the safe and onto the trolley under the loving gaze of Astle. Payne advised officiously on the best positioning of the bags to avoid them falling off. Trott was treated like the Windelton idiot, a role he had no need to rehearse.

"Gently, gently with my… *that* money," Astle said almost reverentially. Meanwhile, Peter Firth had drifted off into one of his many retirement fantasies that punctuated his day and enabled him to survive the tedium of his daily routine.

Firth, who had married well, was familiar with continental travel courtesy of his wife's wealth. He pictured himself seated, on a metal, white painted chair in a bougainvillea scented garden on the shores of a lovely Italian alpine lake. He was reading a rather agreeable autobiography of Ira Malaniuk, the Polish born mezzo soprano singer, a chilled glass of Prosecco was at his side together with a loaded, high velocity hunting rifle. The beautifully marked gun had an excellent Zeiss telephoto lens and the rifle was resting in easy reach on an attractive, white- painted wrought iron table. From time to time, he paused to take a sip of his delicious cool, sparkling Italian wine. Lazily, in a slow, insolently bored manner, he brought the gun to his shoulder, the exquisitely carved walnut stock fitting perfectly, and after taking time to clearly focus the sights of the lens, he softly squeezed the trigger. There was a fat Englishman thrashing about in the middle of the lake. The man looked rather like Astle. He was obviously drowning gently in the warm afternoon sun; no noises of his death throes disturbed the lakeside tranquillity. There was no sound either from the gun as it was discharged, no echo returned across the green water and even the wooded mountain sides made no reply. The only noise was a satisfying thud, like dough being worked on a cook's baking table. It wafted idly across the water as each 10mm bullet was enveloped and swallowed up by the glutinous white flesh of the writhing figure. He was about to reload the rifle's magazine and fire again when Trott's wheezing disturbed him from his reverie.

Payne closed the door on the denuded safe and spun the dial on the combination lock. Astle, Payne and Firth paced out, leaving the still rasping Trott, the smug Simon Seedman and the dutiful Ian to supervise the cash distribution. Next, the trolleys were negotiated into a small lift that took them directly into the

22

banking hall. Ian accompanied the two juniors into the lift to check that they did not make a bolt for the door.

The ritual completed satisfactorily, Astle retired to his office, locked the door and slumped heavily into his sprung leather manager's chair, standard issue to all office managers in country branches. He picked up his Times newspaper and read until nine twenty precisely. The newspaper did nothing to improve his humour. The contents depressed him; he read of strikes, a seemingly powerless government, and the new phenomenon of 'pop stars'. He snorted with derision over the paper's ridiculous infatuation with these young people. There never seemed to be any good news, except the occasional train crash and he enjoyed a good murder trial, the details of which Astle would devour with morbid relish. He put his paper down and pondered his secret past.

Valerie Harper had been Astle's secretary at his previous bank branch in the small West Riding town of Hickleton. It was a little over eight years ago yet the memory of this woman still lingered in his gut. He muttered aloud to himself, a predisposition that seemed to be occurring more and more these days.

Astle shifted in his chair murmuring, "*Oh Valerie, my sweetest. What did you do to me? You ruined everything, but gave me so much; you made me do things that would have horrified my mother…rude things that I'd never experienced before. But you always knew I couldn't go any further… you understood didn't you?*" He plaintively burbled. "*My mother is always watching me, she won't let go…she would never forgive me carrying on with another woman, me, a married man,*" he mumbled on as if in conversation with Valerie. "*She wouldn't have APPROVED.*" He looked upwards at the dulled cornices of the room half-expecting to see a manifestation of his late Mother's loveless face. "*She'd never had time for any of my girlfriends. Even when my poor Daphne came along, a simple and innocuous soul, she even tried to get rid of her. The bitch! No, she never liked other women coming near me. I was hers and hers alone. She would have HATED you, Valerie, my love. She would have sussed you were a minx. Too demure by half, too capable, too bloody WANTON.*"

23

But now Astle began to feel contrite, switching his angry conversation to his all-seeing mother in the afterlife: *"Mother! You have to forgive me, for God's sake!"* He was nearly shouting as he flung himself back in his seat with frustration, the casters of his high-backed chair creaking under the strain of his bulk.

Astle closed his eyes and tried to lock out his mother from his guilty mind as he began to conjure an alternative life with Valerie. Every day he sat in his office hatching more and more dangerous plans, but every possibility he considered was punctured by insurmountable obstacles. Yet, he was unable to curb the restless, rebellious spirit that lurked inside his fat body. He knew that his overpowering and hankering desire to be rid of all that was precious to him would, one day, consume him.

Astle's anarchic flights of fancy went well beyond escaping with his ex-lover. He imagined disabusing his customers that he so despised. The annual Rotary Club lunch was often his chosen venue for his imaginary break out. He saw himself delivering his usual annual address on, *'Banking Today - Much like Yesterday'*. The pleasure surged through his body as he contemplated humiliating his inferiors. His well-rehearsed speech rang in his head:

'Ladies and Gentlemen, I know that there are not many of you here that classify as gentlemen, but I will do my best, eh Sir Toby?' His opening remark is directed at the unctuous, patronising Sir Toby Inchdale, the local squire and near bankrupt land owner and incumbent of Inchdale Hall.

His address would be a triumph of oratory. Nobody would be spared his vitriol: even Marjorie Nelson, his largest customer, the brewery heiress and wife of Windelton's wonder dentist, would get a mouthful of his scorning sarcasm:

'And the ladies don't fare much better do they Marjorie? Your husband's a sex maniac and you've far too much money for your own good! You should be giving back your bloated brewery profits to the battered wives of the drunks who sup your watery ales by the gallon'.

Then there were the uncouth, boorish farmers he had to put up with. He would certainly give them a flea in the ear. They trotted through his office door week after week with unworkable schemes for more intensive farming... and the Town Council would squirm under his revelations of corruption and malfeasance - particularly that oaf of a Town Clerk, Hoskins:

'Ah my dear Hoskins, you thought by blocking my golf club captaincy you'd curry favour with the imbecilic estate agent, Ray Trubshaw. I know he rigged the auction so you could buy "The Rookeries" on the cheap. It's plain for all to see you couldn't afford a fancy house like that on your measly salary. I think the Council's auditors should take a closer look at that transaction, don't you Mister Hoskins?'

Astle smiled to himself as he ran through the speech in his head. It gave him a warm glow of pleasure, it was as if his dreams of personal anarchy were being realised, it was faintly erotic. In reality, it was Valerie Harper who came the nearest to him breaking out of his straight-jacket of conformity, his once-in-a-lifetime moment of passion. She was no fantasy. He had a bastard son to prove it!

"Go away mother!" he scolded aloud as his long dead mother once again peeked at him from behind the net curtains of the afterlife. Astle knew he had already ruined his chances of her speaking to him when eventually he went to heaven.

"I don't want to go to heaven anyway!" he shouted.

Suddenly there was a gentle tapping on the door. The frail Miss Starkey, his timid secretary, slowly opened the door and peered nervously into his office. "Did you call Mr Astle, I am certain I heard your voice?" Miss Starkey was holding the post tray which held a single letter. The tray trembled slightly but the envelope did not move as Miss Starkey awaited her employer's response. Astle snapped out of his mind-whirring trance and turned his attention to the stick-like figure of Miss Starkey. Suddenly he spied the expensive, watermarked envelope. It was marked *'Private and confidential'.* He knew immediately who had sent it. The letter sat menacingly inert on the polished mahogany tray. The beautifully expensive envelope with the bank's embossed motif had the air of weighty importance, despite it containing only a quarto size letter with a few lines of leaden text.

Astle bolted upright: *"Christ! What's this? It's bloody Lombard Street Head Office, they're on to me!"* he thought. Miss Starkey noticed the look of fear pass across her employer's face.

"That'll be all for now Miss Starkey," he said abruptly, leaning forward to delicately lift the letter off the tray as if he was handling an unexploded bomb. As soon as Miss Starkey crept out of the office and the door closed behind her, Astle lifted the letter to his face and sniffed the crisp bond paper, running it over his cheeks hoping to gather some clue to its contents. Finally, he slid his Murchison's Bank paper knife under the envelope back and pulled out the letter. He unfolded it slowly. The contents were shocking in their brevity; it told him nothing yet was full of unspoken meaning. Correspondence from Head Office was rare and generally unwelcome. With trembling hands he gripped the stiff notepaper and read and re-read every word hoping to gain some insight from the typed sentences and the scribbled signature of the secretary who had signed it on behalf of Hector Pym, Controller (North).

Dear Astle,

I would be grateful if you could attend me at a meeting at the Sheffield Regional Office, Ecclesall Road, at 10am on Monday 16th June. You must cancel any other appointments you may have booked for that day to be certain of your availability. Please confirm forthwith your agreement to this request to my personal secretary, Miss S. Howe-Bowden, at the address above. I insist that you did not mention this meeting to other members of your staff at this present time.

Note: your travel expenses will be reimbursed through head office and not the branch.

Yours sincerely,

Hector Pym

Controller (North)

How often did Hector Pym emerge from his lair in London to visit Regional Office, let alone ask to see him personally?

Never!

Astle's mind raced with unpleasant possibilities.

Fact: he had been summoned, without explanation, to attend a meeting in a little over five weeks' time at the Regional Office, with the London-based Controller (North).

"Christ!"

- Chapter 3 -

Pastimes

Astle had few passions outside his banking life. He played golf desultorily. He was encouraged by the bank as it was a good place to meet and hobnob with bank customers. Astle had aspirations to be Windelton Golf Club captain. That was until Hoskins, the Town Clerk, had for some Machiavellian reason blocked his chances. Hoskins had successfully lobbied the committee and convinced them that the sly, self-satisfied Ray Trubshaw would be a more able choice. Astle wondered if a brown envelope had been involved. He would pay Hoskins back. He didn't know how but a plan would emerge. One always did.

One recreational pursuit Astle *did* enjoy (and in which he showed some aptitude) was fly fishing. There was something solitary about being beside a gently flowing river or a quiet lake and casting a fly to a rising trout. It was an entirely satisfying experience. He wasn't quite sure why, probably because he was out of sight of his amenable but dull wife and away from the bank's irritating customers.

Every year Astle took himself off to Scotland to fish for wild brown trout in some remote corner of the Highlands. He always went alone. Daphne would never have tolerated a week away sitting in a cold Scottish hotel waiting for her husband to return from a day's fishing while she knitted and worried about the state of his temper on return. She never knew that Astle never raged about the outcome of his piscatorial labours, just being in the Scottish outdoors had a calming effect on his usual grumpy misdemeanour.

Astle liked to go to different places in pursuit of his fishy quarry. During the winter months he would pore over his fishing magazines planning where he would visit the coming season. He was normally a creature of habit but fishing released in Astle an adventurous spirit that never saw the light of day in his Windelton life. Every year he visited a different hotel. In addition to his fishing log he diligently maintained files of all the hotels he had visited scoring them like a gazetteer, awarding stars for food, fishing, accommodation and ambiance.

It was fortunate that just a couple of days after the arrival of Hector Pym's life-threatening letter he had booked a week's leave. Astle was sure that the distraction of a few days fishing in the far north of Scotland would help him to think clearly and make plans. As soon as Miss Starkey had crept away from his office Astle started to fret about what lay behind his unexpected correspondence. Did it indicate an imminent sacking, a promotion or perhaps some new profit making initiative that the bank was apt to spring upon branch managers?

'*Don't mention this meeting to other members of staff,*' was mysterious; were they going to close or merge with another branch? The letter was worryingly unspecific. It must be serious. Pym was a god, the bank's top man in charge of all the northern region's branches. He had only met him once before at some bank golf match. Astle could tell Pym was powerful; he played golf wearing a pinstripe suit. He handed his bowler hat to the caddy before he played a stroke and replaced it as he strode in the direction of his ball.

Astle racked his brain to think of which customer may have dared to complain. He could barely comprehend anyone having the effrontery to take such an action but you never knew… could it be Ray Trubshaw moaning about overcharging? Had he been exposed by one of his own staff, he wouldn't put it past that wily, old bastard Payne. Astle knew he bore a grudge about being overlooked for promotion. Astle snorted to himself with derision, *Overlooked? He's too small to be even noticed!*

The more he thought, the more he trembled in agitation. Clinging to his manager's chair he gulped for air, his peripheral vision started to close in on him like a vignette circling an old photograph; for a moment Astle thought he might pass out. His mind raced: the meeting was not immediate so it couldn't be *that* serious? Too old for promotion, anyhow regional office normally telephoned first to sound you out. 'Do you want to apply?' All that sort of rubbish. No, it was something else. Something more sinister he was sure. Was now the time to turn one of his fantasised escape plans into something more concrete? Could he persuade his lovely Valerie to flee with *her* boy, *his son*, to a better life, miles away from the damp hills of Whiteley?

"And what about all of my money in the vaults," he muttered aloud?

If Hector Pym was to give him the gentle nudge into premature retirement was there still time to spring a gold-plated exit? If his departure was a disciplinary matter he could be fired on the spot! Out of the door, get your coat, gives us your car keys, goodbye and good riddance! A same day departure would leave him no time to fulfil any of his half-formed plans. If it was *that* serious then Hector Pym would act immediately? Maybe they were still gathering evidence, perhaps they had spotted something when the annual bank inspection team came to pay their Gestapo-style visit three months ago? Since then they had him under surveillance, monitoring his every move. He suddenly thought to himself: *it has to be old Payne*, holed up in his little cubicle, snooping on him, secretly reporting back to Regional Office.

THE BASTARD!

The more he thought about it the more convinced Astle became that it was the extra charges he had added to Trubshaw's account. When he cast his mind back Payne did look a bit pained. *"Why am I joking about this?"* he muttered to himself? He told Payne to charge three extra guineas to Trubshaw's account, for being a 'bloody, cheeky, bugger'.

Astle's feverish imagination spins forward in time. *He sees Daphne, his ever-faithful little wife is in the arms of the awful Trubshaw. They are locked in a passionate embrace. Daphne giggles with childish delight. Trubshaw brays manically and turns to face Astle, "You are in for it, you fat pompous upstart! I have told your superiors everything; your lovely wife and her fortune teller have told me all about your catalogue of shame. The over-charging, your mistress and bastard child, the whole sordid charade of your secret life…" He turns and smiles lasciviously at Daphne. "We have looked into the future too. You are in for the chop! You're going down for a long, long, time. You'll rot in prison, Ha Hah Ha Hah! And when you're locked up Daphne will*

30

come and work for me. She says she can't wait to help me with some of my more personal affairs."
Ray Trubshaw leers knowingly at Astle, meanwhile an enraptured Daphne looks lovingly up into
the blood shot eyes of the claret-faced estate agent. Strangely Daphne is wearing a slinky and
rather revealing black cocktail dress instead of her normal cardigan and sensible shoes.

Astle's mind swims with panic and terrible hallucinations as he foresees his imminent demise;
the final vision is a closing scene from an Edgar Lustgarten film: 'Crime Never Pays'. PC Robson
is pedalling furiously towards him on his bicycle; he is standing up on the pedals to add more
urgency to his crime-busting mission, his handcuffs jangle menacingly on the handlebars. He brings
his cycle to a skidding halt at the bank counter ringing his cycle bell loudly. "Now come with me
quietly Mr. Astle, SIR, you con-artist," he says in a voice of strained politeness. His loyal
customers scatter away from the counter in fear, some freeze in panic, their backs pressed against
the polished mahogany panelled walls, and meanwhile others drop their shopping and put their
hands up in the air as if a robbery is taking place. Miss Starkey swoons and faints behind the
counter. She crumples up like a thin sack that contains only fragments of dust and tiny bones.

"NO, NO, NO, for crying out loud," Astle shouts to himself. "Get a grip man," he adjusts and re-adjusts his sweating under garments. His corpulent body quivers like a jelly.

Suddenly, there is another feeble knock at the door. It is the interminably dull Miss Starkey once again, "Are you alright Mr Astle, it is twenty-five to ten," she asks in an anxious voice, her bony head poking around the door, "I thought I heard shouting?"

This was the first time that Astle had not emerged from his office at nine thirty on the dot. "Thank you Miss Starkey, I will be with you shortly," Astle replied, summoning all his reserves of control. Good God, he thinks to himself, Gerald Astle is *never* late for meetings. As he stands to leave the office he feels like weeping, confessing to someone, anyone to unburden his guilt. The consequences loom over him: the humiliation, the jail sentence, no pension, his life of modest achievement shattered just because he had overcharged a few stupid customers!

31

Now on his feet and charged with the responsibility of dealing with bank matters, Astle begins to see things from a more realistic perspective. His mind, like a film projectionist begins to un-spool one argument and spool-up a new one. He counters apoplectic arguments with reason. He grasps the mahogany door jamb and steadies himself. He pushes his plump shoulders back and breathes in deeply. The panic subsides; his old confidence regains the upper hand. Astle's manner shifts to one of indignant, self-righteous anger. His customers *could* afford the charges; they should be grateful to be over charged by a man of Astle's standing.

He must never forget that he *was* the manager. He brushed his shoulders as if throwing off specks of dust. Now is the time to make plans. *Yes, he would make a plan. A bloody good… no, a stupendous plan. Oh yes!*

"Are you sure you are alright Mr Astle? You look as if you have seen a ghost. I have friend who once saw an apparition in her…"

"Please don't enquire further Miss Starkey," Astle brusquely cut off Miss Starkey's revelations of her friend's spiritual experiences. Miss Starkey revelled in stories from the 'other side' and she frequently believed that she received messages from long dead relatives. The strange noises she heard from under the floorboards of her cottage were certainly coded signs.

"In truth, Miss Starkey, it's an old friend; I have just learned he has passed away. I would rather you kept this between ourselves. Please don't mention it to the staff," he confided to her in a more conciliatory tone, "A little secret, just between you and me," Astle smiled weakly at her, holding her sympathetic gaze.

She'd been right, thought Miss Starkey. It was as clear as daylight, dear Mr. Astle *had* had a visitation of his lately passed on companion. What other explanation could there be for his lateness and him looking as white as death? Of course the poor man was in denial, a common course of events for the unsighted ones. "I do *so* understand Mr Astle, I am *so* sorry. Will you be having some time off for the funeral or will you still be away on your holiday?"

"Oh, I'll be back by then," said Astle brusquely.

"If you're attending the service I'll need to put the details in the office diary. Shall I put it down as compassionate leave with no pay or is it a bank customer? I'll have to inform regional office, you know the procedures about time off," said Miss Starkey in the officious tone which she adopted when discussing matters of bank protocol.

'Let regional office know?' Astle repeated the words in a near choking voice.

"What *exactly* do you mean, Miss Starkey?" he said menacingly.

"It's er... the rules, Mr. Astle?" stumbled the now terrified Miss Starkey as she recognised the signs of Mr. Astle's temper reaching melt-down. He must have been really shaken by the visitation, thought Miss Starkey, he's about to have one of his 'boil-overs' as she privately called them.

It must be her, thought Astle in a flash of inspiration. *She's let on to regional office about the Trubshaw charges. Of course, of course, it all makes perfect sense now. The quisling bitch!*

Astle suppressed his rising anger. "I will let you know in due course Miss Starkey, I am not absolutely certain when the funeral will take place. I am too upset to discuss it right now," he replied, trying to control his indignation. He glanced downwards as if to stifle a tear as he relaxed his expression to a suitably grieving demeanour. He coughed to clear his choked voice and asked in a near-normal voice, "Now, who am I seeing today, I am uncharacteristically late?"

"Nobody this morning Mr Astle. Perhaps it is fortunate you are going to have your break next week. Is it Scotland again?"

"Yes, you're right Miss Starkey; a break will do me good. We all get very tired you know, even us managers," said Astle, trying to add a light-hearted touch to the conversation.

Miss Starkey wasn't fooled, she could tell something had upset her employer, she had never seen him so worked-up.

Saturday morning at the Murchison's Bank returned to its humdrum routine. Well nearly. The word around the staff was that Astle had seen a ghost of a recently deceased friend. He looked completely ashen. Stranger still: he had been five minutes late out of his office – an unheard of occurrence!

- Chapter 4 -

The Inverhapless Fishing Hotel

For Sir Toby and Lady Lavinia Inchdale and their prodigal son, Jasper, it was all a most unfortunate co-incidence. In those days, the far north-west of Scotland was a largely unvisited area of the British Isles. Only the determined and hardy ventured that far north.

Fishing did drive people to extremes and the Inverhapless Hotel was one of them. The hotel's only merit was abundant trout fishing and some good spate waters for sea trout and salmon late in the season. The long two-storey building that had once been an ancient bothy and steadings was set in uncompromisingly remote landscape by the side of a loch and surrounded by glowering, primeval mountains. The roads north of Inverness were mostly single track with passing places and the journey was characterised by hazardous loch crossings on unstable car ferries. These curious craft had all the appearance of overgrown rowing boats with a flat deck thrown on top which is exactly what they were.

It took Astle two days of hard driving to reach the hotel. Sir Toby's entourage travelled in style in their pre-war Rolls Royce. Their journey normally took a minimum of four days and upward of two weeks dependent upon the number of friends they cadged overnight accommodation from en route. They generally had interludes in the Borders, Edinburgh, and Pitlochry area and sometimes they stayed with a distant cousin who had a small castle near Bonar Bridge.

If the local fishing was good the Inchdale party would stay on with the unfortunates they had foisted themselves upon. They frequently had be reminded by their hosts after more than a fortnight's sojourn that they were due at the Inverhapless Hotel sometime that season. The Inchdale's journey to Scotland was a progress, Astle's a dash.

The proprietor of the Inverhapless Hotel was accustomed to the Inchdale's erratic attention to dates and kept a large suite of rooms available for a four week period either side of the due date of their scheduled arrival. Since the late eighteen hundreds generations of Inchdales had successively visited this harsh granite establishment with a corrugated iron roof (the original blew off in a gale in 1928). The hotel was located magnificently on the shores of Loch Orre'ful where the views were either spectacular in fine weather (occasionally) or suicidally depressing in bad weather (frequently). It was rarely in between. The Inchdales along with assorted regulars came like migrating geese in the spring and again in July or September depending on the state of the rivers and the number of salmon reported. The Inchdale consistency had made them akin to family with successive owners of the Inverhapless Hotel. Colonel Cameron McStargs, was the current incumbent, having leased the shabby property from an absent English duke, who owned most of this part of Scotland. Because of their decades of occupation, the Inchdales believed that they enjoyed proprietorial ownership of the Inverhapless, it was *their* hotel. The Colonel was no more than a mere caretaker, and in return he treated them like royalty.

The Inverhapless was typical of Scottish fishing hotels. It was cold, damp and characterised by appalling food served at breakneck speed. Bathing, when the boilers were functioning, meant lying in a deep cast iron bath in soft, brown peat-water in which small pieces of heather could often be found floating. Getting out of the deep bath after a hard day's fishing was a difficult process: fatigue combined with mild inebriation (whisky consumed in the bath was almost mandatory) and stepping onto a slippery, cold linoleum floor was a dangerous process. Death by bathroom was common at the Inverhapless. Once the bathing experience was completed guests attempted to dry themselves with tiny, threadbare hand towels.

The public bar was the focal point of the Inverhapless as it enjoyed an open peat fire that was lit summer and winter. This snug place, lined with stuffed trout of varying sizes, was stocked with a wall of malt whiskies. For those with a taste for a longer beverage there was terrible keg Caledonian ale that only the locals consumed when funds for a nip were in short supply.

It took around a dozen visits before the 'Colonel', as he was universally known, would start acknowledging a guest's presence. The more frequent the visitor and the longevity of years served meant that a reservoir of bonus points was accumulated in the Colonel's inventory of worthiness. This was important as it had a direct impact when he allocated the various fishing beats for the following day. This hand-out of fishing largesse by the Colonel took place in the lounge after the evening dinner had been served (or rather thrown down on the table in front of the guests).

There was no menu so if you didn't like mutton or cod, boiled cabbage and potato you went hungry. The fresh air meant everyone was starving and shovelled down the rations at the same speed that they were served – twenty minutes, nineteen seconds was the fastest time ever recorded for the delivery and completion of the four-course dinner. The food never varied from year to year and day of the week: cod Monday, mutton Tuesday, cod Wednesday and so it alternated. On Sundays there was a choice of cold cod served with salad dressing or mutton as way of a change. The regular guests held a sweepstake every evening on the duration of the meal time. Time started from when the kitchen double doors banged open and the first waitress came running out with the first course, often sardines, followed by some sort of soup, boil in the bag mutton (or cod) followed by either an apple, cheese or occasionally sponge pudding – a big favourite, but this could add five minutes onto the overall meal time.

Guests would sneak into the kitchen to try and find out what pudding was to be served as it greatly aided the chances of winning the bet. Large sums of money were exchanged on this gaming pursuit although the winner had to stand a round of drinks at the bar which considerably depleted any windfall.

It was around six-thirty at the end of Astle's second day of his four day sojourn. He was slumped deep in a lounge armchair when Inchdale's ancient and filthy Rolls Royce lumbered into the car park blasting its horn and scattering guests, domestics and sheep out of the way. The vehicle sat heavily on its springs, weighed down with trunks and fishing tackle; the larger cases were perched perilously on the open boot lid that was held down with thick leather straps.

Astle's fishing had been rained off by mid-afternoon. He had got soaking wet and the loch he had been allocated to fish had been very poor. Wisely, he had decided to come back to the hotel for a bath and to use the time to tie some trout flies. He had successfully completed a couple of Peter Ross flies and was reclining with a glass of whisky and thinking hard about Valerie and the letter he had received from the Murchison's Head Office. At this distance from Windelton the letter didn't seem as threatening as it appeared on first opening; the magic of the Scottish Highlands had been working its calming effect on Astle's fevered mind. Everything was so quiet here, reality far away. If Astle had been back in Windelton he would have been haranguing the Colonel about the shallow, weedy loch he had been given to fish. One look at the hotel's fishing record book would have informed him that nothing of any consequence had been caught there in twenty years. But Astle was a contented man. That was until he suddenly spied Inchdale.

The old Rolls pulled up on the gravel in front of the glass veranda that stretched the length of the hotel frontage. No sooner had it stopped the Colonel emerged from nowhere and was pulling open the Roller's suicide doors. He was kissing Lady Lavinia's bony hand and pumping Inchdale's great big paw as if he had just met Doctor Livingstone in the African bush. At first, Astle couldn't believe his eyes, but then he heard Inchdale's booming, patrician voice and he could see through the grubby windows his trade-mark faded cavalry twill trousers, patched sports jacket and yellow tie. The only difference was that he was wearing a loud tweed cape over the outfit giving him an air of Sherlock Holmes. *Blast! Blast!* He thought.

Eventually the party came barging through the front door. There emerged a streaming babble of obsequious conversation from the Colonel in his best upper class English accent mixed with a strangulated Edinburgh Morningside burr. They marched straight to the bar where the Colonel could be heard ordering large malt whiskies for his newly arrived guests. A group of never-seen-before lackeys emerged carrying trunks through the hall and up the narrow stairs to a suite of rooms at the end of the building where the Inchdale party were to be quartered. Sir Toby Inchdale had swept past in his mass of tweeds and not recognised Astle. Lady Lavinia had followed wearing an ancient fox fur stole and accompanied by numerous Border terrier dogs that had scampered about cocking their legs on the lounge chairs. One approached Astle's seat but he kicked it away before a stream of piss went down his trouser leg. Lady Lavinia pursed her lips as she caught a half-glance of Astle's swishing foot. She hesitated a moment as she scanned the room to see if anyone recognised her before following her husband into the bar. She was accompanied by a good looking young man that Astle didn't recognise but he possessed an air of superiority that marked him out as an Inchdale.

The young man brought up the rear and he scanned the room in much the same way as Lady Lavinia but he was in search of signs of any females to seduce although he knew his chances would be very thin up here. He comforted himself in the knowledge that the Colonel's younger daughter, Hermione, would be available although he heard that she had become engaged to a farmer from Cape Wrath. That wouldn't deter him.

As Lady Lavania went by Astle caught a strong whiff of dogs mixed with tobacco, a cigarette was dangling from her lips and her gravelly voice resounded as she acknowledged the barman, clearly another old friend and part of the Inchdale fan club. Astle fumed to himself. He had come to the Inverhapless Hotel to get away from it all and now the patronising Sir Toby *'en famille'* had turned up to revive all the memories of everything he was trying to forget.

At dinner the Inchdale entourage were allocated the largest table in the window with views overlooking Loch Orre'ful. The previous occupants, a retired minor public school housemaster with a squeaky voice accompanied by a large violent-looking wife had been unceremoniously removed to the back of the dining room near the kitchen doors. She was heard barking in protest to the Colonel while her husband shushed her quiet. He understood the hierarchy perfectly. He accepted his table change like a seasoned stalwart; it was only his wife's seventh visit and she had yet to fully comprehend the Inverhapless protocols of lineage and money.

The Colonel joined the Inchdale entourage at dinner; he had marched ostentatiously into the dining room in full highland dress, his kilt swished exposing his bony white knees while a lone bagpiper played a dirge-like lament on the loch shore. Astle presumed that this was meant to be some sort of Gaelic welcome. It was soon clear that the Inchdale party were eating entirely different food from the rest of the guests. Fresh lobsters appeared followed by sorbet, haunch of venison, a selection of cheeses and finally an enormous meringue bombe that the chef theatrically presented. He was dressed in a clean starched apron complete with chef's hat. Since Astle's arrival the same chef had been spotted occasionally peeping around the kitchen door with a cigarette in his mouth, sporting filthy, blood-stained dungarees.

Champagne flowed followed by Puligny-Montrachet and some decanted red wine that Inchdale kept smelling and swirling around his mouth like a TCP gargle. He kept patting the Colonel on the back much to the obvious delight of the proprietor. Inchdale's booming baritone could be heard around the dining room as they discussed fishing, politics and the state of Highland roads. Lady Lavinia ate sparsely and smoked throughout the meal. The dogs ate most of her food where they lay at her feet. When they had consumed Lady Lavinia's excellent repast they went in search of further sustenance and pestered the guests as they consumed their soup and cod. Astle noticed the young man who was drinking a lot. More and more wine bottles were brought to the table to sustain his apparent unquenchable thirst; they were opened with a flourish by a red haired girl of around twenty five years of age who never took her eyes off the young man. Astle guessed that he must be Inchdale's youngest son, Jasper, who he had heard had recently returned from London. Astle had also gleaned that Sir Toby's boy had made a successful career for himself in advertising. He certainly looked more intelligent than his dimwit elder brother, Courcey.

The meal had taken ages that night as the Inchdale table had been served first and in the process ruined the guests' gambling sweepstake. As the Inchdale troop was retiring the dining room, Sir Toby caught a glimpse of Astle sitting at his tiny single table. He was slurping down the last of his semolina pudding that had been enrobed with a dollop of very nasty looking jam.

"Good Lord man what on earth are you doing here in this God-forsaken place?" cried Inchdale. The Colonel, bringing up the rear of the party, looked crestfallen at this indirect insult. Astle stood up to shake hands with the lion-like figure of Sir Toby. Lady Lavinia proffered a scrawny limp hand in his direction which he grasped, slightly uncertain if he should have kissed it but the overpowering smell of dogs made Astle veer off, instead he bowed very slightly in her direction.

Inchdale introduced his youngest son, Jasper, who looked at him with polite disinterest as if summing him up for any future value. The young man looked as if he was having difficulty focusing. He was undeniably a good looking specimen and bore a strong resemblance to his father in stature but also benefited from some of his mother's fine bone structure.

"So what brings you here Astle, I had no idea that you hunted the silver fish?" boomed the condescending Inchdale elder.

"Brown trout is more to my taste Sir Toby, I come to Scotland every year but it is my first visit to this hotel".

"Absolutely marvellous place Inverhapless, nowhere else like it. My friend the Colonel here will sort out some good fishing for you I am sure?" he said beckoning a thumb in the general direction over his shoulder to where the proprietor was hovering nervously. The Colonel looked suitably chastened as he had given Astle two of the worst lochs to fish on his first two days.

"That would be most acceptable, I have not had much luck to date, in fact none whatsoever," said Astle recognising it wouldn't do any harm to put the boot into the Colonel in Inchdale's company.

41

Inchdale turned to the Colonel: "Cameron, sort something out for this man tomorrow. He's a most important gentleman from where I hail, don't you know! We'd all be buggered without my old friend here! The Inchdales just couldn't carry on; he's the bloody bank manager!" Inchdale roared with laughter and clapped Astle's fat back with a thump that made him gasp for breath. By now everyone in the small dining room was staring at this amusing exchange. Astle went red with embarrassment. He sat down as Inchdale progressed out still laughing to himself. "Bloody bank manager, would you believe it!" Lady Lavinia's loud enquiring voice could be clearly heard as they entered the lounge, "Who *was* that ghastly fat man, he tried to kick one of my dogs earlier. Does he hunt with the Bedale?"

- Chapter 5 -

Trout

Astle didn't sleep well. The Inchdales surprising appearance unsettled him. At least their arrival had brought one bonus: later that evening the Colonel had begrudgingly allocated him an excellent loch to fish the following day.

"You normally have to come here for twenty years before you get a shot at this water," the Colonel had said through gritted teeth, his Morningside accent descending to more like a Govan shipyard worker. But Astle was in no mood to let the Colonel get away talking to him like a delinquent teenager. "Sir Toby *is* a very, long-standing acquaintance and if you're rude to me again I will make certain that *his* cheque for his stay at your establishment bounces all the way to Culloden and back!"

The reference to the infamous '1745' battle stung McStargs, he was at heart a true highlander. The Colonel had lost many of his ancestors to the bloody English army in the last slaughter of the Jacobites. The Colonel's eyes widened but he regained his composure, "Oh come, come Mr Astle, don't be so rash as to threaten me, otherwise I'll have Hamish ma ghillie throw you in the loch next time you set foot on my water!" and with that he stomped off.

As Astle ploughed through his cholesterol-enriched breakfast of black pudding, bacon and fried eggs he pondered his future. When he left Windelton he had nearly made up his mind on a course of radical action but since then, as the miles from home became greater, so his resolve had weakened. Coming to the Inverhapless gave Astle doubts about doing anything; maybe he should just wait and see. But now, meeting Sir Toby Inchdale and his moth-eaten wife and the drunken son, had made him realise that there was no escaping the reality of his predicament. It confirmed that *something* had to be done. He belched under his breath as he tried to digest the last of his gristly bacon. He felt better now; he felt steelier about plotting a final course of action.

43

He returned to his room to collect his fishing gear, went to the rod room to get his fly rod before finally picking up his packed lunch from the hotel porch and set out on his day's mission to fish.

The rain was soft and the gentle breeze gave the loch a perfect ripple, the sky was slightly overcast, ideal conditions to cast his fly. The loch was not very big, five acres at most, dotted with rocky outcrops and islands with birch and rowan trees that grew sparsely. Astle took his time studying the contours and the direction of the wind. The Colonel had offered no advice on the best places to fish but the loch was such a size he could walk its banks in the day easily.

Astle started at the southern end of the loch. The wind was on his right shoulder so it would be easy to cast a decent length of line. Distance was not critical on these little lochs; the fish were invariably close to the bank. It was the ability to gently float the fly onto the water with the minimum of fuss and without spooking the fish that would bring rewards. The first few casts were critical. Astle waded gingerly into the water to above his knees doing his best not to kick up too much sand and silt. A small burn flowed into the loch from his left, it made a restful, gurgling sound and some white spume lines flowed out into the body of water.

On Astle's second cast across the burn mouth the surface of the water erupted next to his fly. He saw a large tail fin of a fish strike the fly and knock it under the water. His line tightened with a strong tug, he waited momentarily before he lifted his rod and the Black Pennell fly barb set itself in to the scissors of the trout's jaws. The fish sensing the control of the fishing line took off and headed for deeper water away from the shores of the loch side. Astle gasped with excitement and let the fish run. It was strong, if he tried to hold the trout his line would break and his prize would be lost. It would need careful playing. The oiled gears of his reel sang in protest as more and more line stripped off the spool. This was a fly fisher's most glorious moment. It cancelled out all the days when nothing was caught. The days when clothing got wet, lines tangled and raging despair on the futility of the sport became overwhelming. A big fish hooked, as yet unseen, twisting and turning under

44

water. Wild animal strength battling against the arched, straining, split cane rod, Astle grimly gripping the reverberating cork handle, hoping, hoping that the fish would tire and can be brought successfully to the landing net. So many fish were lost at the last moment as over eager anglers attempt to land fish before they had exhausted themselves.

Astle was no amateur, he was wary; this was clearly a big fish, perhaps four or five pounds in weight by the feel of it? He had never caught anything so large before, but these wild Scottish brown trout could fool you, they seemed to possess three or four times the strength of the trout he was used to catching in Yorkshire. Astle re-adjusted his footing on the sandy loch bottom and felt for his landing net slung across his back. He touched it reassuringly with his left hand, not needed yet. He was going to have to be patient. For the next ten minutes Astle was completely absorbed with his battle with the fish. His mind so cluttered with worry and half formulated plans had now been emptied as Astle pooled his experience and knowledge of fishing to pursue his goal. The trout had stopped thrashing the water and was now sitting close to the loch bottom in about ten feet of water; it sat gently head into the current as it regained its strength and contemplated its next move. It was a wily old creature, probably eight or nine years old, a predator in its own aquatic environment. The trout had nearly been caught before in its long fish life, but never before had the hook been so hardly driven into its mouth. In the past the trout had managed to spit them out and escape capture. Today was different.

Astle pulled gently on his line testing the pressure, he was worried that he had lost contact with his prey; momentarily, his heart sank as he thought that it had somehow gone. Fish have an uncanny knack of breaking lines or spitting out unset hooks but no, there was still a reassuring weight keeping his fishing line taught. Astle tried to remember the breaking strain of the cast he had attached to his line and fly. Was it two or three pounds? He hadn't been expecting a fish of this magnitude. He was certain that the fish was considerably heavier and therefore stronger than the line weight he had used. Suddenly the trout burst back into life, swimming powerfully upwards it broke the surface of the water and Astle saw the complete fish for a brief moment as it cleared the surface in a flash of black and golden speckled sleekness, his line went slack as it became airborne then tightened viciously his rod bent into a parabola as the fish plunged back into the water, diving deep. Astle hung on, he was still connected. Suddenly the trout felt more pliable and gently Astle started to reel the fish in and eventually he could see the trout on the surface. It was large, very large, probably four pounds, maybe more? It was within fifteen feet of his net and it squirmed and darted away from him again but this time Astle held the line more tightly making the fish fight every yard, wearing it down, sucking out its strength in its last run for freedom. Eventually, the big trout turned on to its back exhausted exposing an off white belly, the last vestiges of strength gone, Astle wound in his line and then passed his net under its body with his left hand, holding his rod upright with the right hand, he gently lifted the fish clear of the water. It was very heavy and wriggled vigorously inside the net, the fish's gills opened and closed starved of oxygen rich water as it went through the fish-equivalent of drowning. Astle staggered backwards under its weight and nearly lost his footing; he waded back to the shore and clambered up into the heather well away from the water's edge before lowering the net and rod to the ground. It was a magnificent fish.

Later as he sat on a rock sipping whisky from his hip flask and chewed on a grotesque sardine sandwich, Astle's mind turned back to Valerie, his son and a new future. The fish lay dead beside him; its beautiful speckled golden colouring dimming as the surface skin dried out and the vibrancy of its long life seeped from its prone body. To anglers great fish caught and landed became defining moments in their lives. Never forgotten. The day, the rod, the fly, the conditions, the location, the fish, the sum of the collective memories were all stored and savoured for years to come.

As the exuberance of the fight and the landing of the fish passed into Astle's memory he realised that if he were to enact his plan successfully he would never again be able to come to this wild place and fish for these wonderful creatures. The thought made his stomach churn, the taste of regurgitated sardine entered his throat and the hip flask in his hand trembled. "Valerie, Valerie" he murmured.

- Chapter 6 -

A Bit Rich

Seven months earlier...

Eustace Hardbottle could see Marjorie Nelson on the telephone from his position in the rose walk. Her face twisted and turned in violent eruptions of powdered, pink flesh. To the untrained eye, she gave every impression of someone in a contortion of rage. Her demeanour suggested that she was spitting every word into the telephone mouthpiece from her gaping crimson lip-sticked mouth. This was the way Marjorie addressed trades people. She believed the only way to communicate clearly with the lower orders was by raising her voice. The greater the volume, the greater the clarity, was Marjorie's maxim. This predilection gave Marjorie Nelson the surprising reputation for being a loud-mouthed snob.

Marjorie resided on the western fringes of Windelton, in a small valley protected from the brunt of Windlelton's winds (although no-one was entirely immune from the wind in Windelton). The Red House was a substantial property built in the Arts and Crafts style of rustic brick with leaded-light windows and deep eaves; it was spacious, comfortable and enjoyed every modern appliance found in prosperous homes of the first half of the of 1960s. Like its owner, the Red House sat confidently at ease in its mature five acres of landscaped gardens and woods. The grounds were meticulously maintained by a staff of industrious gardeners. Early autumn was a busy time in the garden and the workforce were toiling hard, digging and spreading well-rotted compost onto extensive herbaceous borders. Eustace, the head gardener, smiled quietly imagining the poor sod that was on the receiving end of the earful of abuse from 'her ladyship' as she was unaffectionately known amongst the outdoor staff.

Marjorie Nelson was very wealthy. It wasn't quite new money but again it wasn't old money like Sir Toby Inchdale. It had all been bequeathed to her by her late father, Basil Bainbridge, a brewing magnate, who had the presence of mind to make over his substantial assets to his daughter and only offspring well before he died and in so doing avoided considerable sums in death duties.

By Windelton standards Marjorie was by far the richest person in the district. Money that she could readily lay her hands on: cash, gilts, government loan stocks, equities, bonds, Marjorie had them all. On the other hand, Sir Toby Inchdale, the faded, patrician local landowner still had a few bob left despite the excess and mismanagement of his estates by centuries of Inchdale family incompetence. If you had capitalised Sir Toby's ten thousand acres of grouse moor, his dwindling portfolio of investments, the four mixed arable and dairy farms, livestock and machinery, and of course Inchdale Hall - a twelve bedroom, fortified manor house complete with moat, and offset these against his myriad, loans, overdrafts and debts there would be some cash left over. But not much. Such matters rarely troubled Sir Toby just so long as he could continue the life he and his predecessors had enjoyed for the last eight centuries. Liquidity was always Inchdale's Achilles heel; he was invariably short of readies.

If you were to produce an ascending order of Windelton wealth there would appear high on the list one or two canny local farmers with uncalculated accumulations (even to themselves) of the folding stuff who had cash hoarded under floorboards, up chimneys and in mattresses, and other assorted hidey-holes. Their money never burdened Gerald Astle's bank vaults or troubled the Inland Revenue.

But such people weren't of any interest to Marjorie Nelson; farmers did not register on her social horizon and she dismissed Squire Inchdale's so called wealth as, 'ostentatious poverty'. A title well earned, as his appearance was always fabulously shabby in the way that only people who had enjoyed generations of privilege were capable of carrying off.

Inchdale dressed with a scruffy élan and his lion like bearing left strangers in no doubt to his aristocratic lineage. Whatever he wore, however threadbare, his demeanour commanded attention and deference. His clothes were, at the time of

49

purchase by some long-dead relative (they were fortunately all of a similar, powerful stature) of the highest quality. The Inchdales were not quite fallen aristocracy, just stumbling.

Sir Toby and Lady Lavinia managed to maintain a semblance of crumbling dignity and some of the elements of the Edwardian lifestyle that had nurtured them both since infancy. The Inchdales' money flowed out of their bank accounts on a heavy tide of over indulgence; sadly the hoped for returning flood of funds from rents, crop sales, sporting rights, stud fees, gambling winnings, dividends and successful legal actions against poachers never quite covered the high watermark of their outgoing expenditure. Every year there was a shortfall that necessitated selling off some part of the estate. A tastefully written letter from Mr. Astle at Murchison's Bank generally precipitated a liquidation of some assets to return the overdraft to more 'manageable proportions' as the bank manager's euphemistically worded correspondence so pleasingly stated.

The flotsam of the Inchdales decline littered the estate office floor: tradesmen's crumpled-up demands for payment of outstanding invoices at agricultural merchants, grocery stores, wine shippers, and sundry other creditors all bore witness to the Inchdales precarious financial position. The pleading paperwork provided excellent kindling to light the estate office fire on cold mornings. Bills received during the summer months were always more likely to be paid for these could sometimes be located in old shotgun cartridge boxes (an excellent repository for discarded items) or in the cracks of the wall plaster, the paper making an excellent binding material to fill holes in the crumbling daub and wattle walls.

In contrast, Marjorie Nelson's finances were always on the credit side of the profit and loss ledger. Cash flowed continually into Marjorie's many bank accounts from her late father's brewing business, the harvest of his wise investments. Her accounts were engorged with credit balances, yet outgoings, generous as they often were, rarely made any impact on her ever rising tide of funds. A fleet of dividends, bonuses, interest payments weighed anchor daily at the busy harbour of her accounts, unloading fresh argosies of cash.

The result was that Marjorie was Murchison's Bank's most revered, feared and envied customer at the Windelton branch office. Laurence Payne, the deputy manager, could be observed in his mahogany-panelled cubicle, fingering dividend payments made out in favour of Marjorie Nelson. He would have a watery eyed look of wonderment as he pondered the life he could lead with such an annual income. His heart would race and his head swim with possibilities as he reached out to light up yet another cigarette.

Marjorie Nelson's wealth gave her status and importance in the small Windelton community. She was always handsomely turned out in that distinctively domineering, English sort of way. She suffered no doubts about her position and responsibilities. She had strong opinions on most matters and she knew when things were right or wrong. She was always right. And when others were wrong it was her duty to tell them where they had erred. Astle was frequently the recipient of Marjorie's 'advice' and had to sit meekly listening to her explain why Murchison's was the worst bank in Windelton (the only one in fact). She regularly threatened to move her various accounts elsewhere. Astle summoned all his powers of diplomacy when in her presence and smiled good humouredly at Marjorie's many unremitting demands. He continually apologised for the bank's many shortcomings whether actual or imaginary.

Marjorie sometimes felt that people ignored her and was dismayed whenever rebuffed. Despite her legendary wealth she would sometimes be passed over to join a fund raising committee or an invitation to a cocktail party would fail to materialise. Marjorie never took these knock-backs lying down and when an expected invitation was not forthcoming she would phone the 'forgetful friend' to inform them that: "My invitation seems to have got lost in the post." Such was her strength of character that she was rarely refused. As a committee member of the Women's Institute, Marjorie was a wonder of organisational bullying and benevolence; she was always willing to throw open the Red House with its extensive manicured gardens to hold coffee mornings, lunches and every manner of charitable event.

Marjorie's widowed mother, Rose Bainbridge, lived in a small lodge cottage at the entrance to the five acre garden. She joined Marjorie and her husband David at dinner every evening in the main house. When the children were home from boarding school they would be there too and Rose enjoyed their bickering chit-chat. She also found David's quiet, intelligent company was the perfect antidote to her overbearing daughter. Despite her advanced years Rose guiltily found David a very attractive man. She tried to dismiss these secret thoughts from her mind and prayed to the good Lord every night that she might be delivered from her wickedness.

Rose tolerated her only daughter at meal times in dutiful silence. She preferred to listen into the conversation and would only half-heartedly join in when asked a direct question. This enabled Marjorie to talk at length and without interruption. This unfortunate characteristic was a constant reminder to Rose of her late husband – memories she would prefer to forget.

At these evening dinners Marjorie would expound on plans of her busy social agenda; she always had some pet project underway or under development. Recently though, Rose had noticed a certain reticence from Marjorie about what she was scheduling for her next philanthropic, attention-seeking enterprise. Rose was aware that something was being plotted by her daughter and she wondered when Marjorie was going to let the 'cat out of the bag'. Maud, one of Marjorie's maids, who also came and 'did' at the Lodge, had gossiped to her about telephone calls from marquee companies. She had also excitedly revealed how she had taken a long distance call on a crackling line from a strange sounding foreigner asking for 'Signora Marjorie'. Rose decided, as with all things regarding Marjorie, it was better to wait for events to unfold.

To Marjorie, her mother's role in life was to be a sweet, if sometimes tipsy, Granny to the children. It was important that children had grandparents and since

Grandpa Bainbridge had died prematurely and David's parents lived in the south west of England, and rarely visited, the task had fallen on Rose's shoulders to be the doting grandparent to Marjorie's two progeny.

Rose did wonder from time to time why her charming, long suffering son-in-law ever stuck it out with her daughter. It was clear that he was a very attractive man to the opposite sex and she had often seen a lot of women hanging around outside David's dentist surgery and wondered what they were doing. It occurred to Rose that the phone call from the foreigner perhaps signified that Marjorie had another admirer but this idea seemed too preposterous to contemplate. There was certainly something afoot.

~

Every year, as Rose grew older and winter approached, she was already wishing for the following spring and warmer weather. Today there was already a chill Windelton wind assaulting the garden. The autumnal conditions were augmented with bursts of driving rain that penetrated her old frame as she struggled up the washed gravel driveway towards the Red House for her morning coffee. She considered tackling Marjorie about her as yet unspoken of plans, well if not this morning perhaps over dinner this evening... but only then if she could face challenging her daughter?

She passed Eustace Hardbottle at some distance, he was cutting back some roses and she waved vaguely in his direction but he failed to notice. The omens for a peaceful chat over coffee didn't look good as Rose could see her daughter shouting at someone down the morning room telephone. Her right hand was gripping the receiver and pressing to her ear, there were flecks of spittle being sprayed over the heavy damask curtains, her free left hand was jerking about in a series of agitated theatrical gestures and occasionally her hand beat the heavy fabric of the curtains in a smacking gesture. If Marjorie was in a temper it would take time to subside, Rose felt a pang of unease and half thought about returning to the Lodge. Her idea of escape was dashed as Marjorie had seen her mother through the window and sensing her indecision imperiously beckoned her to come in.

Anyhow, by now Rose was feeling rather cold and couldn't face a trudge back to the Lodge. She was in need of a restorative cup of coffee and a nip of brandy that she would sneak from the sideboard decanter when Marjorie had her back turned. Soon, Rose was in the large wood-panelled hallway and the maid was helping her off with her woollen coat as she just caught the final words of her daughter's telephone conversation.

'"Yes, good, that's excellent Signor Fabretti, of course it will be warm enough, and we don't live at the North Pole, THE NORTH POLE!" Marjorie bellowed down the receiver. "Oh never mind, yes, yes, see you in May, Arrivederci, Arriverderci".

"Who was that dear?" asked Rose mildly.

"Oh, no-one of importance Mother, just some ice cream people." Marjorie replied dismissively with a satisfied smile on her large face as she plunged the receiver back on to its cradle with a clatter of Bakelite.

"Now, let's have a nice cup of coffee and a biscuit, I have got something to tell you, providing you can keep a secret!"

"Really dear?" said Rose feigning surprise, "How exciting!"

- Chapter 7 -

A Short History Lesson

Sir Toby Inchdale was a squire of the old school. His credentials were impeccable. Hundreds of years of hopeless land stewardship had brought him to today's state of near insolvency. This minor irritation did not curb his expenditure, retinue of domestics and neither affected his robust lifestyle nor dented an irrepressible, authoritarian charm.

The Inchdale Scottish odysseys were a wonderful tonic from the humdrum life of Windelton social rounds, pressing creditors and the sundry irritations of trying to keep the eight-hundred-year Inchdale dynasty intact.

In the old days they used to spend a couple of months at Claridges during the London season but the social changes afoot meant that presenting daughters at court had all become rather passé. It was also prohibitively expensive. Thus Scotland had come to represent an even more important chapter in the Inchdale year. For Sir Toby it meant that he could forget the estate, the worries over its accelerating decline, avoid his braying daughter-in-law and his useless eldest son with whom he enjoyed an ever worsening relationship. This year he had the added bonus of bringing his youngest, and by far the most successful offspring, with him.

Having Jasper about the place was a real tonic for Sir Toby, particularly as he had only seen him infrequently over the last few years as he had been away working in London and New York. This year's visit was going to be like old times when he used to bring the boys up to Scotland when they were young. Until Jasper's rise to financial independence, commerce had never soiled Inchdale family hands since the times before the knight banneret was bestowed on the family's illustrious ancestor deCoursey Inchdahl in the early thirteenth century. A grateful King John awarded the knighthood as a just reward for seeing off an army of thieving and murdering Scots who attempted to sack Windelton and storm the newly completed Norman castle fortifications. Along with the rank he received substantial parcels of land stretching up to the Scottish borders and eastward towards the North Sea. These lands had been the Inchdale dominion for hundreds of years until the fiefdom had been gradually whittled away and sold off to keep the creditors at bay.

Sir Toby followed family tradition – a governess in the early years followed by Eton, Guards and then gentleman landowner. As a retired major he volunteered to join up at the outbreak of the Second World War. He enjoyed a short and undistinguished period of action before his capture in Northern France as the British Expeditionary Force rapidly retreated towards the beaches of Dunkirk.

Inchdale's brief war experiences had been marked by a series of highly inaccurate and ill-advised stratagems. The last involved the capture of many of his battalion because he incorrectly read a map and sent his force marching into an enemy garrison. In an effort to save the day, Inchdale had rashly set out with Pullman, his adjutant, to reconnoitre an escape route.

Inchdale rarely turned up the opportunity of some 'good tuck'. While his depleted battalion were engaged in ferocious fighting on the outskirts of a small Pas de Calais village he stumbled on a restaurant with pleasant views of the English Channel. He needed resuscitation after his map blunder and decided as it was lunchtime to tarry awhile. The proprietor's devotion to cooking was admirable under the circumstances. Inchdale was savouring the last of a rather agreeable '28 Chateau Lafitte claret when an irritating 8mm German shell landed on the restaurant kitchen. Fortunately this untimely interruption took place just after the main course had been completed but sadly before the cheese and desert menu could be fully explored. Leaving some money stuffed into the dead patron's blood-stained top pocket, Sir Toby hot-footed out of the near-destroyed café. Pullman, his adjutant, who had dutifully remained outside the establishment, was still sweeping bomb-blast dust off the bonnet of the Humber staff car as a slightly dishevelled looking Inchdale appeared.

"Bloody Hun, can't even finish a decent meal without them buggering everything up!"

It was at this moment that a German Panzer tank clanked into view and spotting the British Army Humber car the tank gunner swung the barrel into position and was preparing to blow it to smithereens when Inchdale calmly strode toward to the vast vehicle. The startled tank commander, realising he was unable to fire at such short range, was entirely confounded by the English officer's utter arrogance and stupidity. The tank commander's head popped out of the turret to be confronted by Inchdale who asked in passable German:

"What's the quickest way to Dunkirk Fritz? It's your bloody fault, fouling up the roads with damn traffic, how can anyone be expected to fight a proper war?"

Why Inchdale didn't shoot the tank commander or the German shoot Inchdale dead on the spot can only be divined. After his capture, Inchdale, once it was known he was baronet, was classified by the Germans as a 'special', a part of the aristocratic English ruling class. He was feted by the Germans as a prize; high status prisoners were to be nurtured. Another excellent lunch followed his capture hosted by a member of the German High Command some way behind the lines. This time he completed the pudding course rounded off with an excellent '32 Chateau d'Quem. After a number of toasts he bade the Germans farewell and was transported along with Pullman to a holding camp behind enemy lines. Later he was despatched to Colditz Castle, the legendary high security POW camp, where he joined the other 'notables' and difficult prisoners for the remainder of the war.

On his repatriation Inchdale once again took up the reins of running the estate. Early on in the war, his father Sir Hastings Inchdale, had finally succumbed to madness as a result of the syphilis he'd contracted in an Italian whorehouse during a '30s Grand Tour. With both the senior male Inchdales either dead or locked up, Sir Toby's wife had taken over the running of the estate. During his five year absence the management of the farms, the husbandry of the animals and the welfare of the estate workers were never better served. The books balanced, profits were accrued.

In 1934 Sir Toby had married Lavinia (nee Chivers) a northern socialite and beauty who bore him two sons and one daughter. The provenance of the daughter was never discussed as she was born in the middle of the conflict when Inchdale was residing in Colditz. On his triumphant arrival home he was greeted with a new baby of three years old. A mildly surprised Inchdale thought for a moment, "Oh dear, I see," he said and then turned to his wife with a smile, "Well done girl, good to keep breeding while I was away. She's got lovely blond hair and looks just like you!"

"Tobias, darling, I thought you would never return and it was *so* lonely," confessed Lady Lavinia in a matter of fact manner. "Gunter was a charming prisoner of war and from a *very* good stock. He was *so* helpful running the estate. The German's *are* efficient aren't they? We have a made a profit *every* year. I hope you understand my darling; I had to hedge my bets. I thought it best to have an each way wager, rather like at the point-to-point, don't you see? I had no idea *who* was going to win. You would have liked him, he was an aristocrat, a Baron just like you, with perfect manners and a little schloss in Bavaria... near Munich I think", she continued vaguely, "I hope we haven't bombed it to pieces."

Inchdale accepted this new family addition as if it was his own and no more was ever said about the matter. Ingrid grew up to be a very fine specimen of the Aryan race with blue eyes and white blond hair. She was sometimes teased about her Nordic looks as all Inchdales were without exception dark and Celtic.

~

The sight of the bloody bank manager at Inverhapless had rattled Sir Toby although he did not let his feeling show to his wife or his son. As Inchdale sat up in bed, a glass of malt whisky in his hand, Lady Lavinia snoring next to him, he sensed Astle's presence like a spectre haunting one of his most private pleasures. It was as if the fat man was standing there in his large tawdry bedroom, an unbelievable intrusion. The wind shuddered the window frames and he could hear rain gushing out of a broken drainpipe and water hitting the pathway below. Inchdale wondered if Astle had deliberately followed him to Scotland to check up on him. Why on earth would he come to this out of the way place, known only to a few dedicated anglers? Inchdale had no idea why he had been so cordial to the man, he supposed it most have been self-preservation and of course sheer habit. Manners were *so* important.

Inchdale's relationship with the bank was far from cordial. Bank managers were so dim and unimaginative, puffed up with their own self- importance writing their insipid little letters reminding him about his 'unmanageable' borrowing levels. Astle was in the habit of bouncing cheques every now and then, although the silly fat bugger knew the Inchdale Estate was up to its ears in assets and just short of the folding stuff.

It really was time he thought up some wheeze to generate more cash before the roof fell in. Inchdale was aware that Courcey was ruining what was left of the estate. Perhaps Jasper could save the day if he put his mind to it and stopped shagging every girl he set eyes on? As the hotel generator faltered, Inchdale turned out the flickering bedside lamp before it extinguished itself. He lay back in his back and thought how he could engineer Astle's earliest departure. He would talk to the Colonel tomorrow. Inchdale pulled the fusty, damp eiderdown up under his chin and tried to sleep despite the noise emanating from the other side of the bed.

- Chapter 8 -

Nearly an Injustice

The Following Spring...

Inchdale collared the Colonel in his office after he had finished his breakfast (porridge, kedgeree, bucks fizz, fresh fruit). He explained that there had been an unfortunate 'collision of the planets', as Inchdale euphemistically expressed the situation. Lady Inchdale was insisting that Astle be removed from her presence with all due haste. The Colonel confirmed that Astle was booked for only one more day and was due to leave on Saturday morning.

"Can't you get him out before then?" asked Inchdale. "Surely you can make up some story, say the room has been double booked or something?"

"It's all highly irregular Sir Toby, Mr Astle booked his room over six months ago. I'll have a wee think about it and see what I can do," said the Colonel with some relish.

I'll sort the fat Sassenach out, thought the Colonel, but he'd have to be careful. If the money man sussed that Sir Toby had a hand in his dispatch he'd never get paid.

Inchdale's cheques generally bounced a couple of times before clearing but he always got his money in the end. Mr. Astle could stop him getting any cash at all and the erratic weeks of Inchdale money represented the hotel's annual profit. "Well, whatever you do just keep him out of my way will you; I am trying to have a holiday," said Inchdale grumpily as if it was the Colonel's fault.

"That's easier said than done Sir Toby, we have only got one dining room and eighteen bedrooms I can't put him up the glen in a bothy!"

"I am relying on you Colonel. Lady Lavinia can be very difficult as you know!" said Inchdale giving the Colonel a knowing look as if failure signalled an end to Anglo-Caledonian relations. Inchdale stalked off back to his lair.

60

The Colonel was happy to ignore his guests or treat them with a magnificent disdain but he didn't like throwing them out on some trumped up pretence on the whim of an overbearing English aristocrat. Another bloody Sassenach, thought the Colonel after Inchdale had stomped off.

Despite his verbal threats to Astle, the Colonel would never order his ghillie to really harm anyone. Hamish was useful if you needed to put pressure on suppliers or if a guest had become belligerent in the bar. But Astle had been a harmless enough guest until Inchdale arrived. The fat man had fished the worst lochs without complaint. It was only yesterday evening that Astle had become a wee bit uppity, but on the other hand the Colonel had been insufferably rude.

He suspected that Astle would not go quietly. It was a tall order but that was par for the course when it came to Sir Toby Inchdale.

~

Astle had fished gently for the rest of the day catching two smaller fish but his heart was no longer in it. He had achieved what he had come for. The landing of this massive fish was a talisman, a good omen. He made up his mind to leave the next day.

He left the loch at four o'clock and after a short tramp over the heather found his car and drove back to the hotel. As he staggered toward the weighing room with his catch he thought he heard a girl cry out and a man laugh from somewhere upstairs in the hotel. He weighed his fish and laid it out on a white enamel tray. It was nearly two feet in length and weighed four pounds ten ounces. He entered it in the hotel fishing log noting his name, type of fly and size, weather conditions, weight of fish and loch where it was caught. Scanning the pages in the log for that loch Astle was pleased to see that it was the second largest fish ever caught on that piece of water since records began. Afterwards he went up to his room and started packing and then drew himself a hot bath. The water should be reasonably hot as he was ahead of most other guests who normally returned between five and six o'clock.

~

As Jasper lay in bed he looked out of the window and saw the fat man his father had spoken to the previous evening. He was staggering up the gravel path to the rod store and weighing room. He appeared to be carrying something heavy; it had to be a fish. Interesting, he would have a look later. Hermione pulled on his arm, "Aren't I interesting enough for you?" she whispered in his ear pulling his head to hers and kissing him on the lips.

He grunted, holding her kiss and rolled on top of her again. "Just time for another quickie before drinkies time," he said casually as he arched his back to insert himself back inside the wet vagina of the Cape Wrath farmer's bride-to-be.

~

By the time Jasper went to the weighing room the word had spread around the hotel that a big fish had been caught on the Black Loch. There was a crowd of guests peering enviously at the white metal fish tray. There was a sparse collection of smaller fish on adjacent trays that looked pathetic in comparison with the behemoth that Astle had ensnared. Someone was taking a photograph and people were asking who had caught it. The Colonel came storming in looking red faced and worried. "Who caught the monster?" he asked. Someone said: "The fat, quiet bloke from Yorkshire."

"Entwistle or something he's called?" said another guest. "It's a hell of a fish. Is that a record Colonel?"

"I don't bloody know," said the Colonel, stomping off.

"Cheerful soul isn't he?" said another guest jocularly.

The Colonel would normally be very pleased about a big fish. Word spread in fishing circles and it enhanced the hotel's reputation to have record fish caught. If it wasn't taken home by the catcher it would be 'cased' and put up in the hotel bar for hopeful anglers to admire in the years ahead.

The big fish had given the Colonel an idea that should have Astle out of the hotel after breakfast the following morning. He would accuse him of fishing with a worm or a spinner and not a fly - a heinous crime in fly fishing circles. A fish of that size would not normally feed on flies. To gain exceptional weight trout generally become cannibal and fed mostly on other smaller trout, a diet of flies was not enough to sustain their voracious appetites to enable them to grow to such a size.

He would confront Astle with this accusation, hopefully in the privacy of his room or his office. He didn't want to risk an unholy row in the public areas of the Inverhapless. An accusation of this sort was like striking a doctor off the practice register for some unmentionable lapse of the Hippocratic Oath. If Astle refused to leave the Colonel would feed the rumour amongst the hotel guests so that Astle would be socially shunned and forced to depart, a piscatorial pariah.

The Colonel had a couple of whiskies to fortify him before launching his stratagem. He crept down the corridor towards Astle's rear facing room. He knocked timidly. He was in heavy heart about all this, damn Inchdale, he thought, all for the sake of a bloody day. The door opened quickly, Astle was already dressed for dinner; his nearly full suitcase was lying on the bed.

"Canne spare me a wee moment Mr. Astle?" he said firmly.

"Of course, is it about my fish?"

"Aye. What fly did you use to catch that monster trout that's lying on the tray, you conniving thief?" growled the Colonel making a surprise early attack.

"Black Pennell, size 10. I suspect it might be a record... er what did you say, Colonel?" Astle hadn't quite fully understood the Colonel's gruff Scottish patois. Had he called him a thief? He seemed even more hostile than usual. He won't like it when I tell him I am leaving tomorrow, that's bound to make him even angrier, thought Astle.

Suddenly the Colonel spied Astle's nearly packed suitcase and Astle caught his glance.

"Oh yes Colonel," Astle said thinking he had better get this over with now.

"I was going to mention it to you this evening. Er… I have decided to leave a day early, nothing wrong with the hotel, lovely place… I have some er… personal issues that I must attend to back in Yorkshire. Urgent business, I am certain you understand. I will pay for the vacant room naturally. I'll be gone before breakfast, I have to be away at the crack of dawn," Astle blurted the last sentences out.

The Colonel realising that his unpleasant work was now unnecessary, beamed at Astle in relief, "Oh that's wonderful news, very sensible, business before pleasure eh?"

Astle looked puzzled, "You want me to go?"

"Ach no, it's *grand* about your fish. That's why I came up to see you, personal like. Do you want me to have it cased for you? It's a real specimen."

Astle smiled. "Thank you that would be marvellous? Wouldn't you like it for the hotel bar, Colonel?"

"Well aye, but some guests like to have their fish in their own homes, a wee trophy so to speak, something to remind you of days on the lochs at bonnie Inverhapless?"

"Not where I am going," said Astle, not thinking about what he was saying.

"Och, are you off travelling the ocean wave, the colonies perhaps?"

Astle looked embarrassed and then the Colonel looked sheepish too, thinking that perhaps this poor overweight man had some unmentionable life- threatening disease. It was a strange remark to make and the Englishman certainly didn't look too healthy.

"Och, sorry, very tactless of me, my stupid Highland tongue again," said the Colonel backing his way toward the door. 'Dinnae worry about paying for your room tomorrow night, have it on the hoose. A way of exchange for your cased fish, so to speak," said the Colonel almost apologetically as he closed Astle's door and sped off.

Strange blokes these Highlanders, thought Astle, as he straightened his tie. One moment he is all hostile and unpleasant, next he's falling all over himself. It's a wonder what a big fish can do! Astle finished his packing and prepared himself for the endless round of congratulations that was bound to take place as soon as he reached the bar. Funny really, he didn't really want to face them, he just wanted to get back to Yorkshire.

PART 2

- Chapter 9 -

Café Society

The Previous Autumn...

Every Tuesday Marjorie Nelson held court in one of Windelton's small cafes. The town had many calls for charitable works and the community couldn't afford to be without Marjorie's all-embracing largesse. The equation was not difficult to work out: either people put up with her overbearing manner or missed out on her undisputed ability to conjure substantial sums for whatever cause required her patronage. As the saying goes, 'Money talks' and Marjorie Nelson's money talked a lot.

Her group of acolytes consisted of other wives from the moneyed and professional classes of the area. There was a smattering of wealthy farmers' wives and a jolly owner of an agricultural merchant's business. She had unexpectedly inherited a thriving business on the death of her husband from unexplained strychnine poisoning. There were rumours that their marriage had been stormy.

Other members of this select club included textile factory owners' spouses from the West Riding, the local solicitor's young bride and the Windelton doctor's wife. There was even someone whose husband was in the motor trade. She had only passed the 'Marjorie test' because she drove the latest in a line of rather exclusive luxury cars.

Today the ladies of Windelton had bestowed their considerable spending power on 'Susan's Café, located adjacent to the market square. A dry scone, burnt coffee or an impertinent waitress could see the group of up to a dozen ladies upping sticks and removing their custom to another Windelton coffee establishment. This not infrequent occurrence brought joy to any newly visited coffee house proprietor and despair to those out of favour. In a given year each of the town's cafes received its fair share of custom from Marjorie's bulk buying syndicate. The group moved from place to place like migrating Wildebeest in search of a new watering hole and fresh gossip on which to graze.

The subject matter of these coffee morning covens ranged from the price of vegetables, bargain purchases to be made in the sales and the astonishing achievements of their many offspring. The liveliest discussions often focused on life-threatening illnesses and inevitable death. The more lurid the details the better - growths, seizures, organ removals were debated with the same morbid glee. The ladies vied to relate the most graphic tales of ailments and failed treatments of their decaying acquaintances.

As the conversation moved on to its inevitable conclusion the final forensic scrutiny was given to the quality of funeral arrangements. The number of attendees, clothing worn, coffin design, flowers and all the other sorrowful displays of the final chapter came under the microscope of the Windelton coffee-house morticians; no wreath was left unturned or monumental architecture unvalued.

Whatever the Windelton weather might be throwing at its inhabitants outside, inside the current café of choice a fuggy warmth was being generated by the coffee slurping coterie. Their progress was marked by the application and re-application of lipstick, visits to the lavatory (to check lipstick application), scoff homemade cakes and puff on dozens of Du Maurier cigarettes. Confidently large handbags snapped open and shut as the hunt went on for purses, powder compacts and lighters that had become entangled with the previous week's unsettled bills from the town's merchants.

Marjorie Nelson presided over these meetings in the manner that her late father had run his brewery board of directors - with a warm, ruthless charm. She could maintain control of the group providing the participants were no more than nine or ten strong. She always set the agenda for the conversation and introduced the topics for discussion; she picked the local tradesman for scrutiny, chose the subject for the character assassination of the week, in short, Marjorie held court in the palace of her choosing.

If the numbers exceeded the customary near dozen or so participants, danger lurked for Marjorie; occasionally Mrs Hendry, the industrialist's wife who had a villa in the south of France, had been known to form her own dangerous faction with a breakaway table. This diluted Marjorie's power and her grip on the group.

When the orders had been served the conversation soared to deafening levels. Any other unfortunate occupants of the café could not be impervious to this wall of sound. Inevitably, they were either forced into joining one or other of the rival group's conversations whether they liked it or not. Sometimes they just got up and left holding gloved hands over bleeding ears. Most were generally cowed into silence by the baying cacophony as lighters rasped, handbags snapped, coffee cups clattered, cakes were munched, shopkeepers castigated and children lauded.

When Mrs Hendry held forth her subject matter often fell upon her holidays in the south of France. This alien country had yet to be visited by most other members of the café coven. Her stories gripped most listeners with a genuine fascination although some others were sceptical. It meant that Mrs Hendry could extemporise as much as she liked as there was no way of checking what she said was fact or fiction.

"Does she make this all up?" was an often-whispered question. Surely nobody ate garlic-laden mussels and frogs' legs, sun bathed in a two piece swimming costume (despite the racy holiday snaps Mrs Hendry on occasions passed around the group to solidify her stories), availed themselves of those smelly French lavatories and yet still claimed that this was an enjoyable 'holiday'?

Mrs Hendry's grasp of the French tongue still required some tutelage but to the untrained ear it had an undeniably exotic timbre however unauthentic it sounded to the assembled gathering. Mrs Hendry's Home Counties twang (never fully mastered) interspersed with broad Lancashire was a fabrication not missed by her audience. However much Mrs Hendry would like to erase her loom-working family origins her accent enjoyed a curious combination that melded French, Lancashire and the Thames estuary.

French place-names took on an interesting resonance: Marseilles became a strangulated: "MAsays". "Menton" was articulated as: "Meanton" and "Cap Ferat" was just broad North Country dialect: "Cape Ferret." These renderings did nothing to convince the Windelton ladies that they had been missing out on a glorious holiday experience and only served to confirm their prejudices, that Mrs Hendry was an utter fraud.

On this wet, autumn morning, the discussion was focused on the quality of Barrett's Butchers. In particular the quality of Mr Barrett's lamb had come under the searching arc light of the Windelton shoppers.

In the normal way, Marjorie had lit the fuse: "My last week's leg of lamb was no more Yorkshire than my Afghan Hound!" she had announced with her usual authority. "Mother Rose nearly broke her dentures, the poor woman. And the amount of money I spend at that shop every year, it must be a fortune. I am going to have a word with him next time I am in his shop. *And I mean a word!*"

Everyone knew what Marjorie meant about 'having a word'. There would be even be some people in the room that would feel a little sorry for Mr Barrett for he was quite a pleasant fellow and had been recently widowed ('terrible cancer, riddled with it you know, as soon as they had opened her up, nothing they could do, just sewed her back up and she was dead in a fortnight').

"Frozen I would expect and probably from New Zealand" pipes up Katherine Kingcade, the Irish doctor's wife.

"My lamb chops had a Kiwi stamped on the price ticket", interjected Prudence Hill, a tall, thin woman with a reputation for drinking too many Gin and Italians at the golf club and flirting with the club professional.

"Disgraceful, we should go to Naylor's instead", a faint voice chipped in at the end of the table. Sandra Hoskins was the wife of the Town Clerk. She rarely spoke up, preferring to keep quiet and go along with the others. Sandra was a pretty, petite woman who worried that she did not assert herself enough socially. She had been an aspiring ballerina in her day but her husband had not been keen and her youthful

70

ambition was never realised. *'Ballet was the sort of thing people did down south,'* he had told her. She had decided before coming out that morning she would speak up. Her interjection carried some weight, however faint it had sounded, as the others knew that she rarely uttered a word.

"Sandra's right. It might have been mutton; I wouldn't put it passed him? And another thing, those cottage pies of his – they are dreadful, all thatch and no meat," sneered another voice, which could have been from Mrs. Hendry's table. The cauldron of dissatisfaction was being stirred, a consensus of anger was beginning to bubble nicely; the righteous indignation, magnified as memories of past failures fed on one another - tough joints of beef, thin sausages, and poorly cured bacon were thrown on to the bonfire of dissatisfaction.

"Cured, more like wafted," was another barbed comment heard from Mrs Frobisher, the Solicitor's wife, as she emerged from the ladies toilet, wiping her hands on her camel hair skirt, "There's never any Bronco in that damn lav!"

Mrs Kingcade's Irish burr added to the swell of opinion: "I ask you, do you ever get enough fat with your Brisket to make a half decent Yorkshire pudding mixture? It's a scandal, I should tell the doctor to stop giving the man free surgical spirit, he's forever cutting himself with his meat cleaver. He should just let his arms rot, to be sure!"

Once the quality of the produce had been laid to waste, the inventory of vitriol moved up a gear to embrace slanderous character assassination.

Despite her recent departure, the late Mrs. Barrett's reputation as a good mother, the daughter's drinking problems and Mr Barrett's parentage were all vilified, rumour quickly became fact and speculation was soon historical record. Marjorie's army became a unified body. They moved with a sickening pace from the point of not just removing their patronage to being prepared to storm out of the café and torch Mr Barrett's ancient shop. Their righteous indignation had self-combusted into real anger. The mob was ready to do the bidding of their mistress. The middle ages were never far away in Windelton.

71

There seemed little chance that the baying crescendo of hate that had been engineered so subtly by Marjorie Nelson, punctuated by her timely comments and egged on by her hysterical acolytes, could prevent the mob from committing some foul act of retribution upon the unlucky purveyor of fine meats and pies. Mr Barrett's beautiful grade two listed shop and house, still run by a direct ancestor of the founder, Josiah Barrett, who commenced trading in horses' entrails and sheep offal in 1610, was now scheduled to become a charred ruin.

Marjorie, controlling her timing to perfection, her keen senses attuned to the electrifying vein of hysteria that was verging out of control (yet she was secretly thrilled that she had managed to manipulate two tables of Windelton wives and thus outsmarted Mrs. Hendry), characteristically calmed the fever pitch passions with a dose of practical, economic realism.

"Ladies, ladies, ladies, let's not forget, isn't Albert Barrett a generous donor to our Women's Institute Christmas Appeal – he gave us not just one turkey, but three last December *and* doesn't he always throw in a side of ham too?"

"They are always old birds, he can't sell 'em elsewhere," spluttered Mrs. Hendry wanting to demonstrate that she could take control of the asylum if Marjorie Nelson was now backing down. Her head was giddy with emotion.

"They were *capons* not turkeys," she added desperately wanting to keep the drama alive and lead the assault on Barrett's. "I think we should *confront him with our grievances he needs to know who is in charge!*" she added more firmly, her voice was raised and the accent was all Lancashire now.

Nobody responded. The conversation lulled and fizzled to a nervous halt as the café pondered the two women's differing viewpoints. Facts were facts and those turkeys and the ham were often the most sought after prizes in the raffle. They helped sell a lot of tickets in the draw. A free Barrett turkey or ham was worth having.

Heads nodded, Marjorie was right and they didn't want to have another riot like last year when the owner of the cobblers shop had been nearly beaten to death with

72

his own shoes. A. Barrett & Sons, their property, possessions and physical well-being moved slowly out of the danger zone as the assembled throng assimilated Marjorie's sensible reasoning. Everyone knew Mrs Hendry always went too far and she was lucky she hadn't been prosecuted over the cobbler's shop incident. It had been her idea to tie Mr Snod, the proprietor, to the stocks in the market square and throw shoes at him. Mr. Barrett was once again safe – well, for at least for another week!

Marjorie, the café audience now under her complete spell, could get down to the real business of the morning. Her plans had been in preparation for many months and she had been putting the final touches to it in the last few days, now would be the perfect moment to unveil her coup de grace. Her audience was like putty in her hands, such was her command that Marjorie knew that if had she demanded every woman in that café (with the possible exception of Mrs Hendry) throw themselves from the battlements of Windelton castle and plunge, coffee cup in hand, into the moat two hundred feet below, they would obey. This was to be Marjorie's finest hour; her name would last forever in the town's history as the greatest civic benefactor and philanthropist.

Marjorie rose to her feet, her congregation was hushed in silent awe save for the rasp of Mrs Hendry's cigarette lighter as she scrabbled to calm her shattered nerves and quell her humiliation at being outwitted once again by that Nelson woman.

"I decided many, many months ago," she began in a quiet, almost Churchillian tone, "that this town was going to raise its head high and become a focus for the *arts* in our region."

An audible gasp was heard from Prudence Hill as she thought of the possibility of good-looking actors appearing in Windelton.

"Not just for one year, but every year. We need to attract nationally known artistes from the fields of music, ballet and opera; we need to see writers, painters and poets walking our streets."

"What she say?" whispered Mrs Prendergast in disbelief.

73

"Poets?"

"Oh yes," cried Prudence, "I would *love* poets to come to Windelton, just imagine it, Ted Hu…"

"Shhh!" hissed Mrs Trubshaw.

"So I have decided to create a Foundation."

"Foundation garments make my blasted stomach ache, I can never breathe proper," muttered Mrs Hendry who in addition to her foreign tan appeared quite trim for her years. Her secret was out now.

"Can I have quiet please," continued Marjorie magisterially as chairs shifted uneasily on the stone floor. "I plan to raise many thousands of pounds with your help, dear friends," Marjorie's voice rose, "but how will we raise money for this Foundation you might ask and to what purpose?" Marjorie straightened her back, adjusted her mink stole and removing her pink tortoise- shell glasses, she looked around the crowded café, pausing for dramatic effect to ensure absolute attention. As she stared at her audience a small smile played around her mouth as he savoured the moment. She began: "I plan to stage the North of England's foremost and finest festival of arts," she paused again, it will be known as the:

"The Windelton Festival of Arts."

There was an astonished silence as the Windelton ladies absorbed this momentous news. Windelton and the arts, it was the incongruity of the idea that stunned Marjorie's audience. It was like two planets from opposite sides of the solar system colliding in a freak accident of impossible chance. The 'arts' were for people in Bradford and Manchester.

Windelton's answer to the arts was a Gilbert and Sullivan light opera put on once every two years by the Windelton Players. Not even the senior citizens' painting competition supervised by the art master at the secondary modern school could be regarded as 'art'.

"All the funds we raise in OUR festival, and there is going to be plenty of that, rest assured," another gasp from the audience at Marjorie's sublime confidence, "will go towards a *Cottage Hospital* for Windelton inhabitants that I am going to build."

As news sank in there was hushed silence, nobody could fathom the enormity of the idea of a festival of arts *and* the building of a much needed hospital for Windelton. Only the click of handbags opening could be heard as cigarettes were searched for. Suddenly, Mrs Hendry broke the shocked silence. "Which streets will these poets appear on? We don't want any Byron-type rudery in Windelton high street do we?" she piped up feeling that her knowledge of such works might bring some moral authority to her opposition of Marjorie's annoyingly grandiose plans.

There was a collective sigh from the audience. This was not a time for point scoring. Marjorie's plan was the biggest new idea since the sewage works had been built in 1922.

"Marvellous idea," said, Daphne Astle, completely ignoring Mrs Hendry's ill-timed remark. "It's about time Windelton put itself on the map. Some culture would be a wonderful tonic for us all," said Daphne pointedly looking at a defeated Mrs Hendry, "and the hospital would benefit us all too. I am all for it Marjorie."

"I agree," said Penelope Seedman. "Nobody cares about my Simon's acne. The Windelton wind spreads the most terrible diseases, you just don't know where it comes from do you? We get a lot of Lancashire air here," she said looking pointedly at the deflated Mrs Hendry. "There are a lot of foreigners living over there these days," she glanced over her shoulder anxiously as if expecting some germs to come flying through the doorway at any moment.

"Thank you Daphne and Penelope for your support." Marjorie continued, "My plan is to convert the old TB hospital into the Marjorie Nelson Cottage Hospital. The County Council are behind my plans and have promised to help with the funding."

Suddenly there was a scraping of chairs on the stone floor and three Windelton ladies spontaneously jumped to their fat feet and started to applaud loudly. Then as one with the exception of Mrs Hendry, who had to be pulled up by the diminutive

Mrs Hoskins, who had decided to assert herself once again (twice in one day, she really was making progress!), they were all on their feet.

There were calls of "Bravo," and "She's jolly good lady," accompanied by wild cheering and more applause and some weeping too.

The noise from inside the café was so great that PC Robson who happened to be passing on his bicycle en route to the bank in answer to a robbery alarm call pulled up his machine with a squeal of brakes and put his head inside the front door, "Everything alright in here Susan?" he addressed the café proprietor who had retreated into the café lobby the noise being so great in the central tea room.

"It's alright Constable, everything is safe."

"Thank God for that! We don't want another carry-on like that Mr Snod business last year; he's only just out of hospital."

PC Robson mounted his bicycle with a thin smile of relief and slowly pedalled his way towards Murchison's Bank and his next rendezvous with crime.

As the applause died away Marjorie continued in serious vein. "I am going to need your help in enabling this mammoth undertaking to succeed. I will be in touch with you all soon about forming an Action Committee. In the meantime the press must be informed of my... *our* plans." Another round of applause followed. "But no more questions for the moment please, I have so many important things to sort out."

The Windelton ladies parted as one to clear a path to the café doorway for their hero to exit in a triumphant march. If there had been a laurel wreath to hand it would have been slung over her neck.

"Would you settle my coffee bill please Mrs Hendry, you know I never carry money?" she commanded imperiously as she swept passed her dazed rival.

"There are newspaper editors to brief!" was her parting remark as she strode purposefully in the direction of Harry Webster's office at the Windelton Bugle.

~

By the time Astle had left the Inverhapless Hotel early on Friday morning he had acquired a semi-hero status on account of his magnificent trout and the unassuming deference that he had displayed at this once-in-a-lifetime achievement. He had also acquired a throbbing headache that was a central part of the hangover that would accompany him for most of his journey as he drove southwards.

Astle had settled his bill with the Colonel's red-haired daughter earlier in the evening and before he was waylaid in the bar by the hotel guests. Astle was surprised at his own popularity for something that he had achieved by good fortune and not by duplicity. There was a lesson for him there but he failed to appreciate its significance.

At six o'clock the following morning Astle sped out of the car park spitting gravel and awakening Hermione who was sleeping fitfully in Jasper's bed. She sat up and watched the black Morris disappear into the distance on the road south, the early morning light just touching the slopes of Ben Orr'ful, briefly illuminating the heather and throwing shadows across the high corries. She spied some sheep grazing on closely cropped grass close to the shore of the loch and her thoughts guiltily turned to her fiancée. She knew that he would already be putting out extra fodder for the few animals that he had on pasture close to the headland of Cape Wrath. If he discovered her infidelity he would have most certainly killed them both. He hated the English with a vengeance. She shuddered with fear and got back into bed and clasped her arms around Jasper's naked back and clutched him for warmth and security. She knew he didn't love her but she couldn't help herself. Jasper had been the first when she was fifteen years old and somehow you never forgot that initial moment of glorious pain.

~

Astle was both excited and afraid; the whisky still flowed around his blood stream and exaggerated his moods. He had a rendezvous with a telephone box in

West Bistorp on *Saturday* lunchtime and he had over four hundred miles to drive in a day and a half.

He would just have to surprise Daphne when he got home a day earlier than planned. It was unlikely that either she or her pet poodle, 'Overdraft,' would be excited by his unexpected return. She would be at her clairvoyant's on Saturday afternoon as this was the usual time of her weekly visit to 'Destiny with the Stars'. Daphne liked to go while Astle was playing golf. Despite Astle endlessly quizzing Daphne, the clairvoyant never predicted the result of his golf matches.

As Astle drove over the river Carron at Bonar Bridge, he thought wistfully of his favourite Saturday dinner of sausages and mashed potatoes that awaited him the following evening. It was an oddly comforting thought and a welcome relief from cod and mutton. As the creaking Morris headed towards Inverness his head continued to experience the occasional searing stab of pain. His bowels groaned and a dangerous state of nausea was increasing in intensity by the mile. He would be sick if he didn't eat some breakfast soon. Just on the outskirts of Dingwall he spied a wooden hut sporting a breakfast sign and pulled the car off the road. Forty minutes later, sustained by two mugs of tea, a massive fry up and an extended visit to a filthy outside lavatory that had a large discharge pipe pointing into the Cromarty Firth, he was back on his journey. He felt immeasurably better and he decided he would stay overnight in the Borders. With an early start on Saturday morning he would be at West Bistorp for a drink at the pub where he would put in his call to Valerie.

~

Some days after Astle's departure another hasty exit from the Inverhapless hotel occurred but for entirely different reasons. The Inverhapless barman, enjoying his day off, happened to overhear a conversation between two Cape Wrath locals in a Durness pub. That same evening, back on duty at the hotel, the barman quietly informed Jasper that the Cape Wrath farmer had rumbled his fiancée's activities. Hermione's infatuation was an open secret amongst hotel staff. "Aye you'll need to watch your back, that man has a foul, foul temper," he warned Jasper with a grim expression. Jasper bought the barman a large scotch.

Jasper had not seen Hermione for a few days to verify this rumour as she had been away staying with friends at Brora. He quickly decided that caution was better course than valour. He 'phoned a friend at his office and instructed him to send him a telegram with an urgent request to return to his office. Waving his telegram, he made his fictitious excuses to his parents and dashed to Garve station and the morning train to Inverness. After boarding he caught a glimpse of a burly, flame haired young man in a kilt running up and down the platform. He had a glistening woodman's axe. Jasper hid himself in the train toilet and didn't emerge until he heard the carriages creak and groan as they pulled out of the station.

- Chapter 10 -

A bedtime story

That night as Astle lay in bed his mind was filled with images of heavy trucks lumbering towards him, sheep and lashing rain. He had reached Jedburgh a little after seven. He had been driving for over thirteen hours. At the coaching inn where he was staying he'd consumed a barely passable dinner accompanied by jugs of clear Scottish tap water and then retired to bed exhausted. But now he was too tired to sleep, the heavy venison pie had refreshed his jaded senses and he cast his mind back to his last phone call to Valerie nearly two weeks ago.

On the pretext of buying the Sunday newspapers and having a drink Astle drove each Sunday morning the four miles from Windelton to a pub at West Bistorp. He arrived promptly at 12 noon, drank two half pints of Bainbridge bitter, walked down the road to the phone box on the green and phoned Valerie. He spent fifteen minutes on the 'phone and was back at number 32 Lime Tree Road on the dot at one fifteen for his Sunday lunch. It was as near Astle came to religious habit.

His last call to Valerie was typical in every respect - desultory. It hinted at nothing new, no change in the balance of their respective private lives.

After five rings Valerie picked up the receiver.

"Hello Whitley 236."

"Hello it's me."

"Hello me," she replied. This always annoyed Astle although it was said in a friendly way.

"Why do you always say that, you know I don't like it?"

"Now, don't get in a state Gerald."

"I am *not* getting in a state. How is James, is his cold better?"

"Yes, he is fine. He did well in some tests at school. He's getting very proficient at arithmetic. Must be taking after his dad?"

Astle choked when he heard anything good about his unseen son.

"Oh… that's wonderful!" Astle always enquired anxiously about his bastard son that he'd never clapped eyes on. He didn't even have a picture of him. And his son was blissfully unaware that his father was a respectable manager of a bank.

"You've got your money?"

"Of course! If it hadn't come, Gerald, you would be the first to know." Valerie received a weekly payment from an offshore bank account that Astle set up many years ago. This money was to ensure that Valerie and his issue were financially secure. Astle didn't consider these payments as 'hush money' but a more sceptical observer might draw this conclusion. Their dialogue followed a familiar, well-trod path week by week; miraculously the fifteen minutes passed with remarkable speed.

"Valerie, I will won't be calling next Sunday as I am away fishing in Scotland but I will call again on the following Sunday. Okay?"

"Of course it's okay. Enjoy yourself. Is Daphne going with you?"

"Good God no!"

The routine of these calls enjoyed a sense of timeless permanence, rather like birthdays and Christmases. Their anticipation was more pleasurable then the event. Valerie always sat on her favourite antique ladder-back chair in the dark hallway of her terrace house. The chair was immensely comfortable, the wood worn from age and it fitted her shapely, firm buttocks perfectly. It made her feel enclosed and safe; the hugging contours were faintly erotic and Valerie would push her long auburn hair back behind her left ear, the receiver pressed close and she would shut her eyes to listen dreamily to Astle's slightly breathless, rasping voice as he took her through his week's news.

The tedium of it was comforting and she would occasionally run her hand over her breasts until she felt her nipples stiffen in arousal, she closed her eyes and thought of a gorgeous man she had once seen in Windelton in a little sports car. She imagined him touching her very gently. The man had lovely hands with a light covering of red hair. In this way the time quickly slipped passed, however banal Astle's conversation became.

Over the last eight years Astle sensed that the underlying intimacy to their conversations, that unspoken bond that once existed, had gradually seeped away and their dialogue, whilst friendly, had become more a matter of routine. Astle was tortured by the belief that it was only the necessity of the weekly money that motivated Valerie's muted adherence to the telephone routine. Every week Astle hoped he would have the courage to break free of his shackled conformity, if only briefly, to reawaken the heated intensity that he had once experienced in her bed. He never told her that he loved her or he thought about her every day. Somehow he couldn't bring himself to say the words. As the years passed his resolve became weaker and weaker.

Why he'd never once demanded to see his only offspring and why hadn't Valerie ever offered the infant to him? The answers to both questions were governed by an unspoken mutual fear. The bizarre arrangement they had connived suited both parties and they were both afraid of the consequences if the status quo was broken. Each time Astle inserted his fat fingers into the telephone dial to call the mother of his son he trembled at the danger of his actions.

Astle's secrets were not like those of his customers, tucked away in deed boxes in Murchison's Bank cellars. His hidden treasures were just twenty-five miles away from Windelton in a little terrace house in Whitley.

~

Astle's childless wife, Daphne was a long lost object of desire. She persevered with her husband in a marriage that was as exciting as dry toast. It was a sad, empty existence punctuated by meals, sleep and her clairvoyant. Astle and Daphne were like distant friends that met on odd occasions. An ambivalent tolerance existed between them. She maintained a guarded acceptance of her husband's contemptuous abuse and fabulous indifference. She felt sorry for Astle. He had no real friends and few interests other than the golf club; even there he was always falling out with some club member. And he never spoke about his mysterious visits to the Masonic Hall. She wasn't sure whether he enjoyed whatever they did in that dark building in the market square. He often returned late at night, grasping his little leather satchel, rather flushed and sometimes inebriated.

Daphne had neither the inclination nor the courage to ask. Occasionally he awoke shouting, 'Valerie! Valerie!' when he appeared to have been having some nightmare. Daphne always presumed it was one of Astle's more trying customers. He was always moaning about how demanding Marjorie Nelson was. One of Marjorie Nelson's phone calls guaranteed Astle would come home puce with fear and in a foul temper. On these occasions she tried to keep well out of the way. The Women's Institute was often an escape or perhaps a trip to the good looking dentist. He was very soothing and sympathetic but it was often difficult to get an appointment as he was always so busy. Alternatively, it was a trip to the clairvoyant.

Daphne's father had been a Methodist minister and alcohol was never consumed in their household. He was so strict that he even served Ribena at communion in the chapel. Matters of a sexual nature were never discussed.

She grew up believing that the act of procreation was the joyless duty of womankind and hope it passed quickly. Any suggestion of enjoyment was mortal sin. It had surprised Daphne that at the outset of her marriage she found 'doing it' was not the hideous experience she had been led to believe but quite pleasurable. She felt for the first time in her life, womanly. It had provided her with an unexpected sense of joyful fulfilment. However, even in their salad days she was secretly haunted by the notion that having sex more than once a month was wicked. Astle was never happy to settle for a monthly routine. She believed that her forced compliance would incur God's wrath, either now or at some indeterminate future date. Daphne spent the early years of her marriage in a state of nervous preparedness, always on the alert for signs of her personal retribution.

Sadly Daphne had no-one to discuss these irrational terrors. Astle was uncommunicative and at the same time demanding as he took a vigorous approach to love-making. On one occasion while holidaying in Filey, perhaps charged by the sea air and an unexpected spell of warm weather, they had committed the unmentionable act three times in one week. She remembered being rather sore and uncomfortable by the end of the holiday. The cause was probably a mixture of sand coupled with Astle's exertions but Daphne was convinced that the discomfort was a dire warning from the Almighty. This clear manifestation of sin put her off the idea of love making for weeks afterwards, much to Astle's bafflement and annoyance.

Nobody broached the subject with Daphne that the sexual act could be a pleasurable experience and her worries of turning into some sort of 'doxy' alarmed her. The headmistress of her girls' boarding school had warned her about becoming a 'wanton harlot'. She cringed with embarrassment when Daphne thought what she might have said had she witnessed the licentious pleasures she had experienced during her seaside holiday.

She couldn't remember if it was Astle's reluctance, rather than her indifference to him that slowly turned the tap of their love off from a trickle of affection into the enforced drought. It seemed to Daphne that it all started going wrong about eight years ago. She hadn't the courage to ask Astle why their infrequent love-making had ceased altogether; she thought it might be one of those 'men problems' that she had read about in Women's Realm which seemed to be prevalent with middle aged men. She hoped to succeed in conceiving a child. She visited her local doctor. After the briefest of examinations that had involved taking her temperature and checking her blood pressure, he confidently declared that one day either nature or God would smile upon her and she would be delivered of the child she so longed for.

At the age of forty-one Daphne had badgered Astle into seeing a private gynaecologist who informed her that she had a fallopian tube blockage and there was no hope at her age of curing the problem. Had she been to see him five years earlier the issue could have been sorted out with a routine surgical procedure. "I am so sorry," the consultant had said, "Why didn't you come to see me before? By the way, who is your local GP?"

"Doctor Kingcade at the Windelton surgery," she had replied. The specialist rolled his eyes and politely bade Daphne a sympathetic and hurried farewell.

Daphne's priorities had by now changed; she began to look forward to Astle's pension. She was convinced that he would not live long after his retirement and then she would be free to come and go as she pleased. Her clairvoyant had spelled it all out to her some months ago. "The future looks bright Mrs Astle, your husband will be going away to a far off place quite soon," she had predicted with some certainty, "Oh yes, he will be travelling across the great divide, I can't quite see where yet but it will be quite soon, I can feel the vibrations … there's movement and change ahead for you both. I see a small boy?" The fortune teller seemed to get exhausted at this point and stopped.

Daphne interpreted this vision of the future as a polite euphemism for her husband's demise. "I see a lot of money," the fortune teller suddenly piped up again before finally falling silent. Daphne became excited at this point although she hadn't he faintest idea of what Gerald's pension was actually worth. She rubbed her hands with excitement and shifted her round bottom in the upright chair on which she always sat during her 'readings'.

Daphne knew that her husband needed to reach his full retirement age to be sure of a full pension pay out and Astle needed a model wife to maintain his status and probity within the Windelton community. They both needed one another. It was an image that they played out convincingly in the public arena. A divorce was unthinkable. Astle would be scratched from the golf club, barred from the Masonic lodge and the Bank would retire him early *without* his full pension rights.

~

Astle awoke late and refreshed in his Scottish Borders hotel. After a hurried breakfast of cereals, (he eschewed the kippers) he headed the black Morris southward toward Carter Bar and England.

As he ground the gears and gunned the heavy car up the steep hills of the Cheviots, the phantom of Valerie Harper filled Astle's thoughts. He couldn't deny his carnal longings to recreate the sexual act with her again. The memory of her young, firm-muscled body lingered. It had been the only time in his life that he had been to bed with a woman, that to his astonishment, enjoyed sex. She had wanted him for being him!

"Bugger, bugger and damn," Astle cursed out loud to himself in his frustration for being so cowardly. Some women might be impressed with the trappings of being a bank manager but he knew that was not Valerie's motivation. She had to have felt *something* for him? Whatever Valerie's motivations, Astle now knew he had to finish the weekly telephone charade forever! He was convinced that the portentous letter from Head Office meant that the game was up, they were on to him and time was running out.

As the car descended toward England Astle relived the passion and the abandoned feelings that Valerie had unleashed in that sparse little bedroom in Hickleton. The curtains had been drawn but the strong five o'clock July sunshine had penetrated the thin, unlined fabric of the curtains; he remembered the soft yellow hue that the light cast onto the faded patterned wallpaper. The dying heat of the day, Urdu voices intermingled with the sound of children playing cricket out in the road, Valerie's skin luminescent with a film of perspiration and her shapely, voluptuous body resting against his.

He swerved violently around a bend as the car entered Otterburn narrowly missing a group of cyclists, an awkward tumescence stirred deep down in his twill trousers. Astle couldn't recall the sequence of events that culminated in him being in her bedroom. It was like being the victim of a serious road accident. He sensed that he had asked Valerie to witness some deed at the bank. Somehow he had forgotten to get her signature and her name had been typed in the witness position on the paper. Then she was on holiday at home and Astle needed the document signing for some odious customer.

He'd had to look up her address in the Kelly's street directory. Thinking about it now he would be pushed to remember where it was. It had once been a large Victorian villa now divided into pokey flats. The suburbs all looked the same in those West Riding mill towns. He did remember she was wearing a pretty summer cotton frock and wore bare legs and sandals, quite unlike her normal drab office garb.

At the beginning of Astle's two hour love-odyssey with Valerie he was beset by an all-consuming guilt. Eventually, lust gnawed away its edges until it was replaced by a desire so strong that obliterated everything else. At first, he had huddled, trembling with fright and latent desire between the cool sheets. Gently, Valerie had taken him in her arms, whispered words to him, teased, touched and stroked him; she had suggested sexual acts that she would like to commit with him, acts Astle had never dared think about.

She demanded *his* attention to satisfy *her* needs. This was completely new territory for Astle. Daphne was utterly compliant and completely undemonstrative during sex; she never spoke and only cried out if Astle penetrated her too quickly. For Astle the sexual act with Daphne was like lying on top of a soft, white fish. It was all Astle had ever experienced. He had never participated in the mutual sharing and pleasure of physical contact before. Valerie was affectionate, soothing and later demanding. It was only when she had grasped hold of his straining penis that he realised after all these years of working together that she must have harboured unspeakable longings. She had *desired* him. Even now, he still couldn't quite believe it. At the moment of his ejaculation he thought he would die of joy there and then; life was never going to get better than that moment. And it never did.

What had been the trigger point that had made Valerie flick the switch from formal secretary to ardent lover? He remembered when there had been times when a smile given had been held; when she had shot him a direct look that he had never dared to fully return. Their language had always been formal, controlled like Daphne's pressure cooker, but there had been another currency being traded just below the surface. Sometimes, after dictating correspondence there would be a few moments of conversation; she would ask questions about his home, up-bringing, previous jobs. Valerie never quite flirted; she just showed an interest in the interminable, mundane life that he endured with Daphne.

He could still remember the shock when she took his hand in hers and led him into the bedroom.

"What are you doing?" he said weakly, realising that something uncontrollable was about to happen.

"You are going to do as *I tell you* for a change, Gerald. This has been a long time coming," she smiled at him and led him gently into her bedroom. The yellow curtains were already drawn.

"Get undressed and hurry up."

Astle, wasn't used to obeying women's orders but he complied meekly with Valerie's insistent request. She quickly removed her summer dress to reveal nothing underneath. She slipped under the covers and Astle caught a glimpse of her white firm buttocks and generous breasts.

His mouth was dry as he removed his jacket, looking for somewhere to hang it up.

"Throw it on the floor Gerald, for God's sake!" Valerie said urgently.

He did as he was told but still was struggling with his braces that were tangled around his feet. He fell onto the bed just managing to get his trousers off in time. Laying on the bed with his woollen underpants his cock suddenly flared into life.

"Is that all for me?" Valerie asked with a giggle. "Come here you lovely oaf!"

Astle's eyes half closed as he remembered the moment. Maybe she just felt like going to bed with a man and he happened by? Astle thought as he eased back the Morris to a safer speed.

Soon afterwards a series of events conspired to separate them. Astle was moved to Windelton to take over the branch after the premature death of the previous manager, Mr Prendergast. Then Valerie, in a masterstroke of subterfuge, announced her 'retirement' from the bank. Astle's own departure had made the perfect excuse and she left before anyone got wind that she was pregnant.

Once Astle was installed in his new position he had more time to consider what he might do. He set up the covert payments and arranged to telephone her every week. Then he did nothing.

"How bloody stupid can you be, man?" he said to himself as if he was addressing one of his farming customers at the bank. "All these years of passive exchanges, empty telephone calls…" Would she countenance renewing their relationship and throwing up her life in Whiteley or had he been deluding himself these last eight years?

He wailed in frustration, his eyes welled up with tears as he saw the wasted years that had passed him by, lost because of his straight-jacket conformity to the rules… rules… rules.

"BLOODY MOTHER" he shouted. "IT'S ALL YOUR BLOODY FAULT!"

- Chapter 11 -

Lost on the Golf Course

The landlord of the Nags Head in Windelton knew how to keep his customers happy. He served well kept ales and installed a payphone in the pub's entrance lobby where his regulars could place bets with the bookies in the market square. On Saturday afternoons this kept the clientele in the pub until closing time at 3pm. They sat around or stood with backs propped against the bar wall watching the racing from Sandown Park on the black and white TV in the corner. Their ears tuned to the honeyed tones of Peter O'Sullivan, the BBC's racing correspondent, while they supped, smoked, studied the racing form, swore and occasionally celebrated.

Ian Henderson, true to form, had placed a modest each way bet on the first race of the day and was sampling a creamy pint of Bainbridge Best Bitter. Work was over and his weekend started here. Two pints, a quick punt on the horses, a chat to mates at the bar; superficially life seemed to be treating Ian well. But it wasn't; it was treating him very badly and he didn't know why.

Neither Ian's career nor his marriage was going according to plan.

Well, he didn't really have a plan, rather a rough idea of certain positions he should attain on his career path. Ian wasn't a desperately ambitious man but he did possess a strong competitive spirit and he expected to progress in the things he undertook. Like his golf and his marriage it followed suit that his career should follow a steady upward trajectory. Instead he was becalmed. Everything had been going fine until about three years ago when his promotion prospects seemed to falter.

Ian now inhabited static ground in his banking career. He had been overlooked for a fast track career in a big city office. The promise he had shown in his early 20s, appeared through an imperceptible process of osmosis, to have vanished. Now, after three years of being marooned in his own career Sargasso Sea, he realised that

Murchison's Bank Windelton was a dry dock, a backwater of finance where his tide of ambition was permanently out.

Small mindedness, low esteem and a head-down mentality were choking the irrigation channels to greater things. Often, in the smaller of the bank's branches, a culture aspired to hurry forward retirement and collect one's pension as quickly as possible. With some bank employees this level of insidious thinking started at about age twenty-five and was fostered by longer serving colleagues who were closer to realising the dull glow of their release date. The longer they served, the closer they were to playing golf every day until death parted them from their clubs. Like 'lifers' in a prison, Ian's work colleagues knew how to work the system and were resigned to the institution that was mapping their future. *Better hang on to what you have got rather than kick the paymaster,'* was the prevailing attitude of mind. And once employees were shackled with the handcuffs of cheap mortgages their full term of service was nearly inevitable.

Safe, steady and visionless was what the bank expected of the majority of their captives. It was the mantra of their employment, the unwritten terms and conditions of their contracts. Ian saw it and so did his wife, Dawn.

Two children too late, Dawn realised that her choice of good-looking banker, the popular young man with a three golf handicap who had shown so much early promise, looked like a racing certainty that had suddenly gone lame. His ready laughter and devil-may-care attitude was slowly being worn away by his frustration and failure to progress; he blamed the Bank's shortcomings for not recognising his talents.

Ian's file at the Lombard Street headquarters had identified his potential abilities - good GCE 'O' level passes plus a couple of reasonable 'A' levels that nearly took him to university. These were regarded as above average for a junior trainee in the late 1950s when he joined. The bank's net caught those applicants whose parents were unable to afford either the cost of university fees or to fund joining a professional firm as an articled clerk in accountancy or a law practice. The starry-eyed potential of earning £200 per annum on entering the Bank and rising to the dizzy heights of £350 a year after one year of service was an attractive carrot to a bright young grammar school pupil from an impecunious background. With the benefit of hindsight he should have considered estate agency, it had been his second choice. Quite a few of the candidates that the bank rejected on their 'brighter than average' intake followed this career path; people like Trubshaw's son who was short on grey matter but heavy on bonhomie. Ian never believed that he possessed enough of the chameleon characteristics required to fully embrace the suspect estate agency world.

He was always amazed how some employees of the classier estate agents started to adopt the airs and graces of their wealthier clients. Such was their intoxication with country houses and the landed gentry they started to behave as if *they* owned the properties they were managing or selling. Indeed some were so successful at this ploy that they ended up marrying the daughters of clients they represented and mimicked. As time passed, the same estate agents forgot their humble lineages and started to dress like squires and even bray like them. Some went further and ended up residing in decaying country seats or 'rather agreeable town houses'. And now these same estate agents looked down on the country bankers like Ian Henderson and Gerald Astle. The bankers responded to this inflated snobbery with disdainful envy.

"No better than horse thieves," Astle would say when calculating a particularly loathsome and successful local estate agent's six monthly bank charges. "Bloody… stuck-up… bugger!" was Astle's regular refrain when calculating the six monthly charges on his three podgy fingers, "Add three extra guineas to his charges Mr. Firth."

"Of course Mr. Astle," replied the branch accountant, wondering how he would ever look the senior partner of Trubshaw & Trubshaw (Purveyors of properties of distinction to the gentry and nobility since 1949) in the eye at the next Masonic Lodge meeting.

Early on in Ian's marriage, and at a crucial point in his career when a senior clerk's position was in the offing, Ian had turned down an invitation to join the Windelton Masonic Lodge. Pressure from his wife and the imminent arrival of their first child had been the genuine reasons he had given to the Lodge Secretary. Dawn wanted nothing to come in the way of their married life together; she wanted Ian by her side to help bring up their first baby. She had no idea that this seemingly innocent rejection would be the start of Ian's decline in fortunes.

"What am I going to do on Wednesday evenings when you are out playing secret societies and *our* baby wants bathing?" was Dawn's irrepressible logic. The question seemed reasonable, irrefutable in fact; yet Ian suspected he may be missing more than just meeting a load of blokes in strange clothes in a candle lit hall. There was another dimension to the Masons he sensed rather than understood. There was something more important going at the square Lodge building – influence, recognition, being known in the area as a chap to watch, one of *them*.

The previous manager of the bank was Mr. Prendergast, affectionately known, as 'Old Prendy,' had taken to Ian from the start, recognising the young man's promise – intelligent, personable and keen to learn and with a pretty young wife at his side. He sought Ian out to explain some of the Bank's more arcane procedures, invited him to his exclusive pre-Christmas drinks party at his mausoleum of a house and occasionally asked Ian to join him for a round of golf, although not too often as Ian showed little mercy on the course, irrespective of his opponent's exalted status.

When Prendergast had heard that the offer to join the lodge had been rejected (although Ian didn't know Prendy had initiated the approach) he spoke to him gently asking him to reconsider. It would be of real value in his job, not just in Windelton but wherever he went with the bank. Ian didn't ask Dawn again, as he knew what the answer would be.

Prendy's attitude to Ian slowly changed: there was a polite frostiness between them, the golf stopped and the pre-Christmas drinks invitation dried up. He was quietly frozen out until everything went stone cold when dear old Prendy had a massive brain haemorrhage. Ian's old mentor and patron had now deserted him forever. Friends at the golf club also seemed less effusive although he was hard to ignore. His good looks, easy charm and formidable prowess on the course made Ian someone worth knowing. He played a better game than the resident professional who secretly harboured a grudge against Ian. The club professional refused even to play a four ball against him in case he was humiliated. People talked about Ian becoming a professional player, a secret desire he nurtured but one which he never confided to others and certainly not to Dawn.

As the years slipped by the golf career dream faded away from unlikely to outright impossibility. And with it Ian's frustration grew into a silent, secret rage, thundering underneath his placid demeanour. He controlled his anger, never letting it spill into the public persona of his life. Corking a volcano of impatience and curbing a rising panic contributed to turning his saturnine dark hair to a premature grey. His golf handicap slipped, the career curve got steeper and he felt like a man trying to climb an oil-covered conveyor belt.

He had purchased his house with a low-cost bank loan which enabled him to buy a better property than many of his contemporaries at an equivalent age and career trajectory. Now handcuffed by a cheap mortgage and two young children Ian felt trapped. And few alternative employers regarded the junior management skills acquired in a bank to be of much use. His only transferrable asset was high-speed note counting which might come in handy either working for a bookie or as a bank robber's accomplice.

The birth of their second daughter, Mary, was a trigger point. Ian had estimated a steady succession from Branch Accountant by age thirty, Deputy Manager by around forty, manager of a small branch perhaps mid to late forties and either a city office position or maybe a spell in regional office before his retirement at sixty five. His career mapped out, carry on Henderson your life's all sorted out. But, whoohay, the reality was that he was still only a senior clerk and nearly thirty four!

Panic rose like bilge in his gut as Ian ran through his frustrations in his mind recognising that he was already two postings behind where he ought to be.

~

Dawn realising that her husband's career in the bank was not progressing had gently broached the subject with him but Ian refused to discuss the situation. His pride would not let him admit to Dawn that his career was in a cul-de-sac.

She put it to the back of her mind hoping it would all come out alright even if it took a little longer than anticipated. Dawn was now absorbed by their second child, Mary, then not yet a year old. She loved this precious, pink bundle with her blue eyes and straw blond hair.

Abigail their first-born was three. She was a lively, good natured child but was very much her own person. Ian had already formed a special bond with her. When he was feeling down one glimpse of her lifted his spirits and pushed his worries aside. Ian felt his life was divided and full of contradictions. He had gained two daughters in name and lost a wife in the process. Dawn was entranced with her beautiful girls.

She was an only child, and whilst loved by her parents, had experienced little companionship while growing up. Ian had filled this gap, both as a friend and later as a loving husband. Ian had awakened passions she hadn't realised she possessed. And that arousal in turn agitated a desire in Dawn, triggered soon after she first met Ian, and finally confirmed at the birth of her first child, for a better life from that of her parents. Dawn's father had been a railway signalman and her mother worked part-time in a wire making factory; neither desired to be more than they were, nor did they bear malice at their lot in life. When Dawn was growing up her father worked industriously during the summer evenings and at weekends in his allotment to supplement the meagre post-war rations. They were a contented family, channelling their love and energy to their only daughter. They had wished Dawn, rather than steered her, into taking a secretarial training course. It was Dawn that really made the choice; her strong desire to get on and move herself up a notch in life motivated her ambitions.

She had met Ian at school but he was two years her senior. She had goggled at him from afar without him being aware of her presence. She passed the eleven plus and after grammar school enrolled on a typing course and went to College to complete an advanced Pitman secretarial course. Dawn courted success and love in equal measure. She saw it as a rite of passage. She wanted to replicate the unconditional love that her parents had given her. But she also desired something else. *Respect* was what Dawn craved: for what she was, what she had achieved, she did not want to lord it over others but she also hated to be patronised or ignored. She was proud of her husband and her children; Dawn Henderson was not just a secretary who had married a handsome banker with a great golf handicap, she was a person to be noticed in her own right. She was a successful mother and homemaker.

But the banker had surprised her by not fulfilling his part of Dawn's own ambitions. Suddenly the prospect of being the successful 'Bank Manager's Wife,' began to look a long way off. Her children sustained her but as time moved on Ian's salary failed to match all their needs. At first Dawn cut down on unnecessary luxuries: new clothing for Dawn was forfeited to pay the costs of private ballet lessons, swimming and birthday parties. She gave up smoking.

As Ian's employment grades failed to go up, so his salary increases were only inflationary; occasionally the bank trade unions won some paltry increase in basic wages or secured fewer working hours. But working less didn't help pay the bills and only left Ian more time to think why he was failing to climb the management ladder. Ian's annual golf subscriptions fell under Dawn's scrutiny:

"Why can't you become a weekend member? The money is for *your* children you know." The thought was too horrendous to consider, he had had a seven day subscription since the age of nine.

The pressure made itself felt in the bedroom too. Ian's passion for making love wearing his golf shoes was a privilege withdrawn. "Grow up Ian, we can't afford more ripped sheets," was Dawn's tight-lipped reply to his Saturday night ritual.

Trips to the Golf Pro Shop at the club became less frequent. Ian always liked to browse around the little shop that adjoined the clubhouse as much to marvel at the absence of any decent stock than to make any purchases. The club professional was not only a very poor golfer but an even worse retailer. His modest store often lacked even the most basic equipment like golf balls or tees. Occasionally, some really good brand name items would appear in the shop at bargain basement prices that made members suspicious of their provenance. Ian couldn't stand the inconsistency of everything and was obliged, like most of the other club members, to purchase much of his equipment from a major golf shop inconveniently located twenty-five miles away.

Ian was amazed by the demands of providing an ever expanding inventory of toys, dresses, riding lessons and special outings that Dawn insisted that their children should have by right, irrespective of costs. She was always meticulous in itemising the children's needs and the associated costs were planned in a weekly budget. The problem was Dawn's beautifully coherent plans always exceeded Ian's meagre income.

Ian tried to face up to his own shortcomings. He seemed to be hemmed in by the tyranny of modern living in the 1960s - the sudden abundance and the necessity for endless new consumer goods. The only way that Ian could possibly afford to fulfil his wife's dreams would be to resort to living on secretly arranged credit along with the rest of the population. And it was only a few years ago that the Prime Minister had been telling him, "That you had never had it so good." Somehow it didn't seem that way to Ian.

~

At just before five o'clock Astle had parked his car discreetly off the village green of West Bistorp, just around the corner from the telephone box. He stiffly emerged from the Morris, its bonnet was hot to touch after the long trek south but the old car had served him well. He was going to telephone Valerie. He had formulated a plan for them both but now faced with the reality of communicating his coup de fou, his stomach churned and he felt light headed. His hands shook as he grappled the heavy GPO telephone and started to feed the coins into the box. He dropped two pennies on to the concrete floor and spent some minutes bent uncomfortably trying to retrieve them. Finally he dialled the number.

- Chapter 12 -

The Vulgarity of Commerce

Jasper Inchdale, Sir Toby's second son, recognised that the family seat would never become his inheritance nor would family money sustain him. He had two options: marry someone rich or get a job.

The former alternative was not promising. The pools of nubile girls in the Windelton district with sufficient money to sustain any half-decent lifestyle were few and far between. There was no shortage of thick-set, earthy 'gels' that had enjoyed a private school education rounded off with a spell in a Swiss finishing school. The problem was that the majority of these worthy and well-bred contenders would fail to get 'best in class' in the dray horse competition at Windelton show. As Lady Inchdale would often perceptively remark, "Lovely family dear, but the daughter's rather plain."

Jasper decided to break with eight centuries of family tradition and make his way in the world of commerce. It was a move born out of necessity. This blinding realism pleased Sir Toby and appalled his mother. She regarded the idea of work anywhere other than the estate, the army or the Church, as unspeakably vulgar. She was a massive snob, and there were no bigger snobs than those from Yorkshire 'county' families.

Jasper was fortunate enough to have inherited his father's charm and his mother's superb bone structure; it was conversely unfortunate that he also inherited the lineage's lack of brains. One rather unkind Headmaster suggested in an end-of-term report:

"Jasper has innate charm and excels in all fields of sport. However, his lack of application in the classroom leads one to wonder that if he had possessed one chromosome less he could have been a vegetable. His career prospects in the normal fields of academia and the professions seem limited and it is recommended that he seeks employment in the motor trade where his undoubted persuasive abilities may come to the fore (or forecourt!)."

Despite the Headmaster's witty sarcasm and damning school report Jasper's sense of determination was undiminished. At school his warrior ancestry and occasional lack of sensible reasoning made him a formidable sportsman. He excelled at rugby, cricket, tennis, athletics and drinking.

Academic work required long periods of concentration that bored the pants off him. His status as the school sports ace bestowed upon him a heroic hue that helped mask his lack of application in the classroom. His good looks and open friendly manner also aided the cover up process. On reaching his teens, girls became an additional potent distraction. Even at this young age he determined that marrying for money alone may be a folly that was unlikely to last the test of time. A university education was beyond his academic reach. The idea of a city job with one his father's broker acquaintances seemed interminably dull. He was looking for a career where his God-given gifts would be appreciated and lack of intellectual assets could pass without too much close scrutiny. Above all Jasper was seeking *fun*. He was a born hedonist.

Good fortune often smiles upon the most undeserving: the father of his best school friend owned an advertising company that superficially (and what better way to come to any judgment?) seemed a career that could generate ample funds. This was evidenced by the Bentley that his friend's father drove ostentatiously to school sporting fixtures, parking it with a flourish dangerously close to the cricket pitch boundary.

The son of the publicity mogul regaled Jasper's dormitory with stories of his father's work place which was characterised by endless parties, days on location 'shooting' TV commercials and as much drink as one could possibly consume. And the best part of it all was that this largesse was paid for by witless clients.

Well, that was the son's interpretation of his father's illustrious career mostly garnered from overheard, heated rows between the boy's mother and father. The son's impressions had been confirmed on visits to his father's smart Mayfair offices when he was a child. While he sat dutifully at an artist's drawing board and painted with beautiful fine brushes, he was attended by pretty, blond, secretaries who provided him with endless glasses of excellent squashes and the occasional sip of Pol Roget.

Jasper sat at the feet of his friend lapping up his stories. This sounded the sort of life that Jasper could warm to even if his friend was prone to a little exaggeration. Surely some of it must be true? In his last term at school, with an uncertain future looming, Jasper badgered his good friend into securing an interview at the London offices of Walt Holt & Bolt (known universally as WHB) the establishment of his friend's father. The process was arduous but fun and consumed a whole day and one evening. It was run by the advertising company's head of personnel, Carolyn Hardy, and involved putting applicants through a series of tests. These involved working in teams, creating advertising campaigns, solving inexplicable business problems and filling in forms that were meant to plumb Jasper's deep-rooted, but latent, mental abilities.

His psychometric tests, devised by the company's psychoanalyst, showed Jasper to be arrogant, untrustworthy and excellent company – at least some of the basic raw material needed to have any hope of qualifying as a cut-and-thrust advertising man. Working in teams, Jasper demonstrated his excellent leadership qualities and the creative test revealed an anarchic, witty and appealingly naive imagination.

His creative proposal for 'Parsons,' a popular brand of vinegar, excited him to crudely draw an illustration of the crucifixion where the Christ figure was seen to refuse the offer of vinegar and wine with a caption stating the simple but memorable message:

'Heavens! I would rather die unless it's Parsons'

Business problem solving quickly brought Jasper's Machiavellian tendencies to the fore. He was quizzed what action he would take if faced with an intransigent client who refused to pay a TV commercial invoice that had gone heavily over budget. He was faced with a number of options from which he had to choose the most appropriate:

a) Agree with the client and tear up his invoice

b) Discuss with the client the reasons for the excessive expenditure but at the same time point out to him what a great commercial it was and agree to some form of minor reduction or offer 'free work' on a future project

c) Develop a strategy of your own to solve the problem always bearing in mind the best interests of the client and WHB.

Jasper chose option c) ingeniously suggesting that he should dine with both the client and his wife at an extremely expensive restaurant. This would enable Jasper to discuss the issue 'man to man' in an informal and relaxed environment. However, over the meal Jasper would concentrate all his attention, charm and persuasive skills upon the client's wife. He would reason with her that the invoice should really be paid in full while explaining what an electrifying affect her husband always had on the leading ladies in all the commercials they have made together. The unspoken innuendo would be enough for the client to quickly agree Jasper's terms and change the subject.

Finally the candidates were taken for dinner at the Ritz to gauge their social skills – Jasper's strongest suite. His offer of a trainee position at WHB, (there were only two positions for the six applicants) was sealed after Jasper returned with Carolyn to a slightly lesser hotel frequented by WHB personnel. Here, he exposed to her his many years of athletic schooling in the lift, on the hotel bedroom floor, in the shower and finally in the large bed kindly provided by the directors of WHB. The hidden camera in the bedroom ceiling made a low cost movie for WHB's Chief Executive to peruse at his agreeable Nash country house nestling in the Berkshire countryside. Jasper's position was sealed when Bill Walt phoned Carolyn and instructed her to make certain that Jasper was one of the names to be hired. "That guy's got real creative talent and stamina too. Hire him," he had stated emphatically, "And you take a pay rise too, Miss Hardy!"

Bill Walt and his wife had not had such an enjoyable evening's viewing for years.

~

Jasper's eight-year sojourn at WHB included a two-year secondment to the company's New York office. Jasper turned out to be a natural at his job and his career thrived.

It had been unfortunate that his New York adventure had been brought to an abrupt halt. New York was a city that appealed to his reckless, devil-may-care attitude and it was a place where he hadn't been judged by his upper class accent – to Americans all limeys sound the same –funny! It was also a time when it was 'hip' to be English, everyone wanted a bit of it, the Beatles, Carnaby Street, cute old London, all the usual sixties clichés applied.

His Manhattan decline was sealed after a difference of opinion over a bill in one of New York's more notable eateries patronised by WHB worldwide President, the venerable Walt Walt and father of Bill Walt. An irate phone call from the restaurant owner to Walt Walt's third assistant's assistant had brought Jasper to Walt Walt's attention that some unpleasantness had ensued with the maitre de cuisine of Club 58 involving a number of bread rolls and a four hundred dollar unpaid bill. It was not the first time that this had happened as Jasper was a frequent customer. In the past it had been overlooked but this time the restaurant owner was not prepared to let it pass. The diners demanded better behaviour and so did Walt Walt. He was incandescent and decided that it was time for the aristocratic, rugby playing Englishman to return to his native country despite his artistry in the bedroom (the President was on his son's home movie circulation list too). Jasper's bread roll kicking days were over.

Jasper's next two years of indulgence back in the WHB London offices had started to wane. After his sojourn in New York the new challenge of seducing a fresh supply of secretaries, bar maids, clients' wives and assorted personnel had sustained his interest. However, recently during a lean period when his gambling

103

had temporarily denuded him of ready funds, he had had to live for a couple of months in his old Bentley parked on the Thames Embankment. But as quickly as his fortunes evaporated so they returned (a hundred to one win at Haydock Park) and he had managed repossess his old flat once again.

The appeal of Jasper's tiny Bayswater apartment had begun to lose its original allure and like a germinating seed waiting for spring sunshine, there was something nagging away at Jasper for a change of scenery and pace; something more than dodging rent and other tiresome bills. It never ceased to surprise him how overdue bills turned with such rapidity from an angry solicitor's letter to a court summons, or worse: ugly, hard men on his door step. He always paid up, eventually. Why didn't trades' people understand this simple logic?

Serendipity played its part in realising Jasper's subconscious objectives. An old friend with an advertising agency in a thriving commercial city close to Windelton suddenly offered him a senior position. Jasper didn't have to think twice about it. His moonlight flit from London was beautifully executed; he saved nearly a year's rent and untold household bills including a wine merchant's account that was as magnificent in proportion as it excelled in good taste. Sir Toby would have been proud of him.

The move up north beckoned a life of even less work and a nearly comparable salary. Irritating debts would vanish (or a lengthy postponement until he was located again) plus all the added glamour of being a 'London type' in the provinces. And of course a new supply of 'top totty' as he liked to refer to his unsuspecting paramours. Jasper's arrival home was greeted with undisguised pleasure by both Sir Toby and Lady Lavinia. The latter having relinquished her reticence to people 'in trade' on discovering that her son had ample supplies of cash and sported a beautiful E-type Jaguar.

"Too, too vulgar darling," she would shriek as she clambered into the small bucket seats and demanded to be driven into Windelton to anoint the local tradesmen with her weekly grocery orders. For Sir Toby it was simpler than that: he just liked having his favourite son about the place to share their joint passion for betting on the horses, shooting and sharing a bottle or three of excellent claret.

Jasper's elder brother, Courcey, didn't embrace with the same enthusiasm this outpouring of joy on the prodigal son's return. He secretly feared that his upstart brother might start to interfere with running the estate for which he was now entirely responsible. What Courcey didn't know was that Jasper hadn't the faintest interest in trying to keep the Inchdale estate solvent. He had decided long ago that he would leave that task to someone even more stupid than himself. Even Jasper divined that his sibling was nearer the headmaster's description of himself in the brain cell department and that in a few years' time Courcey and the estate would be flat broke.

Sadly, like many of the great English estates they were doomed to be sold off piece by piece. Once Sir Toby died the death duties would effectively bankrupt the estate. Unless Courcey turned the place into some sort of ghastly theme park they would never generate enough income to keep it going. Jasper couldn't see his brother as a fairground proprietor; the chances of his wife serving 'country house teas' to the great unwashed was even more remote.

Griselda, Courcey's wife, enjoyed horse-like proportions and appropriately equine teeth. Jasper thought that her only money-raising abilities might lie in becoming an attraction in her own right. Filial loyalty prevented Jasper from being openly uncharitable to his brother's spouse, but search as he did, he couldn't find any redeeming feature in the woman. Griselda enjoyed a diabolic combination of misfortunes: she was ugly, smelly and boorish.

But she did have one extraordinary quality: her laugh. It started with a gurgling rumble in her bowels that eventually rolled up through her massive torso and heaving breasts and culminated in a donkey like braying that caused the air to be sucked out of her lungs exposing her massive teeth and food-deposited gums. The noise could be heard above the strongest Windelton winds and people would halt in

105

the town's streets over a mile away and listen, wondering if it was an old Lancaster bomber taking off from a nearby aerodrome.

Jasper was only interested in creating a life that revolved around Jasper: a world of pleasure and the pursuit of enjoyment. He already had his eye on a cheap estate cottage that would make his homecoming complete. He had just one small obstacle to overcome: he would have to persuade Courcey to evict Walter, the retired gardener, from his home of forty years.

~

'Old Walter' as he was affectionately known had lived at Gardener's Cottage for nearly four decades. Sir Toby hadn't the heart to move Walter out when he retired. The poor man had recently lost his wife when one of the estate's prize bulls had gone on a rampage at the Windelton show. The beast had somehow slipped its handler and ran amok in the show ground knocking down a number of stalls before finally trampling 'Mrs Walter' to death. After the tragedy the old squire forgot all about Walter's occupancy of Gardener's Cottage. Courcey was equally hopeless and could never face any embarrassing hassle with the tenants and so never got around to moving him on.

His tenure after retirement had never been discussed and Walter wasn't going to remind them. He continued to tend his well-kept kitchen garden and poach the odd rabbit or pheasant when he wanted to supplement his meagre diet. Now with his wife gone he needed even less money and with no rent to pay he could get by nicely on his old age pension. However, Jasper was not so sentimental. He reasoned that the cottage was owned by the estate and it was time Walter was moved off to some old folk's institution. He wanted the cottage for himself.

During the war Windelton had a POW camp located down by the river. Once the last of the POWs had been repatriated (including the energetic Bavarian Baron), the Council had converted the asbestos and corrugated iron Nissan huts into what were euphemistically called, 'retirement hostels'. One of these would be the perfect place for Walter to spend his final years. They were poorly made, single-storey dwellings prone to dampness in winter and flooding at any time. They were considered ideal accommodation for pensioners and cheaper than council houses.

Jasper resolved to tackle Courcey about it once he had got himself established in his new job.

- Chapter 13 -

Bogey Man

It all came to a head one Saturday a few weeks before the great Windelton Festival. Dutifully following Dawn's request for punctuality, Ian had arrived home at six o'clock sharp after his customary game of golf. Dawn was busy making a dress for her daughter to wear at her mother's sixty-fifth birthday party. The embroidery anglais on the collar was causing bother and her patient nature was being tested to the full.

Ian had played a hard eighteen holes of golf and had been unexpectedly beaten by Jasper Inchdale in the final of a club cup match. He had been the favourite to win by an easy margin. There had been something very irritating about the nonchalant, self-deprecating style of young Inchdale that had irritated Ian throughout the game.

"I'm completely hopeless at golf, rugby is more my bag," said Jasper on the first tee as his first drive went straight down the fairway landing within an easy chip shot of the green. "Absolute fluke I've got this far," he continued breezily.

Ian sliced his first drive and it landed in some rough grass about thirty yards behind Jasper's ball. Losing the first hole by two shots was not the start Ian had anticipated. By the eighth hole he was three shots down but by the sixteenth Ian had pulled the match back to evens. The small crowd following the match murmured in excitement as the flamboyant squire's son seem to be giving the club's star player, and thrice past cup winner, a run for his money.

"Women golfers in the US, you should see them Ian. Competitive as hell," Jasper continued to chat aimlessly about the prowess of American lady golfers who were formidable opponents both on and off the course. "They shriek like hell if you beat them and shriek like hell when *they* win. And they shriek even louder in the sack!"

Superficially, Ian had tolerated this stream of jocular banter with the occasional nod of sympathy and strained half-smile at his opponent's good fortune. Secretly, he was seething at this self-satisfied prig who seemed to bowl through life without a care. Jasper gave the appearance of having no malice in him but Ian wondered how deep this ran.

The game began to personify the wrongs and sleights of Ian's current humdrum life. Was young Inchdale doing this to wind him up or was he always such a garrulous buffoon, he thought to himself? The trouble was that Inchdale *was* quite clearly an accomplished golfer. He had a natural swing, a good eye and a steady temperament. He was not thrown by dropping two shots on the tenth.

"I told you I was no bloody good!" he said with a laugh as his green shot bounced off the far edge of the green and rolled into a bunker. As the match drew towards the closing stages Ian's normally unruffled demeanour became frayed as the desire to beat his opponent grew and grew. The thought of losing was unconscionable; he *had* to beat this clever-Dick newcomer.

On the seventeenth Ian won the hole by a shot. The eighteenth was a difficult four hundred and ten yard par five hole which held a hidden pond, a stream and finally a notorious L shaped plantation of birch, holly and oak - the 'Killer Copse' as it was known to the club regulars. To achieve par on this hole you had to be a good player. There were always mutterings in the committee rooms to make this hole a par six as every year the trees grew taller and the challenge harder. Playing around the small wood inevitably meant dropping a shot.

Ian's first shot hurtled off the tee and disappeared over some gorse bushes, the first of its many hurdles. The ball rose promisingly, if a little too steeply. Clearing a bluff of land it headed on an upward trajectory toward the descending land of the fairway below. From the tee it looked a copybook shot. However, just at the moment the ball reached the zenith of its climb, the gentle Windelton breeze turned into a brief violent blast.

"What the bloody hell happened there?" said the normally placid Ian as his perfectly judged stroke was transformed from triumph to disaster. "Bugger me!" Ian exploded loudly. There was some tittering from the crowd as swearing was not approved of anywhere in the precincts of the club. The ball veered off its perfect forward direction and plunged into some rocky scrub before finally skittering under a large outcrop of millstone grit. Once the ball was nestling in its inaccessible resting place the wind returned to leaf-wafting normality.

Jasper's No 7 iron shot off the tee looked dangerously low. It shot through the tops of the gorse but landed true onto the fairway bouncing downhill stopping obligingly at the dogleg point in front of the 'Killer Copse'. Blast, hell-fire and damnation, Ian mouthed to himself managing to curb speaking out loud. He was seething with inner rage, exasperated by his own bad luck that Windelton's malevolent wind had conspired to play havoc with his game. He desperately tried to chip the ball back onto the fairway and finally succeeded in overshooting the dogleg, dropping a shot in the process and leaving him no option but to play around the small wood.

There was a sudden gasp of surprise from the crowd as Jasper took a wood from his golf bag rather than an iron to do battle with the copse. It was typical of Jasper to take a daring but calculated risk. He secretly enjoyed the mutterings and murmurings emanating from the spectators. If he could achieve enough height to clear the wood he would be on the green in two and hole-out for a stunning eagle. The amazed group of followers and an equally awe-struck Ian, who was now standing some distance behind, watched Jasper execute a powerful downward stroke that removed an enormous divot of grass. The ball lifted into miracle flight. Like a jet aircraft on take-off it roared over the copse and landed within eight foot of the hole. It was a finale worthy of a British Open Championship. An eagle at the eighteenth was nearly as noteworthy as a hole-in-one.

Ian struggled hard to conceal his wrathful admiration for his victorious opponent. "Bloody miracle of the gods," Jasper exclaimed with a laugh.

As soon as the cup ceremony was over, Ian forfeited his post-match drink at the bar as he needed to get home for his mother-in-law's visitation that evening. Dawn had sternly reminded him not to be home late. Ian was only too pleased to have an excuse to get away but on parting the club lounge Jasper stopped him: "Look old boy, sorry you have to scoot off now, but why don't we meet up for a drink somewhere on another day? We could celebrate our great battle of the fairways. Have you got a girlfriend, we could make up a foursome, it would be rather jolly?"

"I am married," said Ian sullenly.

"Oh come on, she can't be that bad, surely?" replied Jasper with a grin, "You are a good-looking bloke. I bet she's a belter! Wheel out the beautiful bride, she'll be pleased to get away from the housework for a bit of laugh. Quite frankly I am finding this place a bit dull since I came back from London."

This was of course one of Jasper's fibs as his feet hadn't touched the ground since he got back. The social grapevine was alive with gossip that Windelton's most eligible bachelor was back in the district. "How about the Nags Head on Wednesday, say 7.30'ish?" Before Ian could splutter an excuse, "Right, that's it, Wednesday it is then... and well played today, bad luck about that blasted wind. Bloody unfair, I would have called the club referee! Lucky you didn't have a bet on it! Hah, hah but I suppose all's fair in love and war! Toodle'oo for now," and Jasper was out of the door heading toward the members' bar with a purposeful stride and the grin of a champion.

Ian's humour didn't greatly improve as he tore home in his little Austin Mini. He meshed the gears and raced the small engine, enjoying punishing the machine for his own misfortune. *Jasper-poncing-Inchdale,* he thought to himself. *Who would have thought that I would lose out to that toff?* He murmured to himself as he screeched the car into his street. *Why was Inchdale trying to be so bloody nice about it?* Ian knew that he could tell Inchdale was enjoying every moment of the drama, particularly that last hole. What a bloody shot he played! Ian had to acknowledge it *was* one hell of a stroke, risky in the extreme but still it was a piece of masterful play. And where did all those people come from following the match? He had never seen so many at a club cup and the cheer that went up at the eighteenth. *And what's his game, he wanting to have a drink with me? Patronising bugger, I'll phone and cancel it,* he thought as he locked the front wheels of the little car pulling it up within inches of the garage doors.

"So who's rattled your golf bag?" said Dawn looking up from her sewing as Ian banged his way into the front room with a flushed expression. She could always tell when Ian was in one of his moods, his forehead crinkled, eyes narrowed and his cheeks were flushed. "You look as if you have been robbed of your life savings... if you had any darling!" she added in a sympathetic voice.

"Ha, ha, very funny, I got hammered by that supercilious Jasper Inchdale in the cup match. You know the squire's younger son, the one who has just come back to live on the estate."

"He's rather dashing I hear. I presume he'll be like his father, a law unto himself with the ability to charm the birds out of the trees," said Dawn.

"Oh yes, he's a charmer alright. Pretends he can't play golf but plays like a professional. And he knows it. What gets me is that he makes it seem so ruddy effortless."

"Isn't *that* the sign of a professional? Making it *look* easy"

"Don't *you* rub it in!"

"I am sorry Ian, but you have won the championship before, you can't win *every* year."

"I know, but I didn't like losing to HIM!"

"You sound terribly jealous darling, I hope you are not getting embittered in your old age, raging against your contemporaries. I suspect this is more than just about golf isn't it?"

"Perhaps it is, perhaps it isn't," said Ian, annoyed at Dawn's perceptive jibe. "Jasper Inchdale is one of a type. He waltzes through life as if he has a God-given right to succeed at everything he does, enjoying himself along the way and somehow earns oodles of cash. Why is that? It just doesn't seem *fair!*"

"Ian, you are impossible, you sound like a whining child! How do you know he hasn't got any worries? He might be covering up all sorts of insecurities under that attractive exterior. For God's sake with a father and mother like Sir Toby and Lady Lavinia, well I ask you, how can anyone be normal growing up with them as parents? Would you like a mother like that? She's a powdered old hag who smells like a dog kennel," retorted Dawn indignantly. "She'll barely speak to anyone she thinks is from the hoipoloi."

"Sir Toby's okay. He's a pleasant enough buffer, if a little eccentric. He's as nice as pie when he ever comes to the bank," said Ian in a more conciliatory tone.

"So he should be if his debts are as large as you say! Whenever I have seen him he struck me as a bit of a letch. I bet old Astle bows and scrapes whenever he sees him; he does that with anyone with any real money. I saw him meet Marjorie Nelson the other day on the high street, he practically curtsied," said Dawn.

"Yes that's true about Astle; it's the poor sods like us that he looks down on. There's something not quite right with old Astle. I can't put my finger on it. I think he's got some dark secret hidden away, which is maybe why he is so overbearing with customers. It is as if he's trying to over-compensate."

"He's wife is rather sweet," said Dawn," she always seems in a bit of a dream. Somehow, she doesn't seem bank manager wife material. She never appears as if she's in this world. Astle could be an undertaker or a burglar but she wouldn't notice, or I suspect, give a damn."

"*Jasper bloody Inchdale, Jasper Inchdale!*" Ian roared in annoyance returning to his bad tempered theme.

"Oh for goodness sake Ian, grow up, it *is* only a game of golf. You should be concentrating on your career at Murchison's Bank instead of whingeing about your punctured pride."

"That's easy for you to say," snapped Ian.

"BUT what are you going to do? We have got Abigail's schooling to consider and I want her to go to Oak Tree Preparatory when she's six and that's next year!"

"I don't know. I'll sort something out."

"Precisely how, Ian?"

"I told you, *I will sort it out*," said Ian in exasperation, his voice becoming deeper, as he tried to control his rising fury.

"You'll just have to give up that golf club membership; it's not doing you any good judging by your mood tonight. It must cost as much as Abigail's fees," replied Dawn testily now rising to her well-worn theme for family rows.

The golf club annual subscription was a burning fuse for Ian. Golf was his passion, the *'petite amie'* of his existence. However, it was a line of argument that he consistently failed to defend with any conviction. On the golf course, he could shine, he *was* someone. He was on equal terms with the best of them. He wasn't just a bank clerk. He was a scratch golfer, good enough in many people's opinions to become a professional. To remove this element of his life would be to emasculate him, a devastating blow to his self-esteem. But despite the emotion he couldn't refute the logic of Dawn's argument.

"What's wrong with the local primary school down the road?" his customary rebuttal came trotting out like a jukebox replay.

"You *know* my views about *that* place", emphasised Dawn, "we have had this conversation I don't know how many times. I want the best for Abigail, not *second best*. The primary school has children from families I don't much care for."

"How do you know, you've never met any of them?" retorted Ian.

"I HAVE!" she shouted.

"You're just being a bloody snob!"

Ian's normally calm nature was evaporating fast as the all too familiar argument unfolded. He knew the only way out was an orderly withdrawal before he or Dawn said something they both might regret. He turned on his heel and headed off to the kitchen with a loud "hurrumph!"

Dawn could hear him draw the water from the kitchen tap, it rattled as he filled the kettle followed by a bang as it was slammed down onto the cooker ring; the sound of matches being broken followed by the scratching sound of a match box as it fell to the floor followed by muffled expletives. Eventually she heard the soft reassuring 'crump' as Ian finally lit the ring. At least he hasn't stuck his head in the oven, thought Dawn.

The obnoxious smell of escaping gas and the battered kettle shuddering on the ring had a soporific effect on Ian and his shallow, anxious breathing became deeper and more regulated. He began to regain his composure as some of his feelings of self-righteous indignation ebbed away. He made two cups of tea and took one into Dawn who had placed her embroidery on her lap. She had sat back in the armchair, head on the seat back with her eyes closed, her light brown hair resting on the side of her face, her flawless skin slightly flushed, waxy in appearance. Ian thought she looked like a beautiful corpse that has been carefully made up by an undertaker. The thought of her dead made his heart stab with imaginary grief and his body surged with an overpowering sense of love and an almost primeval desire to protect this beautiful woman, the mother of his children, the anchor of his life.

The presence of Ian and the smell of strong tea stirred Dawn from her torpor, her brown eyes flickered open and she looked sadly at Ian's white, drawn face, the lines around his eyes seemed more deeply etched than they used to be and his chin was jutting out caused by the tension of clamping his back teeth together. "Thank you," she said quietly, taking the mug of tea, "you mustn't get so worked up darling, I am certain there is a way we can work things out. And I *am* sorry about your golf game." She took his hand in hers and gave it a little reassuring squeeze as you would a small child who had taken a tumble.

"How's the dress coming on?" he asked with a faint smile, his voice breaking slightly, the matter-of-fact question could not disguise the emotion bubbling under the surface of his troubled life.

"Getting there, but it's a very difficult collar. You know mother is coming around in half an hour?"

"Yes, I remembered, what's the reason for the visit?"

"Oh, she wants to run over the arrangements for her party and she needs you to give her a hand at choosing the wine for the birthday meal."

Ian's mother-in-law, Bessie, had a real soft spot for Ian, which he found mildly irritating. Bessie's husband had died four years ago and now she was unable to make a decision about anything without referring to Dawn or Ian. Ian had become surrogate husband in Bessie's life. Bessie had come from one of those marriages, common for pre-war couples, where the husband of the house did everything relating to finance, house maintenance and garden. Meanwhile Bessie had cooked, kept home, was lover in residence and brought up the children. Her husband's untimely death, just prior to his retirement, had left her rudderless. Her sixty-fifth birthday loomed and a party was being planned to celebrate this milestone; it would be just a small gathering of family and a few friends. Ian and Dawn's was the only place large enough to accommodate the party. Bessie also wanted to show off to her friends her daughter's attractive home, charming husband ('he works in the bank you know') and their two perfect children.

Wine was a new experience to Bessie; her husband had preferred a bottle of stout, she a glass of sweet sherry. Wine was what young successful people drank these days and she wanted some at her party. Now her husband had died Bessie wanted to exercise her newfound worldliness and sophistication.

Her late spouse wouldn't have approved.

- Chapter 14 -

The Chameleon

Valerie Harper never had any desire to marry the man who had fathered her son. Some days her attitude to men was at best ambivalent. On others sexual desire was the most important thing in her life. Its overwhelming power amazed her.

As she got older the 'mad dog' of her needs, as she called them, seemed to be more in balance and she could see her life in a clear mirror. Now she had what she wanted: James, her adorable son, and a steady but modest income to bring him up. She put all the money that she made from her special evening work into a savings account for James which he would receive when he was twenty- one. It already amounted to a tidy sum.

After the 'Gerald moment' and her shock pregnancy Valerie had surprised herself by the way in which she quickly adapted to her new way of life. She had hurriedly moved from her flat in Hickleton and purchased a solid terrace house in Whitley, a small West Riding town ten miles away from her old place of work. After resigning from the bank, her new location turned out to be an unexpectedly agreeable place to settle down and make a new life. It was quieter and away from the prying eyes.

It didn't take long to find a part-time job in the typing pool of the thriving Sweet Tooth confectionery company in the town. Nobody ever questioned her suddenly widowed status. Her quiet, private manner put people off enquiring too deeply about her past; her dowdy appearance and sensible dresses successfully belied her age and outside interests. Valerie concealed her smouldering beauty better than any actress. She was an exemplary employee: prompt, polite, efficient and rarely off work. Out of the office she kept herself to herself. She made casual friendships with the other girls in the typing pool. Valerie was solicitous about her work colleagues' welfare and always had a kind word for others. Any enquiries about her own life she just shrugged off with a smile. "My life is far too dull to be of any interest to you," she would say with a shy smile. It was her stock answer and it invited no further comment to the curious. After the first few months the other girls in the office gave up probing. There was no point in asking Valerie to the bingo or a party as they would always be met with the same polite, stone-wall response.

"Thanks girls, but bingo and partying just isn't me!"

Because of her interest in others she became a listening post for the younger girls. They would confide their problems with boyfriends or parents. Valerie surprised her confidants with her practical, worldly counsel. The wisdom they received was not what they expected from this drably dressed widow. She became a bit of an Agony Aunt in the office.

In less than a year Valerie had been promoted out of the typing pool to become the buying director's secretary. Three years later when the business owner's personal assistant retired, Valerie was the natural choice to take over the position. Working as Reg Grimston's personal assistant was an exacting task and perfectly suited Valerie's efficient and discreet temperament. He was a chaotic, ambitious confectioner who thrived on conflict. She was peace-maker, unobtrusive and quietly efficient – a perfect match.

Valerie's parents had been both tragically killed in a train accident long before her mad moment with Astle. Her parents were spared the embarrassment of an illegitimate child, a fact that made Valerie shamefully glad they were no longer alive. As an only child from a small family, she had no relations with the exception of a cousin somewhere in Australia whom she had never met. To the outside world, Valerie Harper was the apogee of a genteel, struggling lower middle class widow. A woman who has been delivered a series of bad turns in her life. Not only had she lost her parents but her husband had been killed during the Korean War, doing his duty for King and country. The fiction perfectly fitted the brave, tragic and quietly resilient Valerie.

It was her pregnancy and a desire to create a home for her unborn child that had made Valerie decide to use the proceeds from her late parents' estate to purchase her stone built Victorian end terrace house. It sat on a curving hillside street, one of thirty or more properties. It had white painted sash windows, a blue slate roof and a stout polished pine front door which led out directly on to the street. There was a small yard and patch of grass out at the back. A gate from the back garden opened on to a side alleyway at the terrace end that led back onto to the street. The old outside privy has been converted to make a respectable garden shed. A redundant blackened range once used for cooking was now a 'feature'. It had been usurped by a gas cooker and eye level grill. The open fire still heated the water and made the breakfast kitchen cum-living room a cosy central focus for the house.

The house perched on a south facing side of a steep valley overlooked textile mills and related industrial warehouses. A car park and a newly constructed concrete shopping complex were also in view a little further away. The tall stone factory chimneys were still very much in evidence but only a couple of them still billowed black smoke. The view from the front rooms gave an expansive south-westerly aspect. In the far distance were glimpses of heather clad moor tops, purple in late summer months. To the right of the house and looking north, high on the moor top was the Stapleton Obelisk, a folly of grandiose proportions. This curious half-temple, half-tower, was the Stapleton family homage to nearly two centuries of human exploitation - the time it took four Stapleton generations to weave a fortune in worsted cloth and lose it all.

Conversely, the back of the house looked onto a weeping rock bank where dampness and moss were evident even on the warmest of summer days. Twenty feet above this wall of sweating millstone grit was another tiered street of identical properties rising higher into the arthritic, raking hillside.

Astle's monthly allowance was like a war widow's pension. It enabled Valerie to live comfortably but not extravagantly when added to her secretarial wages. It provided extra funds for a few small luxuries in which she liked to indulge herself.

She had a passion for silk lingerie, Sobranie Black Russian cigarettes and decent hock, providing it was served chilled. She kept a Triumph Bonneville 650cc motor cycle in her garden shed which she only rode at night when her son James was safely tucked-up and asleep in bed. She loved to creep out of the house dressed in her black leather biker's gear and roar up to Whiteley Moor Top, leaving her daylight life behind, letting the powerful machine take control of her as she swooped across the moors and winding fell roads. It willed her to drive on faster and faster until the goggles on her face pressed so hard against her delicate skin that her cheeks hurt and she thought the white crash helmet would be ripped from her head. Her bike was so like many things in Valerie's private life: secret, unpredictable and full of abandonment.

Having no husband, Valerie and James spent so much time together that they had become like a married couple. Although he was only eight years old he provided an anchor to her life as well as valued company. James rarely questioned her about his fictitious father. The snapshot of a man in a suit and waistcoat didn't look like the military heroes he had read about in comics. These and other questions, Valerie knew, she was going to have to face one day.

Despite her feelings towards men that fluctuated wildly from the reticent to the unhealthy, Valerie harboured a child-like romantic vision of 'innocent love'. Deep down she still believed that one day she would encounter her 'prince' who would emerge out of the night's blackness and whisk her away to a new life of companionship, true love and fulfilment. These fanciful and long buried desires were a long way from the Valerie characterised by the efficient, demure secretary witnessed at Sweet Tooth Confectionery. In private, Valerie fuelled her idealistic ideas of romance by consuming the serials in Woman's Weekly and Mills and Boon novels. Valerie couldn't get enough of the latest heady cocktails of trysts and tragedies of gifted but bad tempered surgeons, widowed ships' captains and helplessly good looking airline pilots that these novellas served up. She recognised these publications for what they were, however ludicrous the storylines. But it never stopped her from dreaming. And of course there was Thursday nights at the 'Bridge Club'. That made up for a lot. It was the pressure valve she needed releasing; although dangerous it fulfilled her strong need for uncomplicated sex. She had been a stalwart of Madame Romanji's Bridge Club for five years. This very discreet and highly exclusive brothel was strictly a members' only establishment and boasted many of the great and good from the northern region. It enjoyed the patronage of the judiciary, high finance and a smattering of visiting minor royals. Bridge was played but not in every room. The elegant Victorian building on the outskirts of Bradford provided haute cuisine, an enviable wine cellar and luxurious sleeping accommodation equipped to satisfy most men's tastes, however bizarre. It was presided over by the daughter of an Indian Maharajah who had impeccable taste and ruled the establishment with a rod of iron.

In schizophrenic contrast Valerie looked forward to Astle's drab Sunday telephone calls. They provided a link with the past and moored her week to a comforting familiarity. She never really understood why Astle kept up this charade; they hadn't met face-to-face since she conceived. Valerie had considered telling him to stop but the money *was* useful. She had no anger for Astle only sorrow and regret. Regret more for him not herself. She had a child, he hadn't. He had never been brave enough to claim her and his son. At first this really hurt. Now she recognised that he was thwarted by conformity. As time moved on she realised the advantages. It suited her to maintain the status quo. The moment hadn't come yet to sever the umbilical cord but she knew that one day it would.

- Chapter 15 -

Magnetic North

Settling into his northern career, Jasper found time to involve himself once again in Windelton life. Eventually, his brother Courcey had begrudgingly evicted Walter to free up Gardener's Cottage and leased the cottage to Jasper at a peppercorn rent.

This insensitive act had not gone unnoticed in Windelton or with other estate workers. Jasper was asked to help ease Walter's undignified departure by trying to find him suitable alternative accommodation in the town. He had lamely suggested to Walter that he should move into one of the council's old folk's homes down by the river.

"What the bloody hell has it got to do with me? Jasper had argued. "It is our family's bloody cottage and he's been ruddy lucky living in it for sod all rent for decades! Anyway, he's your bloody tenant, aren't you supposed to be running the estate?" Jasper had shouted at his ineffectual elder brother when the matter seemed to be getting nowhere.

Eventually, Walter retreated to his daughter's house with subdued rancour and the Inchdale family brushed the unpleasant memory aside by conveniently forgetting all about him.

Jasper was now able to reinstate himself back into the social rounds that he had once occupied before his departure to London. Nothing much had changed except that he was now transformed into an eligible bachelor, a bit of a 'catch'. This was some rehabilitation from his previous incarnation of being the impoverished squire's second son with few brains and no likelihood of any inheritance – the old principle of primogeniture, 'eldest takes all,' still being the Inchdale tradition. To all appearances Jasper now appeared to have his own money and was worthy of a second look by parents of the landed Yorkshire families with a spare daughter to marry off.

Invitations to drinks parties, dinners and balls were soon dropping through his cottage letterbox. One day, a short note arrived from Jasper's mother with an accompanying advertising flyer promoting Marjorie Nelson's forthcoming Festival of Arts. The carefully planned day of artistic enlightenment was to conclude with a disco and a barbecue. This was to be, *'especially for the younger elements of Windelton'*, Lady Lavinia had scrawled in a spidery hand on the leaflet:

Dearest Boy

Why not spend the weekend up here for a change and come and have Sunday lunch at the Hall? We are having the Forrantes over with their youngest daughter, Lucia. You might remember her? The family is frightfully well off. Thankfully she has turned out less plain than the rest of the family, some of the Italian blood coming out methinks!

His mother had spiced-up her missive with the enticing note: *'There will be popular dancing at the Festival too'*, as if this tempting morsel would tip the balance in favour of acceptance. Jasper groaned inwardly. He imagined some ghastly quartet playing their idea of pop music while a load of drunken old farts from the golf club would be doing their version of the twist.

The prospect of lunch with the Forrantes was an even worse prospect. The lure of their unseen daughter did not excite him. He remembered the two older sisters being absolute horrors. Maybe Lucia had undergone surgery in Switzerland? Her father was wealthy enough, he thought, he had armament factories and sold ordnance to emerging African nations.

But Jasper was forever the diplomat, particularly when it came to keeping in his mother's good books. He recognised that he had not seen his parents since their Scottish odyssey at the Inverhapless Hotel. This weekend could be a bridge building moment he thought. On their return to Inchdale Hall his mother had expressed in no uncertain terms her displeasure over his unexpected Scottish departure. After Jasper's hurried escape there had been an unpleasantness in the hotel.

After their return from holiday Lady Lavinia had hectored him over the telephone: "A mad Celt turned up on his tractor shouting and swearing in the most

123

uncouth way. He threatened your father with an axe and tried to ram the Rolls. The police had to be called and had it not been for the Colonel and his gun we could have all been murdered. It was all terribly embarrassing, something to do with the Colonel's daughter. I think you know what I am talking about, you are *impossible* Jasper!" Jasper said nothing and tried not to imagine what might have happened if the wronged Highlander had got hold of him.

To exasperate his mother even more Jasper had strenuously, however plausibly, refused the last three invitations for various 'social' events at the Hall. The date was set for a month ahead, was he free that weekend? He had flipped open his diary and oddly enough it was blank. Nothing new in that: Jasper's social life happened on the run, rarely was anything planned - spontaneity was everything. Situations presented themselves, dinner invitations, parties, sailing weekends, shooting, something *always* turned up.

This one he realised he couldn't avoid. Jasper phoned his mother: "Mater darling? Everything okay at home on the range? Good, good, yes…. I am fine, busy as always. Yes, the cottage is fine, bloody cold but never mind. I'd love to come for lunch with the Forrantes. Who knows the daughter may not be a dog after all!"

"Jasper, don't be so nouveau. Jack and Florina are very dear old friends and I think you might be surprised at how Lucia has turned out. She is training to be a doctor. Frightfully brainy, just finished medicine at Edinburgh University, I hear."

"Lovely, I am sure she will be great company, looking forward to it already."

"No need to lay it on Jasper, I am not entirely gaga." Lavinia replied waspishly.

"Many thanks for the tip-off about the Festival too," said Jasper steering the conversation away. "Sounds frightfully jolly! Please tell the Nelson woman I will be coming, get me half a dozen tickets and I will try and rope in some pals."

"Marvellous news, darling! The Forrantes *will* be pleased you're coming to luncheon. They do *so like* meeting *young* people. Florina says it keeps her young. She always has had a bit of wandering eye. I don't think her husband is at home often, always gallivanting off, selling things that go bang to the natives. All work and no

124

play makes for a dull do, I say. So do promise to behave yourself Jasper, no more scenes pleeeese," she said in a wheedling voice. "Must go now, your father is expecting the bailiffs. We are *definitely* out *all* day. Dear Courcey will sort matters out, he'll probably let Griselda loose on them so that should frighten 'em 'orf. Some silly misunderstanding about a wine bill that goes back centuries, it's all *so* bourgeois! Pip."

That was a job well done thought Jasper. He was enough a politician to recognise that he needed to keep topping up of his reservoir of brownie points with his mother. Even though he was 27 years of age, there was a time and place when it was better to obey the royal command. There were all sorts of reasons why it was important to keep on the right side of the old girl. You never know when she might come in handy – like fighting his corner at the Inverhapless Hotel!

Despite him waving an axe about, she had evidently given the poor Cape Wrath farmer a terrible flea in his ear. She had got on to the Procurator Fiscal to have him removed from the hotel grounds. Evidently, he had threatened to crush the old Rolls with his tractor. Seems a bit extreme thought Jasper, but Highlanders have never been the same since the Clearances - always got 'The Scottish Grudge'.

- Chapter 16 -

The Best Laid Plans

Marjorie Nelson's festival of arts was taking shape. Success was never in doubt. She would build her hospital. Marjorie had decreed it, therefore it would come to pass. After some months of agonising over the title a decision was finally reached. The printed flysheets had been delivered to every Windelton household and the large posters had started to appear around the district. It boldly stated:

THE WINDELTON INTERNATIONAL FESTIVAL OF ARTS AND CRAFTS
In Aid of the Cottage Hospital Appeal

The 'international' title had been an inspiration of Mrs Hendry. Marjorie had to admit it was a good idea, even if it came from *her*. The 'crafts' had been added at the last moment as a number of the district's potters and artists had booked stalls although Marjorie had fretted that they may lower the tone of the occasion. On balance, the thought of the additional revenue swayed her decision.

Harry Webster had been 'persuaded' to run a four-page preview in the Windelton Bugle. Ticket sales were going well and the quality of performers was drawing people from all over the West Riding.

The ambitious programme was to begin in the early afternoon with a procession by the Reverend Max Headcase and his Angelic Boys Choir. The Reverend Max and his heavenly acolytes were to march down the High Street accompanied by the Boys Brigade band. Windelton's eccentric vicar was of the evangelical persuasion. His particular wing of the Church of England enjoyed spectacle and the Reverend Max was not going to let them down. He was a determined man and had agreed to open the proceedings on the proviso that he could hold a torch lit procession. The Reverend Max insisted on "full editorial and choreographic control over my angelic boys". The fact that they would be marching in broad daylight did nothing to curb his enthusiasm. The white-cloaked choir boys would sing rousing spiritual hymns. These were composed by the Reverend Max and turned out to have rather questionable lyrics. The Festival March of Love and Hate had a rousing Negroid quality blended with music adapted from a popular Tamla Motown hit tune of the day.

The march would commence in the market square and proceed through the town to culminate in the Red House's fields. At which point the children's flaming torches would ignite a pre-constructed cardboard and wood tableau, liberally doused in paraffin. The structure boldly featured the Windelton coat of arms, some mysterious heraldic and religious imagery (the meaning of which was only known to the Reverend Max) and the words, 'God Loves Windelton and Hates Sinners'. The tableau would be consumed by the conflagration and finally doused by the Windelton Voluntary Fire Brigade at which point the proceedings of the International Festival of Arts and Crafts will officially open. This was scheduled for twelve noon.

"The symbolism of the flames of hades being extinguished by the waters of the Jordan (river Win) and the souls of the people being cleansed by our own courageous firemen will not be missed by the Windelton people!" roared the Reverend Max to Marjorie with a strange glint in his eye.

"Maxwell," Marjorie always called the Reverend Max by his full Christian name, like addressing a recalcitrant child, "Maxwell, are you sure you know what you are doing, we don't want any children becoming burned or property set alight?"

"I assure you Madam Marjorie that I know *exactly* what I am doing. The Windelton people need a sign that God is amongst them and this celebration will be a manifestation of the Good Lord in our presence. The all-consuming fires of hell that on the day of judgement…"

"Yes, yes, yes Maxwell," Marjorie cut in before the Reverend Max went off on one of his evangelic rants, "but I need to see what this tableau is saying about my

Festival. I want sight of the hymns you plan to sing, the music score. I don't want you turning this into one of your political rallies."

"Of course, of course Madam Marjorie," he nodded vigorously in agreement knowing full well that Marjorie would forget all about it in the rush that would overwhelm her in the days leading up to the opening.

Marjorie had heard the rumours that the Reverend Max was once a regional organiser for the Brown Shirts during the war. His 'hell fire and damnation' sermons on the vices of youth and the voodoo power of bus drivers who plied the streets of nearby northern cities were legendary. His charismatic Sunday services caused many elderly female parishioners to slump full length onto their hassocks in a dead faint. The church ushers had to be trained in first aid and a St John's Ambulance was in attendance every Sunday outside the church.

The span of Marjorie's ambition for the festival was wide. In addition to the crowd-pulling 'arty' elements, the festival programme was to include a range of refreshment tents offering locally produced food, a tea tent, a large and extensively stocked bar. There was to be arts and crafts stalls, raffles and a 'posh' tombola with luxury prizes. Everything had been designed to extract the maximum amount of cash from the pockets of the Windelton townsfolk and the many expected visitors from further afield. The ballet, a book reading by a famous female author and the musical events were all to be held in one large marquee that would have a raised stage with special sound systems and lights provided by the local theatre (at no cost).

"Neville, I need your lights for my festival," was Marjorie's uncompromising telephone call. "You can call it sponsorship, if it makes you feel any better."

"But, but…"

"No 'buts' Neville, just do it or my annual donation to your 'Theatre Fighting Fund' stops today."

'Click' went the phone, conversation over.

The theatre director sat at his desk holding the phone, "Bloody blackmail," he exclaimed. Neville realised that to shun Marjorie's patronage was tantamount to financial suicide; the thought of losing Marjorie's annual donation made his veined, artistic hands tremble.

The admission costs had been set at the high price of three guineas per head and one pound for children under sixteen (more than three children in one family and the fourth child goes free). The steep entry price bought an all-in-one ticket that would entitle holders to see every performance and gain free admittance to the evening disco. Marjorie was not without some of her late father's business canniness.

Marjorie also had the presence of mind to engage the services of a pop band that had been in the hit parade within living memory. This was to prove to be a winning formula at drawing in the younger crowds for the evening part of the festival.

~

"We have to meet." It was a demand not a question.

"Aren't you meant to be in Scotland?"

The telephone call came at just past noon on a Saturday.

Astle's voice quavered, on edge. Valerie could hear his shallow breathing.

"There are some *problems… changes.*" Astle's breath sighed down the telephone wires like a Windelton wind. His voice lacked its normal commanding cadence. The calmness and reason of Scotland had deserted him. His good intentions of a rational discussion, a coherent explanation of his plan had evaporated. Instead he resorted to garbled hints and innuendo. "We have to meet," he repeated, "It's got to be by chance. Can you get to Windelton the two weeks today, the Saturday?" Gerald continued, ignoring Valerie's question.

"But *why* Gerald and after all this time? You must tell me. Why can't you come here?"

"I can't explain now. Have to see you. There's a big festival on in the town. It would be easy for us to meet by chance."

"Why all this cloak and dagger stuff in your home town with other people about? This doesn't seem at all sensible Gerald! Can't we meet on another day and somewhere in private?"

"No, no, it *must* be in two weeks' time at the festival." Astle insisted, his voice rising to a near suppressed shout.

"Are you sure you are not ill Gerald, this sounds a ridiculous request?"

"No, of course not," he said.

"The important thing is that you are there to meet me." His voice lowered to a near rasping whisper, uncertainty tainted his tone.

"Valerie *please*, my love, *please* come along and then I can tell you my plans. It'll be alright, everything is going to be alright. You and me, James, it's all going to be wonderful," he blurted.

"But for heaven's sake Gerald, you've positively avoided me for the last eight years," said Valerie feeling hurt and exasperated with Astle's incoherent demands. "You've had all this time to meet and now you are asking me, no demanding, that I come to your home town and risk everything? And what is all this about everything 'being wonderful' for me and James? *I am happy as it is.* Gerald, you seem to have taken leave of your senses."

Astle was incapable of answering Valerie's questions. Even he couldn't fathom why he had never visited. Now he was desperate. He ploughed on: "We need to plan ahead; I want to do more for you…. both……us." Astle's voice trailed off. Still he couldn't articulate the proper words.

"You're not planning to do anything *stupid* Gerald, *you're not are you, for God's sake?"* cried Valerie in real alarm. "What we had arranged these past years has worked *so* well for us all. Don't go and spoil everything now. You have to think

130

about *your* son too. When James gets older he'll have to know the truth but *not yet*," she said, pausing. She could hear Astle's heavy breathing.

Valerie carried on trying to adopt a more reasoned tone: "I know when you retire I'll have to manage on my own financially. I have been saving for these times Gerald, I am not stupid you know? Do you want to reduce the monthly allowance, is that what's worrying you?" she asked hoping that this might be the reason behind Gerald's sudden need to meet and talk.

"NO, no it's much more than that. It's about US!" declared Astle in a stifled shriek.

Oh God, thought Valerie, her worst nightmares were about to come to true. "What exactly do mean, Gerald?" she asked trying to sound calm. Valerie was trying to take in the implications of Astle's unexpected U-turn from passive benefactor to sudden claimant on her ordered life.

"Well us - you, James, me," spluttered Astle.

She tried to steer the conversation in another direction. "What about Daphne, have you mentioned 'us' to her? Are there problems at the bank?" she asked.

Astle ignored both questions. "Valerie, just listen to me," said Astle, trying to sound more composed. "This is important; it's about *you and me*. You've *got* to come. It would be quite natural to bump into one another at some pre-arranged spot. After all we are old colleagues. Afterwards we can find a secluded spot to talk."

Astle's whispered plan didn't sound in the least convincing.

"I will need to get away afterwards; it will be my last chance to speak to you for a while.

"What do you mean *last chance?*"

I can't explain over the phone, people are listening."

"Who's listening?"

"*People.*" They are listening all the time."

"Gerald, I think you are having a breakdown. Where are you going to afterwards, what's all the mystery?"

"Can't talk about it now. I'll tell you when we meet."

"Who says we're meeting?"

There was silence; all Valerie could hear was Astle's laboured breathing.

"Are you still there Gerald?" asked Valerie worried that Astle might be having some sort of seizure.

"*We have to meet,*" said Astle emphatically. "I am going to call off now," he whispered. "It's too dangerous, people at the telephone exchange; they know everything that goes on around here."

Valerie felt a strange wave of sympathy for Astle. He sounded if he was going mad. After all, he had given her precious James, albeit by some terrible mistake. He had been such a sweet, repressed man. She remembered the day he had turned up unexpectedly at the flat with some boring papers to sign. She had a sudden and inexplicable desire to sleep with him; one of her 'black dog' moments. She had had thoughts about him before, curiously attracted by his ridiculous shyness and obvious loneliness. Today he was lonely and vulnerable again and now perhaps about to self-destruct. She would have to help him in some way or it would be disaster for everyone.

Astle realised that he was sounding hysterical and he tried to inject some reason back into the conversation. "I couldn't call tomorrow because the all-seeing Daphne," he managed a little joke about his clairvoyant obsessed wife, "has invited some friends around for drinks, around lunchtime."

But Valerie didn't see at all. She could tell Astle was lying. She knew Daphne well enough after eight years of clockwork Sunday conversations that she would not invite people around when Gerald went out for his Sunday pint. This call was not of Daphne's making. "You know I don't mind about James, you've always looked after us, there is nothing to feel ashamed about Gerald," Valerie's tone was conciliatory.

"*You need a proper life, money to spend, James needs a father figure,*" he gushed. "*I have been weak ...utterly hopeless,*" Gerald's voice choked.

132

"Well that's all a bit late now?" said Valerie, frightened by Gerald's garbled proposal. "You can't just phone me up and come out with this end-of-the-pier confession after all these years? Valerie's sympathetic feelings for Astle dissolved and she finally erupted into rare anger at this mad intervention. How dare him, after eight years of pathetic bleating, start to talk about a new life. James was *hers* and she was not sharing him with anyone, father or no father. "Gerald, I will see you but on my terms. Phone me again in a week when you've come to your senses and we'll discuss where and when."

The realisation that his blurted confession had been badly received finally dawned on Astle. His attitude to all people, and especially women, had always been command and control. He was not used to being rebuffed, however bizarre the request.

"Okay, I'll call again a week tomorrow to fix things up," he said curtly. "This could be the break we all want for a new life. We'll have plenty of money, sunshine and a carefree life," he continued as if explaining the terms of a bank loan to a customer.

"What *are* you talking about Gerald? If you expect me and James to suddenly up sticks and disappear with you, then think again. *Where are you getting the money from, what about your wife, your job, the bank?"*

It was worse than Valerie had suspected, Gerald had flipped.

Astle, realising his monumental blunder, decided his best strategy was to get off the phone as fast as he could; the whole conversation had gone completely wrong, wrong, wrong.

The phone went click, brrrrrrr. Valerie stared at the neutered telephone hand set in disbelief.

~

Marjorie had planned the festival meticulously. It would be both a celebration of her benevolence and a carnival of unremitting exploitation of the Windelton community. Nothing on this scale of municipal robbery had been experienced in Windelton since the great coronation mug scandal back in 1953.

On that occasion it was Windelton's enterprising but unscrupulous Mayor who had orchestrated the crime. He managed to coerce nearly every rate paying member of Windelton into to buying a celebratory mug from the Borough Council at a grossly inflated price. The discovery of the Mayor's secret mug kiln, his mysterious death and the ensuing publicity turned the value of the mugs into collector's gold. Despite the mugs' poor manufacture - many were misshapen, had handles missing or featured the Queen's head upside down, they had become collectables and limited edition china enthusiasts traded the mugs at up to ten times their original price.

Marjorie's festival plan was nearly as ambitious as the Mayor's scam. She aimed to clear a total of ten thousand pounds profit from the whole event. Marjorie in her own generous and philanthropic way would match any funds raised for her Cottage Hospital Foundation.

The planned evening disco would complete the fund-raiser on a less high- brow but equally popular note. Marjorie conceded that the disco and barbecue tickets could be sold separately; these had been fixed at an outrageous nine shillings and sixpence to discourage the 'riff raff' from nearby villages. Windelton's precincts were invaded on Saturday evenings by roaming gangs of youngsters from the outlying rural areas in search of strong ales and spoiling for physical violence. There was also a practical reason for the high ticket prices as the pop group hired did not come cheap and profits still had to be made.

Marjorie's surreptitious forward planning had reaped rewards. Nine months ago she had reserved a northern choral group and orchestra; such was their popularity that forward booking was essential. A small Florentine ballet company with a formidable reputation had reluctantly agreed to perform three extracts from celebrated pieces - Swan Lake, Giselle and The Nutcracker Suite. Marjorie had used all her powers of persuasion to overcome their doubts about performing and she had agreed to install a specially sprung, outdoor stage in the Japanese garden. The only proviso from the dance company was that the temperature must not drop below sixty degrees Fahrenheit otherwise the dancers would be unable to perform. Cold toes meant loss of flexibility and movement. As this was a distinct possibility, even during the month of May, Marjorie installed under floor heating to avoid any last minute dramas.

Her final 'pièce de résistance' was to secure Denise Sowter, the celebrated author of popular romantic fiction who had agreed to come and read extracts from her latest novel, 'Other People's Husbands'. She would also give the audience tips on writing and reveal some 'hidden secrets' on how she created her chaste but passionate blockbuster romances. Denise, who wrote under a number of pseudonyms, turned out to be a friend of one of Marjorie's coffee morning syndicate.

The friendship had started when the unknown Denise worked as the tea trolley girl on a weekly newspaper located further north. Providing this part of her early career was not mentioned, she had agreed to grant Windelton an audience. She had also been coerced into undertaking a charity auction, the star items being a number of her own signed books along with other precious artefacts that Marjorie has expropriated from the good and great in the Windelton district. Marjorie had ordered Ray Trubshaw to stand at the back of the marquee and make false bids (no change to a normal day's work for him) to 'get the prices up'. This charade would conclude the afternoon's activities before the barbecue and disco started the evening's entertainment.

The date was set for the last Saturday in May and Marjorie had ordered the Reverend Max to pray his hardest for good weather. Marjorie was far too busy to pray herself but she wanted to leave no stone unturned just on the off-chance that the Reverend Max did have a direct line to the Almighty. The marquee installers had been instructed to double up on the key guy ropes to ensure that Windelton's unpredictable winds did not rip the tents from the ground. The local magistrates gave the nod to granting a special alcohol licence. Sir Toby Inchdale was the chairman of the bench and Marjorie had phoned him prior to the hearing to ensure that he understood what he had to do. Sir Toby hadn't the energy to disagree and the idea of a new hospital was laudable enough. He wasn't getting any younger himself.

The special licence would be the first one granted since the VE Day celebrations. It allowed intoxicating liquors to be sold and consumed from two in the afternoon until midnight. The Methodists and most of the town's thirty or so landlords had vigorously objected; the Methodists cited moral corruption and the landlords claimed it would cripple their Saturday night trade. These were dismissed by Sir Toby from the bench as 'complete nonsense.' Any ensuing rude comments made in court were issued with on the spot fines and the proceeds put towards the fund raising appeal. Over one hundred pounds was raised by the town's generous publicans and ten pounds from the Methodists for singing Wesleyan hymns in court.

Now all Marjorie had to do was to ensure that anyone that was anyone attended. In early April, Marjorie sat down at her Louis XV escritoire, took out a new pad of Basildon Bond notepaper with the Red House embossed in blue, charged her fountain pen with crimson ink and commenced putting pen to paper. Her offensive had begun.

~

Astle dropped the telephone receiver onto its cradle like a defeated man, he sagged sideways, leaning against the red framed windows. He stared at the graffiti scrawled on the notice board in front him. 'Dick's knobbed Suzy,' claimed the writer in a crude hand. 'Gerald's knobbed Valerie,' thought Astle.

He realised he had completely messed everything up. He would have to think of a different approach. If he couldn't possess Valerie and James, then what? He was convinced he was going to be dismissed from the bank so what were his options? Retirement with Daphne; buy a bungalow in Scarborough and disappear anonymously, drop dead in a few years. God what a future, he would rather die now.

With barely enough strength he pushed open the red 'phone box's heavy, metal door and staggered out. He was having difficulty breathing again. What a fool he had been, he thought, blurting all that out to Valerie over the phone. He was tired from his long drive and needed a drink. Valerie would not be his accomplice but maybe he could persuade her to join him later. Yes, he thought, that was a more realistic approach. Why hadn't he considered that before, instead of going the whole hog?

For a man who had spent his life going out of his way trying never to shock anybody, Astle was having a vintage day. The landlord at the pub was nearly as surprised as Valerie when his two-halves-of-bitter Sunday regular lurched into the pub on Saturday. Astle was white faced with perspiration beaded on his forehead. He looked terrible.

"Good morning Sir, didn't expect to see *you* on a Saturday," greeted the landlord. He was taken aback again when Astle ordered a large gin and tonic instead of his customary half pint.

"Everything alright sir, you look a bit peculiar, do you want a seat?"

"No, no just get me my drink, don't hang about man."

The landlord busied himself with Astle's G&T. He was alarmed at his Sunday regular's agitated manner; this fat middle-aged man had been coming to his pub all the time that he had held the tenancy. Over the last few years they had exchanged no more than the usual pleasantries about the weather and the latest trade union strike. In all that time the landlord considered Astle had been calm, guarded and uninvolved. Quite frankly a bit of a bore! Now he had turned up on the wrong day, sweating like a pig, his hands shaking like a leaf and with a face as ashen as a cadaver.

Once the gin started to work its magic, it dawned on Astle that he had been behaving in a highly conspicuous manner. Although he didn't normally give a damn, his instinct for self-preservation warned him that he'd better pull himself together. The gin had liberated his spirit a little; his conversation with Valerie, however rambling and incoherent had released from him a heavily laden burden - he had nearly spoken the truth for once in his life, however badly it had turned out. He also had the terrifying realisation that she didn't want to hear what he had so unsuccessfully tried to articulate. Now when he realised that his plans might be impossible to fulfil the realisation overcame him that *he really did want Valerie and his son.*

This inescapable truth came over him like a tidal wave of regret. "Damn, blast and bugger," he muttered to himself under his breath.

"What was that sir?" asked the landlord gently.

"Oh nothing, just a thought," Astle said attempting a more cordial approach.

"I am so sorry; I don't know what I was thinking. I have just been visiting a relative nearby, she is very, very ill. It's all been a bit of a shock."

"Did she live in the village?"

"Er, er yes... I mean no... no, down the road," Astle was caught completely off guard. He thought desperately where the next village was but his mind was blank. "Basingstoke," he blurted, "on the phone, you see" his voice trailing into a mutter, "it's about money... money, my son... he is going away you see."

The landlord was now convinced that his Sunday customer was having some sort of 'turn'. What was he rambling on about? He decided to keep a watchful eye over him. Perhaps he'd been cut out of an inheritance, he didn't appear to be grieving, more aggrieved? He was obviously upset about something. For years he had been coming into the pub, calm as a lamb, everyone locally knew he only came to the village to use the 'phone box. The fat man from the bank had become quite a fixture. Locals no longer tried to make calls on Sundays around midday.

The landlord studied the grey hunched figure at the bar with his trembling drink. You get them all in a pub; the bar was often better than a confessional box. Customers came in and told bar staff things they wouldn't tell their closest mates. This one looked like he could admit to murder at any minute!

"Another G and T sir?"

"No, better not, but I will sit down for a minute and catch my breath."

Astle shuffled off into a window seat that overlooked the village green. He looked wistfully out onto a tranquil late spring scene. Wild cherry blossom was being wafted from the trees in a gentle breeze (no Windelton gusts here), the hawthorn hedgerows had burst into flower and birds darted about searching out nesting materials.

The landlord could see the fat man's lips moving as he continued a muttered conversation with himself. Sometimes he appeared to smile, occasionally a frown crossed his brow and he twisted in his seat while he tried to readjust some under garments that seemed to be bothering him. The fat man's flabby hands kept returning to his fly as if he was trying to push something large down his trousers. The landlord hoped he wouldn't have to call an ambulance, it always upset the other customers.

- Chapter 17 -

Making a Play

He didn't quite know why but Jasper rather liked Ian Henderson There was something about his boyish charm and the obvious embarrassment that Jasper was not his usual social company that he liked. Jasper tried not to be patronising about Ian's evident vulnerability and chippiness. Ian had every right to be annoyed about his golf game, he really had had bad luck; providence must have summoned up that sudden blast of wind.

But Jasper hadn't invited Ian for a drink because he felt sorry for him, rather he felt some affinity between them, something beyond golf, maybe it was an age thing. Anyhow he got rather fed up of his usual circle of friends who could be a complete bunch of Yorkshire hoorays when they were fuelled up with claret.

On the contrary, Ian was baffled why he had not made an excuse to duck out of his drink with young Inchdale. It must have been Dawn's curiosity and perhaps his desire to heal the scars of their post-match row and show her that he didn't bear Jasper a grudge. That he was man enough to accept defeat and sup with his rival. Their meeting was going better than expected. It hadn't taken long for Dawn to feel perfectly at ease chatting away to Rachel, Jasper's beautiful girlfriend. Considering that Dawn rarely ever visited the Nags Head nor had ever met Jasper or Rachel before she was enjoying the relaxed sociability of the evening.

"Another pint?" asked Jasper.

"I'll give you a hand," said Ian

"Same again girls?"

The two men got up and headed toward the bar.

Although Dawn was a little older than Rachel and despite the differences in their lives and social backgrounds she quickly clicked with the younger woman. Rachel's father was a successful lawyer in Bradford and since she had returned from a finishing school in Switzerland she was expected to find herself a suitable husband

and start producing some progeny. Her father expected her to maintain the family line of lawyers and judges. This was not Rachel's idea at all. She didn't tell him this while he was shelling out a generous allowance to keep her socially mobile.

Rachel had other ideas how to best maximise her one 'O' level in domestic science, the only dividend of her expensive education. Her alpine tan could be clearly seen above the thigh length suede boots and below her tiny matching mini skirt as she crossed and uncrossed her long legs. Rachel had clear ambitions but they didn't involve boring lawyers. She wanted to make it with a rock star, anyone would do; she had recently seen a picture of the Rolling Stones and thought that their lead guitarist would make a good sleeping off point. Rachel's idea of a 'good bloke' was the one most unsuitable to her parents' idea of 'the ideal man'.

Jasper was too much a chip off the old block she confided to Dawn, drawing heavily on a Chesterfield un-tipped cigarette which she devoured one after another. Only twenty-one years of age, Rachel already had the gravelly laughter and rattling cough of a veteran smoker. Dawn and Rachel were discussing the possibilities of arranging this meeting with the dark haired guitarist as the group were due to play the Excelsior Ball Rooms, York, in a few weeks' time.

"Two pints of bitter, a dry martini and soda and a Babycham please," Jasper tried not to wince when ordering the Babycham for Dawn but the barman seemed completely unfazed by the order. "Dawn's a nice looking girl Ian, you sly old devil, where on earth did you find her, not in Windelton surely?"

Ian was taken aback by this backhanded compliment but at the same time annoyed at being patronised by Jasper. He tried to make light of the remark and breezily replied:

"Oh, you'd be surprised at what you can find knocking about in Windelton, you can't have been looking hard enough!"

"Obviously! I have to drive thirty five miles into darkest Yorkshire to find a good-looking girl and thirty- five miles back to find a good pub and all Rachel wants to talk about is pop groups and kinky boots".

"But she *is* gorgeous Jasper."

"They are all the same horizontal!" he replied arrogantly with an accompanying conspiratorial wink. Ian winced at this disparaging remark about such a beautiful girl.

Returning to the table with the drinks, Ian appeared crestfallen as he looked at the lithe, beautifully groomed, suede suited and booted girl; a rich girl in a rich girl's outfit. How could Jasper be so dismissive of such a delicious beauty?

His momentary gloom lifted as Rachel's perfectly shaped face looked up at him, her thick lustrous blond hair moved like a TV commercial for shampoo. It settled naturally on perfectly shaped shoulders, strands of hair caressing her neck and the suede of her jacket.

"You look as if you have just lost another round of golf," she said brightly smiling at Ian. "Has Jasper been teasing you with one of his tactless, misogynistic remarks?"

"Oh no, it's nothing", he stammered uncomfortably and thinking that she was more perceptive than her appearance would suggest.

"Ian always get moody about his golf, don't take any notice of him", chipped in Dawn. "He doesn't like losing".

"What man does?" said Jasper.

"I don't know how the hell I beat him. Ian is loads better than me. You just have to see him hold his clubs and watch his action, he's an absolute natural," Jasper continued looking directly at Dawn his eyes widening in a smile.

"You married a talented man, Dawn!"

"I know, but he doesn't realise it half the time, that's Ian's biggest problem".

"Why the hell do you work in that stupid bank, you should be doing something that interests you?" said Jasper.

Ian looked up into the thick, boozy haze of the pub as if in search of some profound answer. He knew he had no plausible response to Jasper's question.

After a long pause Ian looked at Jasper in mock seriousness, "You know," he said, "I don't bloody know! I could tell you that the bank's okay, you get a cheap mortgage and I'll end up being a manager one day." Then Ian mimicked a funny old crone's voice: "*And just when I am about ready to drop off my perch I'll get a wonderful pension. Then I'll snuff it and my wife will travel the world as a merry widow with a young man thirty years her junior in her bed every night!*"

Everyone laughed but Dawn gasped, "Is that what you really think Ian?"

Jasper roared, "Lucky man, can I apply?"

"*You'll* be too old by then," replied Dawn looking up at Jasper's confident smile and seeing the funny side of Ian's self-deprecating view of the future. The problem was that Dawn could see that Ian *did* really think that this *was* his future.

"You'd better hurry up and kick Mr Astle out then; your wife and family could do with a pay rise, sharpish?" Dawn added, just a little too tartly.

"Oh stop getting at him you two," interjected Rachel.

"Let's change the subject and discuss the Excelsior concert. Dawn and I are going even if you two stick-in-the-muds don't want to come."

"Who said we don't want to go?" retorted Jasper. "I am up for it and Ian was telling me at the bar that he was as keen as mustard."

Ian nodded in solemn agreement with this blatant lie as he suppressed his anger at Dawn's barb about money.

Dawn cheered up immediately and looked across at Jasper's cheery smile wondering why Ian wasn't more like this charismatic and carefree man. He seemed to ooze a love of life and enjoyment. He was very good looking even if he was beginning to look a bit bottled scarred by his high-living ways. Dawn rarely thought about men. Looking at Jasper and Rachel it suddenly occurred that life was passing her by and there seemed little prospect of change. If they hadn't come out this evening, what would they have been doing? More as likely nothing, certainly not talking, not even arguing! She was often too exhausted by looking after the two children and having the responsibility of running the home; while Ian would be sitting in silence, his frustration of work gnawing at him. Love-making was invariably off the agenda these days, what was the expression? *'One year of sex for a lifetime of marriage!'*

Jasper persuaded Dawn to try a martini and soda. After two more she agreed with him that they were the best drinks she had ever tasted in her life. The bar seemed to be getting noisier and Jasper more and more attractive. Even Ian seemed to be loosening up; he was engaged in earnest conversation with Rachel. Although it seemed more like he was doing the listening and Rachel doing most of the talking.

Little did Dawn realise that Rachel was explaining the finer details of what little English 'madams' did while away at expensive finishing schools in Switzerland. Being locked up in a beautiful ski resort with no men and spending her days learning how to arrange flowers and walk correctly were not high priorities on Rachel's agenda. She preferred to party.

Ian's imagination had by now started to wander, fuelled by beer and the close proximity to this vision of beauty, his mind was carrying him away across snowy landscapes and mountains of hot buttered breasts, many bearing an uncanny resemblance to the shape and alluring curve of Rachel's skinny-rib sweater.

Dawn realised she needed to go to the lavatory. Now!

She felt light headed and rather hot, a change of air and a splash of water over her face would do the trick. She excused herself and negotiated her way to the ladies loo without getting lost or falling over.

Jasper casually looked at his watch. He was becoming seriously aroused by the twin notions of Dawn's innocent, womanly beauty and the knowledge that within the hour he should be running his hands over Rachel's delicious brown thighs and removing her mini skirt back at Gardener's Cottage. But like most men, Jasper always wanted more. He didn't want to just drink from the trough of indulgence; he wanted to stand in it. Now on his fifth pint he felt the world was a silver dish of the most succulent oysters and they were all waiting for him. All he had to do was choose. But Dawn would need some preparation before he swallowed her whole!

Six minutes into Dawn's sortie to the lavatory (Jasper timed ladies loo visits very carefully) he made his move. Jasper calculated he could intercept Dawn on her way back and before she reached the bar. There would be ample time for a comforting word, a kiss, the promise of a future, clandestine meeting. Married girls always fell for it. They couldn't believe their luck that someone had taken an interest in them, just when they thought that they were getting passed their best.

"I am just going to buy some fags," he announced to Rachel and Ian and darted off. Ian was engrossed with Rachel and hardly noticed his departure.

Jasper's timing was impeccable, near military planning couldn't have coordinated a better rendezvous. Dawn was gingerly feeling her way out of the ladies' lavatory, the fingers of her right hand gently trailing the panelled corridor walls that linked the ladies lavatories and the bar. This steadying action gave her reassuring contact with something solid, it would help keep her upright and avoid wobbling too much. The bright lights of the ladies ablutions had had an unpleasant effect on her and the water splashing hadn't helped at all. In fact she spilt most of the water down her dress and there was only a soiled towel for drying off. Overall, she felt worse than when she went in; she was feeling light headed and nauseous.

The Babycham followed by successive martini and sodas had caught up with her. She was not used to drinking this amount of alcohol. She was elated by the company and attention of Jasper. But Dawn had enough common sense to know that by now she had drunk more than enough. Just as she was thinking she must tell Ian it was time to go home, the figure of Jasper appeared out of nowhere walking straight towards her. Instead of him standing aside to let her pass, she suddenly realised that his hand was on her shoulder and he was looking directly into her eyes. His face looked a bit flushed with tiny red veins showing up on the surface of his boozy cheeks. Funny she thought, I hadn't noticed them before. He seemed very close, she could feel his breath on her face and there was a smell of beer and an underlying aroma of expensive cologne. It was a smell she hadn't experienced before. It was nice. It must be especially for toffs she thought, 'Old Toff' maybe? She pondered drunkenly, amused at her own mental joke.

He was speaking to her quietly but she couldn't quite work out what he was saying. It was coming to her in snatches, she really shouldn't have drunk so many of those martini things, it was a bit like listening to Radio Luxembourg when the sound wavered, always at the best part of the song: "Beautiful, meet again, you're lovely." Suddenly his face was in front of hers, it was so close she could no longer focus. She closed her eyes and there was a hot feeling on her lips. Losing her balance she stumbled forward, her arms around his body to stop falling headlong onto the floor. She realised he was trying to kiss her – she pulled her head back, shaking it from side to side in a determined effort to say something coherent. "No Jasper, I am married. I am flattered but ...no!"

He gripped her gently and let her rock back in his arms, studying her flawless face as he murmured "I am not in the habit of kissing married women." This was a complete untruth as Jasper had made a career out of fornicating with other people's wives. "But you are *so* beautiful. If I can't kiss you, can I at least call you?"

Dawn had by now gathered enough wits about her to start to feel embarrassed about the situation. All her married life she had never considered another man, with the exception of the dentist, but every woman felt the same way about him. She was annoyed finding herself in this position and felt mildly alarmed by the overpowering proximity of his presence. She was in a tender trap. On the one hand she just wanted to get back to Ian and to feel normal again, but on the other she didn't want to stop this bizarre fantasy. In an instinctive move for flight she leant forward, kissed Jasper's cheek and gently pushed him out of the way.

"If you want to see me again, you'll have to search the telephone directory," she slurred and was gone.

~

Valerie sat perched on her favourite chair in the hall. She felt cold and afraid. She stared incredulously at the mouthpiece of the black telephone receiver. Had she really had that garbled conversation with Astle or was it a terrible dream? The Bakelite telephone was heavy in her hand and she replaced the receiver with deliberate care hoping that he was still not on the other end of the line.

She felt a mixture of genuine anger and alarm at having her ordered life so strangely interrupted. Astle was always *so* predictable, *she* was the unpredictable one. He must have had some sort of breakdown. The ideas he had tried to express were the ones she dreaded that one day might arise. The situation was volatile; her well-hidden secret could be exposed. How could she shield James? If necessary he would have to be told now, rather than later as planned.

Astle's bumbling could undermine her plan of disclosure. This infuriating thought crowded her mind creating a cocktail of sensations. She felt sick. Was it the worry or the thrill of being discovered? Valerie thought of the few moments of genuine excitement she had experienced over the years. The occasional Thursday evening client that had satisfied her gnawing needs for sexual pleasure, a handful of sensational orgasms, even Gerald's. Then there was that beautiful man she had once followed on her motorcycle. Someone said that he was a dentist. She had quite forgotten about her high-speed chase after him near Windelton. He had given her the slip. That town seemed to have a hold over her when it came to men crossing her path. That had been the last occasion she had got astride the Bonneville during daylight hours.

- CHAPTER 18 -

A Festival of Drama Begins

Finally the day of the great festival arrived. Marjorie Nelson's philanthropy and the hectoring prayers of the Reverend Max had been rewarded. A gentle breeze blew fluffy white clouds across a duck-blue Windelton sky. For once the wind moderated and warm May sunshine prevailed.

The opening procession made a spectacular sight: the Boys Brigade drummers in their black and white uniforms thumped their way down the high street. The virginal purity of the angelic boys' choir touched the hearts of all who heard them. Fortunately, the words of the Reverend Max's spiritual compositions with questionable lyrics were lost to many, drowned out by the band. Their lit torches were held aloft and the Reverend Max looked resplendently sinister in his hooded, woad-stained gown and flowing train. The druidic symbols woven into the coarse hair-like fabric were embedded with garish jewels. They flashed dangerously in the bright sun giving the Reverend Max the appearance of a medieval Inquisitor.

As the procession reached the market entrance and opposite Murchison's Bank, one of the torches brushed the awning of Mr. Wheelwright's wet fish emporium. The Windelton volunteer fire-fighters immediately sprang into action dousing the conflagration with buckets of water. Crowds stood on the pavement three deep. Young women hung out of the windows of high buildings and spat spent chewing gum into the horns of the trombone players and onto the stretched skins of the Irish drums. Everyone cheered and waved union flags liberally. These had been issued by Marjorie at modest cost to all the town's retailers and sold to the public at extortionate prices. Publicans stood in their doorways booing. Their antics were drowned out by the celebratory carnival noise and the spirit of goodwill that permeated the whole town. Hoskins the Town Clerk noted down any trouble-makers in his black notebook.

The great wooden tableau was positioned some distance away from the main marquee and myriad side stalls in the Red House lower garden. It was lit to a fanfare of trumpets while the choir sang halleluiah choruses. As the flames leapt heavenwards the Reverend Max loudly invoked the Windelton community: *"To follow the good Lord in all his ways and save themselves from eternal damnation."*

At one critical moment of the opening ceremony, the Reverend Max, charged high with emotion, his voice hoarse from shouting above the roaring fire, swayed dangerously close to the leaping flames and was only saved by one of his church wardens grabbing him from behind and throwing him backwards to the ground. This saintly gesture saved the Reverend Max from pitching into the flames of purgatory. Only the ends of his magnificent, voluminous robes were singed and scorched a hellish ruddy-brown colour indicating his brush with the inferno.

Once the drama of the opening had become a smouldering heap the sweating crowds dispersed into the grounds and headed for the licensed bar and much needed refreshment. The first concert of the afternoon commenced at two-thirty and the main marquee quickly filled up as the Windelton brass band groaned through its repertoire of popular classics. Marjorie's great festival was underway.

~

Gerald Astle had been busy. He spoke once again to Valerie on the following Sunday.

"Hello Valerie, sorry if I sounded a bit odd the other day. I was feeling very tired after my long journey back from Scotland. Did I sound off my rocker?" Astle sounded back in control.

"You sound better today, Gerald. What was all that nonsense about us all getting together? You sounded as if you were planning to disappear into the blue yonder?"

"Well in a manner of speaking I am, Valerie."

"Are you *really* going on an extended holiday then?"

"Yes, yes, you could call it that", he replied with a forced giggle.

"Is Daphne going with you - Gerald, how exciting, are you going to retire early from the bank?"

"Sort of, I am going to South America."

"Crikey, that's a long way off, the other end of the earth."

"What does Daphne say about this wild suggestion?"

"She doesn't know."

"Why not Gerald?"

"Because I have bought tickets for you and James too", he whispered conspiratorially.

"What? To go to South America, you must be joking Gerald. How could I find the time to go all that way?"

"Well, only for a holiday, two or three weeks, as long as you like."

"Gosh, that's very generous of you."

Valerie realised there was more behind this suggestion of a 'holiday' so she thought it would be better to try and reason with him.

Astle went on. "You must get a passport and then a visa for you and James from the Argentine embassy in London," he said, his voice becoming more strained.

"Why, when are you planning to go?"

"Very soon. I have got your tickets already. They are open returns. First class BOAC Heathrow to Madrid then on to Buenos Aires. I want to give them to you personally."

Valerie was both stunned and frightened at this crazy suggestion from Astle. "But Gerald you have not answered my question about Daphne? When are you going to tell her that you are going off on this jaunt to the other side of the globe? And why Argentina of all places, couldn't you have settled for Spain or Portugal, somewhere a bit nearer home?"

"No extradition treaties in Argentina."

"What does that mean?"

"Oh, never mind."

"How long will you be gone for?"

"A long time I would expect. That's why I have to see you both before I go. Please, please come along to the festival. I am going to send you details of how we can meet so it looks like we have just bumped into one another."

"Hey, who said I was going?"

"We have so much to settle up before I go," Astle said heavy with emphasis.

"Gerald are you going forever, is that what you are trying to tell me, are you cutting me and James off?"

"No, no, I am NOT saying that, quite the opposite. I want you and James to come and have some holiday with me at some time in the future. I just want to give you the tickets and to finally see my SON before I go!"

"I don't think that's a very good idea."

"Valerie, I won't tell him I am his father but I would at least like to meet him. That's not an unreasonable request, surely?"

Valerie thought for a moment. I suppose as long as James has no idea who Astle is it should be okay. It was perhaps better to see him now and get it over with if he is really going away. "I will agree to meet you at the festival on one condition Gerald. You have to pose as his long-lost uncle NOT his father. If there is a hint of any scenes or public confessions I will tell all and that includes Daphne. Will she be there?"

"God no, she'll be at the clairvoyant for her Saturday afternoon session. She'll not miss that for the world!"

Astle let out a large sigh of relief.

"Okay, I promise to be a pretend Uncle. You'd better call me 'Uncle Gerald' then."

"Okay, Uncle Gerald it is. But no going back Gerald, I am warning you, I will spill the beans if there's any funny business. Understand?"

"Understood."

Valerie thought the unorthodox way in which Gerald was behaving meant that he was capable of doing anything. She would have to be very careful. The idea of presenting him as a long lost uncle solved the immediate problem and Astle had readily accepted the 'Uncle' ploy. He had seemed to become more rational once Valerie had made the agreement to meet.

It confirmed her reasoning that Astle was heading for some sort of breakdown. However, she had to try and secure James's future for as long as she could if he *really* was planning to disappear. After the call, Valerie dug out her Readers Digest World Atlas and was astonished to see how far Argentina was from Whiteley.

He's going for good, that's for certain, she thought.

~

In Astle's own mind everything had finally become crystal clear. He had convinced himself that he was about to get the chop from Hector Pym. The meeting was scheduled for the week after the festival. If he was to make a bolt, it was now or never.

Astle had already thought long and hard where he would go; he had ruled out Europe as being too close for comfort. South America was a place he knew harboured lots of Nazi fugitives from World War II. It was a country with no extradition treaties with Great Britain so he should be safe there once he was ensconced. If it was good enough for the blasted Hun it would be good enough for Gerald Astle. In the end it was an easy decision to make. His planning over the previous months would now pay dividends for time was short.

It was clear from his telephone conversations with Valerie that enticing her to join him on the day his new life would begin was not a feasible option. He could now see how fraught with danger this idea was. He had to concentrate on managing his own exit and then use his energies to persuade Valerie to follow him at a later date. His new plan would be a softly-softly approach. He would invite her and

James on an extended holiday to his imagined, luxury hideaway villa complete with swimming pool and servants. Then they would all be thousands of miles away from tedious Windelton and its ghastly inhabitants. They would spend day after blissful day of indolent luxury. Then, once captivated, how could she refuse to stay on indefinitely? He would have his beautiful wife and his son by his side, life would be perfect.

His woollen underwear started to itch.

~

Valerie pushed her auburn hair under the crash helmet and secured the clasp under her chin. Despite the warm weather she had donned her all-in-one black leather motor cycle leathers. She dressed James in his best school clothing. Valerie wrapped his winter coat around him tightly securing the cloth belt with a strenuous tug on the highest eye hole; she had invested in a new child's crash helmet for him to wear on the journey.

"Are we going to do a ton-up?" he asked excitedly, thrilled to be going on his mother's gleaming black and silver motorbike with its glossy chrome and roaring engine.

"No we *definitely will not,*" said his mother firmly. Valerie was already tense about this meeting with Astle. She had not seen him for so many years, would she even recognise him? James was excited and a little scared too. He had never been on a motorcycle before. He would be able to tell his friends at school that he had done a ton-up down the Whitley by-pass whatever speed his mother reached!

As it turned out they arrived at Windelton early; not because of Valerie's excessive speed, but because in her nervous state she had misjudged the distance. Whatever, the journey had been a real joy. Despite Valerie's worries she dismissed them from her mind and concentrated on controlling the big machine. James clung onto his mother's leather clad waist. It felt like they were going a hundred miles per hour all the time and on occasions he was afraid he might fall off as the machine tilted and bended to counter the curves and twists of the road. When James became tired he rested his head on Valerie's taut back.

Mother and son headed over the high moors out of Whitley, bonded by the throbbing machine, exhilarating in the experience of being together in the open air, the feel of the tarmac under the wheels and the throaty roar of the engine as Valerie kicked up and down the gears. They shared the clear views towards the North Yorkshire moors and the coast beyond as the bike swooped over the high moor-top roads. Soon they descended down into green vales and gradually distanced themselves from the rugged Pennine country that was their home. The weather was warm as the sun climbed and they neared their destination. As the bike slowed they both could feel a gentle balmy breeze play over their faces.

James tapped his mother's shoulder and shouted, "Are we nearly there, Mum?" She signalled with a thumb's up of her leather gauntlet and soon Valerie was manoeuvring the heavy machine on to its stand in the festival car park.

"Phew, I am hot. That was the *best* thing I have ever done!" James exclaimed as Valerie helped him with off his coat and tied both their crash helmets to the handlebars of the Bonneville. Valerie gave him a big smile and a pat on the back.

"You are quite the experienced biker now!" she said before her mind returned with a sickening jolt to her meeting with Astle. There were already many vehicles in the Red House field car park and queues of cars and other motor cyclists were edging into the field. Large charabancs packed with visitors were arriving too, their liveries sported names from towns and villages from all over the north of England. Many of the occupants were music and ballet lovers, some held entire societies of enthusiasts who had travelled from far and wide. The swell of excited, chattering people, the breeze cracking the marquee flags and the sound of the brass band warming up with the odd discursive trumpet note all added up to an atmosphere of anticipated jollity and well-being.

"Can I have an ice cream?" asked James.

"Yes, but let's get in first."

"What are those flames and smoke for?" asked James as they spied sheets of flame and a pall of black smoke rising rapidly into the clear blue sky from inside the gardens.

"I have no idea, but we'll find out soon. I hope a tent hasn't caught fire," Valerie replied gripping his hand tightly.

"Ow!" he cried, causing a large fat woman to scowl at Valerie as if she was treating him cruelly. Valerie smiled at her as if to say, 'What can you do? Kids!'

Everybody seemed happy but Valerie was gripped by nerves as she tried to straighten out the crushed curls that had formed under her tight-fitting helmet. She felt nauseous with apprehension.

What would Astle look like? Would he do something stupid when he met James for the first time? It was going to be a highly charged moment for all of them although James, hopefully, should not be aware of the significance of the meeting. He thought he was just going on a fun outing with his Mum with the added treat of travelling on her motorbike.

Valerie had arranged to meet Astle in the Women's Institute tea tent at three o'clock. It was two fifteen and so there was plenty of time to wander around and look at some of the stalls. They would have an ice cream and try their luck on the tombola. As they walked into the lower gardens they passed a smoking heap of burnt timber from which emanated a terrific blast of heat. It was the remains of the fire they had seen earlier, funny thing to have a bonfire on such a warm day, thought Valerie.

Valerie cut a striking figure in her tight fitting biking leathers, she had put on black mascara around her eyes and had applied red lipstick; the outfit bore a striking resemblance to some of the clothing she wore at the club except this costume didn't expose her firm uplifted breasts or reveal the cheeks of her bare bottom. Whilst applying her make up that morning she had tried to conjure Astle's appearance in her mind. Would he be wearing a suit? He always did; his uniform of

155

respectability. She imagined he would be fat by now; he was plump eight years ago. God, I hope he is not going to make some awful scene after all this time? Why couldn't he have just left things as they were?

After browsing the Northern Watercolourists' tent they moved on to the tombola where James failed to win a prize despite digging his hand up to his elbow in sand for some minutes. A dreadful feeling made Valerie think that perhaps there were no prizes in the tub at all. James looked crestfallen.

"Never mind darling, we'll have an ice cream in a moment," she said to comfort him. Valerie then became absorbed by a Civic Society stall featuring old sepia tinted photographs of Windelton.

"James come and look at these old photographs of Windelton," she called.

"They're boring," he said as he briefly pondered a series of interior and exterior pictures of Murchison's Bank.

"Mummy used to work in a place like this once."

"Were you there when these pictures were taken?"

"No silly, these are nearly one hundred years old. I am not *that* old".

There was a charming photograph of a groom leading a horse and trap into a stable at the rear of Windelton bank. Looking at the pictures brought memories of working in the bank at Hickleton. The interiors had hardly changed since these photographs were taken; the people were dressed differently and the gas lights had been replaced with electric ones, the striking thing was everyone wore hats even the small children, and the men looked very severe in their long dark frock coats.

One of those would have probably suited Astle she thought smiling to herself. It would have made him look even more self-important. She asked herself again why she had ever seduced this man in the first place. What had come over her? He was so much older and married too. She had broken all her own rules. But to have *slept* with him was *her* particular madness. It must have been his look of hopeless resignation, the result of an unhappy marriage to dreary Daphne, and then all the years of working together, where she had witnessed at first hand, his suppressed yearnings. This must have been the spur that had driven her to offer herself to him for those few moments of pleasure and release from his conformity. And it hadn't worked.

Valerie had become so absorbed with her thoughts, studying the photographs that a number of minutes had passed before she suddenly realised that James had slipped away into the throng of festival goers and was now nowhere to be seen.

- Chapter 19 -

Hangover Caller

Dawn Henderson hadn't expected the telephone call.

She had tried to put the evening at the Nag's Head out of her mind but it kept on creeping up on her at unexpected moments during her day. She had been sick in Ian's car on the way home and he had been furious; she could hardly remember Ian carrying her into the house passed the startled baby sitter and upstairs to bed.

The next day had been difficult; a fierce headache combined with the half remembered shame of her flirtatious behaviour with Jasper had haunted her. At the same time she felt a tinge of excitement about what had happened. Jasper was an obvious rogue but there was still something appealing about his worldly charm and flattery. When she ran over the events of the evening it gave her butterflies which didn't help the hangover at all. God, she thought to herself, I am worse than a gauche teenager after having been kissed for the first time. She was struggling to hang out some of Mary's towelling nappies on the clothes line, battling one of Windelton's customary winds that were trying to wrench the damp washing from her unsteady grasp when she heard a distant 'phone ringing from inside the house. Blast! She thought, who could that be now? Dawn ran inside. Mary was asleep in her Moses' Basket in the hallway next to the telephone.

"Hello darling, how is Windelton's most attractive housewife today?"

"Who's that?" she replied, fully recognising Jasper's voice but feigning confusion.

"Jasper... Jasper Inchdale, *you clot*, remember, the Nags Head? You *did* ask me to look you up in the telephone directory!"

"Did I? *Me*, are you sure... *what* about?" Dawn tried to sound innocent, surprised. There was a mild irritation to her voice.

"Oh come on Dawn, you weren't that tight," Jasper laughed down the phone, not fazed by this initial brush-off. "Stop being a little minx! Anyhow I was wondering if you were going to the festival disco. I thought we might meet up for a drink with you and your golfer hubby before we went to the dance?"

There was a silence as Dawn tried to think of an excuse why they weren't going but her mind was blank.

"You *are* going aren't you?"

"Well er… yes I suppose so, I think *everyone* is going, the whole of Windelton I would imagine."

"That's great, we'll meet at the Heifer. It's closer than the Nags to the Red House."

"But…"

"There are no 'buts' to it, I am not asking you to go to bed with me, just to meet up for a cosy drink with your husband. Nothing naughty about that?"

Dawn was so shocked by Jasper's presumption and mention of 'going to bed' that she just stuttered a response. "Oh… well, I suppose that will be alright, I will have a word with Ian."

"Let's say around half seven. I am really looking forward to seeing you again."

Dawn didn't reply. There was an awkward silence.

"That's okay then?" he continued nonchalantly as if this was an ordinary conversation about the weather.

Dawn simply couldn't find the words to reply. Her throat constricted, her heart was racing; she had not been propositioned by a man for over six years and she felt utterly helpless, embarrassed, a tongue tied half-wit.

"Saturday it is then. Love for now."

The phone clicked and Dawn stood by the telephone with a handful of clothes pegs in her hand wondering what she had agreed to. Mary woke up, gurgled and smiled at her. It was amazing what some empty flattery did to your spirits.

Dawn smiled back at her daughter.

~

159

Walter brooded over a mug of tea at his daughter's kitchen table. His eviction from Gardener's cottage had been a terrible betrayal by his old employer. He still couldn't quite believe that it had happened.

His departure had been announced by a curt letter from Courcey Inchdale from the estate office:

For the attention of W. Tindal Esq.

As you are no longer an employee on the Inchdale Estate we are unable to provide Gardener's Cottage rent free. Should you be interested in renting this property the cost is five pounds seven and six pence a week. You will have to buy your own coal for the fire. Trubshaw and Trubshaw, 42 High Street, Windelton, is dealing with the new lease on behalf of the estate. Should you wish to stay in tenure you should contact them with immediate effect. If not please vacate the property within two weeks from the date shown on this letter.

I have asked my brother, Jasper Inchdale, to make himself available to you in helping find alternative lodgings if you have no other accommodation in mind. He has some good contacts with Windelton Borough Council who have retirement properties for the old and needy. I am certain that he can 'bend the odd ear' with the relevant council official to ensure that you can be housed somewhere suitable.

Although you officially retired some months ago and in recognition of your long contribution to the Estate it has been agreed to pay you two weeks' back pay calculated at the rate of your last wage. This will be sent on to you once you have vacated Gardener's Cottage. Please let me have your forwarding address.

On behalf of the Inchdale Estate may I wish you a long and happy retirement and thank you for your many years of servitude.

Yours faithfully,

Courcey Inchdale, Estate Manager.

Courcey Inchdale knew damn well that Walter did not have a hope in hell of affording the five pounds or so a week in rent. He was effectively throwing him out on the street.

160

Walter tried 'phoning the estate office to talk to Courcey but had been politely told that he was not available. After the third attempt his coins had run out in the phone box and he had given up. Finally, he decided to confront Courcey at the ramshackle estate office and have it out with him. He duly turned up but Courcey was nowhere to be seen.

He went back on another day and caught a fleeting glimpse of Courcey roaring down the estate drive in his battered Land Rover, careering his way through slushy snow as his vehicle bumped out of sight. Someone must have spotted him approaching on his bicycle and tipped Courcey off. After nearly forty years of working for the squire this was no way to be treated. His daughter wrote a letter to Sir Toby on Walter's behalf which Walter had signed with an illegible scrawl. After nearly two months Sir Toby had replied:

My dear Walter

I was distressed to learn that you are no longer part of the estate (he had crossed out 'a serf' rather badly). *As you know I relinquished the running of the estate some years ago to the younger generation and these matters are now sadly out of my hands.*

I would suggest that you take this matter up at the earliest opportunity with my eldest boy, Courcey, who is responsible for all estate matters. He is a kind hearted soul, if sometimes a little dim, but we have to do our best don't we?

I hope you are in good spirits. It's infernally cold up here at the Hall and Lady Lavinia is suffering horribly with her chilblains. Do try and keep warm.

I have taken the liberty of enclosing a small donation to your retirement fund. May I wish you and your good lady wife my very best wishes and enjoy your well-deserved retirement.

Yours sincerely,

Inchdale (Bart)

Walter discovered a crumpled ten shilling note at the bottom of the envelope. The death of his wife under the hooves of one of the estate's bulls had conveniently slipped Sir Toby's memory.

Towards the end of Walter's two weeks' notice period Jasper Inchdale had turned up in his flashy sports car.

"Walter, old boy," he started as if he was addressing his oldest friend, "You'll be pleased to know that with a bit of wangling with the town council I have managed to fix you up with a new home," he continued with empty brightness.

"It is all arranged for you to move into the splendid River View Room at the Council Retirement Home – no charge, free gratis! Waddya think about that old chap?" he said, as if handing Walter a priceless gold artefact.

Before Walter had the chance to splutter out an exclamation of disgust, Jasper continued in full effusive flow. "And what's more if you want to keep on the cottage garden to grow some vegetables and the like you are most welcome!" Seeing that his five carat offer was not being well received Jasper went on in a more conciliatory tone, using all his legendary powers of persuasion and charm. "I do hope you understand that *this* cottage," he said pointing at it as if coming across it for the first time, "is owned by the estate and we've now *other* uses for it."

Walter was not going to be sucked into this obvious conscience-assuaging offer of keeping his garden in exchange for moving into the arthritic, one-room riverside council flat. Walter was far too proud to take up either offer although the cottage garden would have been useful. He had enjoyed tilling his small piece of land and he'd made it an abundant source of vegetables and soft fruits, it had been his fiefdom, however small the domain.

"No thanks squire, all the same. I think it's time for pastures new," he replied drily, through gritted teeth. His eyes refused to catch Jasper's eager look. It was all too clear that Jasper was the one that needed the escape route to cover his guilt. Walter wasn't going to let him get away with this scandalous eviction with the measly offer of his old garden and a fly-blown, damp hut. Stuff his garden, stuff the bloody lot, he thought!

"You can keep your bloody garden and that dump down by the river. And that's flat. Good afternoon squire."

"Please yourself, it's a good offer," said Jasper lamely, as Walter stumped off into his potting shed before his fury got the better of him.

Some weeks after Jasper's visit, and after Walter had moved out, he happened to pass by his old cottage while on one of his rambles around the estate; he was surprised to spy young Inchdale's brightly polished sports car parked in the muddy yard at the side of the cottage. Suddenly, it all fitted together.

The BASTARD! Walter mouthed in anger. The bloody cheek of it, 'needed for the estate' my arse! The whole thing was a pack of lies. Trubshaw and Trubshaw were never letting his cottage; it was earmarked for that young scoundrel from the start. They had the cheek to try and conveniently shunt him off into that damp old codger's home.

After his eviction, his daughter and son-in-law had kindly come to Walter's rescue and squeezed him in to their semi-detached house and at the same time Walter had quickly taken on a small allotment garden. Most days he busied himself there and brooding on the unexpected turn of events that had brought him to invade his daughter's house. It wasn't the same as Gardener's Cottage and he still felt like an intruder in his daughter's cramped little semi. It was a new experience being surrounded by screaming grand-children and piles of damp washing. However much his daughter and son-in-law denied it, he knew he was getting under their feet. But anything was better than being shoved off into the old folks' home to die of rheumatic fever or be swept away in a flood.

Despite being nearly seventy years of age Walter was still fit and healthy and determined not to give up life just yet. As he hoed the weeds between his runner bean plants and seeded rows of lettuces he had pondered a number of courses of action. He was determined that those damned Inchdales wouldn't get away with it; somehow he would get his own back. He would bide his time, the right moment would come. In the meantime he remained cordial and continued to greet the Squire and family with a deferential touch of his cap. It might have appeared to the unseeing that all was well with Walter. Good old Walter, the faithful old retainer, accepting his forced retirement with stoicism and dignity.

But nothing could be further from the truth.

- Chapter 20 -

A Robbery, No Violence

Like all good plans Astle's was simple. And like all deluded people he believed them
to be fool-proof.

An hour after the bank closed on Saturday morning of the great festival day he
had slipped into the branch. If spotted he would just say that he was catching up on
urgent paperwork. When the following week's safe codes had arrived on Friday by
secure messenger he had noted Laurence Payne's own code numbers before
handing them to him. He apologised to Payne on their being opened, explaining he
had mistaken them for his own. This had happened before and didn't excite Payne's
attention.

Armed with the codes for the week, Astle calmly entered the bank from the side
door. Before descending the cellar steps, the Windelton festival parade marched
passed the bank's front door and Astle witnessed a heavenly glow permeate the
frosted glass windows and bathe the empty banking hall in an ethereal light; the
parade's flaming torches spilling their message of joy and blessing Astle's final bank
transaction. Once in the bank's vaults, the Reverend Max's Angelic Boys' Choir
could just be heard singing their messianic chants of spiritual hymns with
questionable lyrics. The sounds were just audible, and Astle paused for a moment
from his dreadful felony, as he strained to hear the words:

> *'Fight the good fight, vengeance our duty, hatred our right*
> *Fight the good fight, vengeance our duty, hatred our right*
> *God loves Windelton and hates all sinners*
> *With God on your side there can only be winners*
>
> *'Fight the good fight, vengeance our duty, hatred our right*
> *Fight the good fight, vengeance our duty, hatred our right*

Where wickedness abides there will only be travails
Hark the heavenly Word and expunge Calgary's nails'
'Fight the good fight, vengeance our duty, hatred our right…..'

As the voices faded, Astle couldn't be quite sure of what he heard but the Reverend Max was capable of a bizarre turn of phrase at the best of times. Such was the commotion and merriment on the streets that a little while later no-one noticed Astle loading the boot of his car with two worn, black leather Gladstone bags.

For some weeks Astle had deliberately not requested any new bank notes from the central treasury. Customers were inclined to complain when they were issued with old notes when asking for withdrawals. It was a process that Astle had postponed despite frequent reminders from the ever-interfering Laurence Payne. This had achieved Astle's aim of building up a larger than average proportion of old notes to the new traceable variety. Astle was careful not to add any new notes to his horde.

The cash would be mere pocket money in comparison with the funds he had already misappropriated from Marjorie Nelson's various accounts. He had already secretly transferred vast sums to a number of offshore bank accounts. So on this festive sunny Saturday morning Astle was already a very rich man. He didn't need the cash and he was not quite sure why he had gone to this subterfuge to take it. Perhaps it was because it was there and it was so easy? Or was it that deep down in Astle's psyche he rather liked the idea of rubbing the bank's nose in it? It added certain piquancy to his already enormous crime. This was now a genuine robbery, not just a paper swindle. In Astle's warped code of conduct stealing by bogus transactions seemed a less honourable theft. However, taking the hard cash was just returning money to its rightful owner. Him.

Taking actual money meant that he could feel the worn notes in his hands; it comforted him just looking at the bundles. He caressed them as he stacked wad

166

after wad into the leather bags. He made sure they fitted perfectly laying them in six rows on the base of each case and then stacking them up one on top of another. There was approximately thirty thousand pounds in each case. He took three of bundles of fivers and placed them inside his linen jacket pockets. Once the cases were filled he closed the brass clip mechanism, the levers slipping home with a reassuring 'clunk'.

The calmness he felt while redistributing Murchison's assets was in stark contrast to the anxiety he was to experience later that afternoon.

- Chapter 21 -

Uncle and nephew

Astle recognised his son as he saw him pick up a piece of iced sponge cake and try to force it whole into his mouth. The boy gripped the slice with three fingers and thumb leaving the little finger of his right hand erect and free of the sticky concoction. It was the same gesture that Astle employed when scoffing one of Daphne's home-made cream cakes. Unfortunately the cake wouldn't all go in one piece and half of it broke off like a ship being split apart by a torpedo. The cake's back broke as it sank below the table into the grassy depths of the Women's Institute tent floor.

A beaky-faced woman started to scold him from behind the trestle table.

"Have you paid your threepence, young man?" she demanded in accusatory tone, "You shouldn't be so careless, there's five eggs in that cake, I'll have you know!"

The boy dived under the table in search of the sunken morsels and out of range of the beaky woman's vision. Astle handed the woman a six-penny piece and placed two more cake slices on a plate. As the boy emerged from under the table he softly took the boy's hand and said in a friendly voice, "It's alright James, come with me and we'll sit down here and eat these new slices of cake together." He gently steered James back to the table where he had been seated.

"My mummy told me not to talk to strangers," James said as he sat down although the thought of the cake was testing his will power. James looked at the fat, perspiring figure smiling at him and thought that he recognised him from somewhere.

"I know your Mummy," said Astle, she is an old friend, we worked together many years ago. I am your Uncle Gerald," continued the fat man hesitantly.

168

James thought he looked a bit like the man in the picture that Mummy had in her bedroom, except that he was a lot fatter. He didn't look much like a war hero either, so it couldn't be him. Anyhow he was dead.

He bit off some of his cake half hoping that his mother wouldn't appear until he had finished his new slice. James's mind kept going back to that picture his mother had of his father. People in wars wore caps, had badges and things he thought. James was still worrying that he was disobeying often-repeated instructions from his Mother, 'never to talk to strangers or take sweets from anyone'. Well, cake wasn't sweets and this cake *was* delicious. Funny, he thought, he hadn't seen his mother for ages, not since he had been to the Punch and Judy show.

Then the fat man said quietly, "You *are* called James aren't you?"

Astle suddenly worried that he might have mistaken the boy in his eagerness to spot his son. Although he had been certain from when he first saw him, he still couldn't believe that his own flesh and blood was sitting in front of him eating a large piece of cream cake. And where was Valerie? She shouldn't be letting *his* boy wander about unsupervised in a busy place like this. It was lucky *he* had found him.

"Yes *of course*", James said.

"Where is your mummy?"

"Dunno, she will be here soon. We are going to have an ice cream."

"How do you know my name?" enquired James.

Astle already flushed went even redder. James thought that the fat man might start crying or explode, or perhaps both.

"Because I am your Uncle, silly," Astle managed to reply as he tried regaining his composure.

James started to fret. His mother's words kept coming back to him. The fat man seemed quite harmless but he did seem to be staring at him a lot. He thought about running off but there may be a chance of more cake - an opportunity too good to miss.

Astle started to enjoy himself. He was quite happy sitting next to James watching him eat.

"Do you want some?" asked James gesturing at the cake with a sticky finger.

Astle smiled broadly, "No thanks I have had enough now. Would you like another slice?" he asked.

James thought the fat man didn't look quite as frightening when he smiled. The creases on his face seemed to nearly swallow up his eyes and his shoulders shook a like a jelly. "YES please", said James his eyes shining with excitement.

When Astle returned with yet another slice of cake he said gently, "Your Mummy worked for me, a long time ago, before you were born. She is a very nice lady."

"I know that," he said matter-of-factly, "I came on Mummy's motor bike, we did a ton-up," he added more thoughtfully, as if this was a demonstration of her boundless kindness.

The fat man's face looked shocked.

"Are you *sure* it was a motorcycle?"

The boy thought for a few seconds as if pondering this important point.

"Yes, it's got two wheels and big engine that makes a loud noise."

The boy did a very good impression of a motorcycle starting off. It was so authentic a number of the Women's Institute tent occupants looked around half-expecting to see members of the Windelton Hell's Angels chapter ride into the tent in dirty black leathers and accost them with oily bike chains.

"I had no idea that your Mummy had a motor bike, whatever next?"

James tucked into his third slice of cake with relish and Astle sat quietly watching him eat.

"I am feeling thirsty. Shall we have a glass of orange squash?" Astle asked cheerily just as James was licking the last morsel of cream cake off his fingers.

"Rather, YES please Sir!"

Astle got up and returned to the beaky-faced woman at the serving table.

"How is Daphne, Mr Astle?" she enquired finally recognising Astle in this unaccustomed environment. He didn't look himself thought the woman. What on earth is he wearing under that linen jacket? It looks like a shirt with beach umbrellas on it and is that a sombrero hat he is sporting as she espied a large hat that Astle had placed rather self-consciously on the table next to his chair? Entirely unsuitable and garish, after all he *is* the bank manager not a Mexican cowboy. I wonder if Daphne has seen him in that outfit. She is probably too embarrassed to be with him. Poor woman! "Isn't Daphne coming to support the good cause Mr. Astle? What a shame and such a splendid occasion?" the beaky woman continued with heavy innuendo that Astle had let the side down by not bothering to bring his wife.

"Oh she's coming later, loves the ballet you know, in fact we both do. Unfortunately, Daphne had a prior appointment."

"Oh, I see" said the beaky woman, not seeing at all and thinking to herself what is Astle doing with that young child. He shouldn't be stuffing so much cake and squash into him, the child will be sick. All very odd.

Astle hadn't lied. Daphne *was* at a prior appointment but he was not going into the details for the benefit of the nosey-parker Women's Institute woman. Daphne had received a telephone call that morning from her clairvoyant who had insisted she call in for an urgent consultation. Although Astle didn't know it, the clairvoyant had been in a state of near apoplexy, claiming she had been getting strong messages from the 'other side' about her husband. Daphne had not confided to Astle the details of the clairvoyant's desperate call. Astle thought it was all a load of baloney and just another of Daphne's many eccentricities.

"Now who is that young man with you Mr Astle? Is he relation of yours, he's got a look of you?" enquired the beaky woman.

"Well actually I am his fa…, Uncle," he blurted. Astle was both flattered and alarmed simultaneously. He had nearly let the cat out of the bag. He was so proud of his son. He'd have loved to declare his rightful relationship there and then. Astle contemplated the beaky woman's reaction if she had any inkling of how this innocent child came to be here. Well, she wouldn't have too long to wait. Astle was already regretting not being able to see their astonished faces as they "oooed" and "aaahed" while they slurped their foul-tasting coffee in the cafés of Windelton!

He sat down and placed the orange squash in front of James smiling at him with genuine pride. James returned it with a shy grin. It was a moment Astle wouldn't forget.

~

Suddenly there was a terrible kerfuffle at the tent entrance as a woman in a motor cycle suit came bolting through the tent flaps, pushing people aside. She charged forward and then stopped to scan the packed tent. She had a fearful look, her large eyes roving over the busy tea tables. She shoved her way through the munching Windeltonians towards the centre of the assembled throng. Suddenly, she spotted a small boy sitting next to a fat, perspiring, old, man.

Valerie let out an anguished shriek of relief, "JAMES, JAMES, where have you been?"

In her panic Valerie failed to recognise James's father. She forced her way through the tables towards where James was sitting. Just when she had nearly reached the boy Valerie finally recognised Astle and she gave a startled shout: *"What the hell do you think you are doing with my son?"* at which point she suddenly swooned and slumped sideways across Mrs Hendry's table.

There was a tremendous thud as tea and scones cascaded onto the laps of astonished tea-supping ladies. Valerie's inert body tumbled off the table, dragging the linen cloth with accompanying cups, saucers and cup-cakes before crashing onto the grassy floor in a heap of tea-time delights. A number of the Women's Institute members thought that the long-feared motor cycle rampage really had begun and two of their number let out small screams of alarm.

Astle was equally astonished to recognise Valerie clad in her tight fitting motorcycle leathers, her auburn hair tousled and heavy black mascara running down her cheeks. He stared open mouthed at the carnage at his feet. There was a brief moment of horrified silence as the onlookers tried to take in what had occurred. More women screamed as James leapt to his feet and wailed, *"Mummy, Mummy!"*

David Nelson, who had witnessed the drama from the tent entrance, was the first to leap into action, thrusting aside the paralysed tea drinkers he rushed forward to take charge of the situation. "All of you stand back," he said with the quiet determination of a man who was in command of the situation. Everyone silently obeyed, standing back as he knelt down and felt Valerie's pulse.

"Don't worry, it looks like she has just fainted," he said looking up at the waiting assembly who had drawn back to form a circle around the scene of the drama. The crowd gave out a collective sigh of relief. The handsome dentist had rolled Valerie into the recovery position and was briefly feeling her legs and arms for any fractures. Soon Valerie started to regain her senses and as her eyes fully opened he scooped her off the grass, slinging the leather clad beauty over his shoulder and marched toward the tent entrance. A number of the women swooned as he made his way forward with the blessed Valerie, secretly wishing it was them that had fainted. David shouted, "Make way, make way,' as he headed for fresh air and space away from the stupefied crowd.

Astle and James followed in quick succession, a soft, small hand and a podgy red hand gripped together in united fright.

~

The first thing that Valerie could remember was someone gently unzipping the top half of her motorcycling jacket; it was not an unpleasant experience. She looked up to see blue sky and the underside of tree boughs. Then she saw a concerned, attractive face of a man. Somehow he looked familiar. The outside edges of her vision were framed by a worried looking James and the perspiring white face of Astle.

"It's alright, you just fainted," said the familiar face in a quiet, reassuring Scottish accent, "It was a wee bit hot in that tent and you were wearing these warm clothes," said David Nelson, his hand pulling open wider the top half of her tunic to let more air circulate, his other hand held hers in a gentle but comforting grip.

After a while someone brought a glass of water and Valerie sat propped up against the trunk of a large tree. She started to re-connect with the living world again; she felt a little nauseous but otherwise alright. Valerie couldn't remember where she had encountered this very attractive man before but she didn't want him to leave. She needed shielding from Astle who seemed to becoming more agitated as the minutes passed.

James sat down next to her and put his head on her shoulder. "Are you are alright Mummy?" he said tearfully. She nodded her assent and smiled at him, his head on her shoulder felt light and comforting.

David Nelson introduced himself to everyone: "Hello, I am David. I'm not a doctor, I'm a dentist but understand first aid." Looking at Valerie he said: "I would suggest that you stay here under this tree in the shade for a while until you feel better. I can ask the St John's ambulance people to come and look you over if you like? I am sure it was the heat in the tent and your leather clothing that caused you to pass out. Fortunately, nothing appears to be broken. Are you sure you are okay?"

"I'm fine", said Valerie quietly. "I feel such a fool, causing all this fuss." She smiled at the dentist, her eyes lingering on his strong jaw and perfectly shaped face. "Thank you for your help."

David slipped his dental business card into her hand, "Anything you need or if you want to talk about what happened when you are feeling better, just give me a call." He looked directly into her eyes and Valerie felt that he was climbing inside her whole being so penetrating was his gaze. Finally, he sprung to his feet and shook hands with the sweating Astle. "Are you okay, you look a bit shaken up too?" he enquired.

Astle smiled vacantly at David and said, "No, no I am fine. I think the heat must be getting to me as well."

David recalled having seen Astle about Windelton and then remembered he was his wife's bank manager. Bit of an odd ball according to Marjorie, he looks very unhealthy, he thought. I wonder why he's hanging around this beautiful woman with the little boy. Perhaps he's some sort of family friend? Anyhow, he wasn't being much help, stamping his feet and mopping his brow. Astle was giving every signal of wanting to get rid of David as soon as possible. In contrast, this demure but oddly wild looking woman, seemed to be willing him to stay, he thought.

Just as David turned to leave he looked down at the woman again, the colour was returning to her cheeks and he looked directly into her eyes, "Do you ride a Triumph motorcycle by any chance," he asked.

"Yes," she replied meekly.

"I thought I had seen somewhere before," he replied with a smile. "Are you feeling a bit better now?" He continued seeking a reassuring sign that she was okay.

She returned his smile and nodded a gesture that said, *it's okay, I am alright…really.*

Then he was gone and Valerie was faced with Gerald's sweating visage.

~

"You have met James?" Valerie enquired a little later, looking at Astle.

"James this is your Uncle," she continued hoping that Gerald had not said anything different.

"We were chatting about you before you arrived," said Astle.

"He said you worked together," piped up James.

"Yes, that's right darling, a long time ago, said Valerie, "you've not…?" she looked at Gerald pleadingly.

175

"No, of course not!"

"He bought me some lovely cake *and* squash," said James shyly.

"He's a wonderful chap, a nephew to be proud of. I would love to spend more time with you both but unfortunately I have to go very soon," said Astle sadly.

"Why are you wearing that silly hat?"

Astle ignored Valerie's question and grappled inside the pocket of his linen jacket. He produced two long thin booklets with BOAC written on the outer cover.

"Here are your tickets," he said in a hoarse whisper, looking around him to see if anyone had noticed. "When I get to Argentina I will give you a call. You must use these to come and see me," he said in a hoarse whisper pointing at the tickets as if they were gold bars.

"They are valid for up to six months."

"But Gerald, what about your wife?"

"I'm leaving her, she'll be better without off without me. She'll be able to see her clairvoyant every day once I am gone. My life is finished in this place. I'm going to make a new start, *with you and James I hope.*"

Valerie felt dizzy and she thought she might pass out again, James grabbed her hand.

"Mummy?"

"It's alright James, I'm okay", she said closing her eyes briefly as if to summon up strength to carry on.

"I don't understand why you're going? If you care about us both you should be staying here. We could arrange to see one another more often and James too."

"The die is cast," said Astle dramatically.

"What on earth do you mean: 'the die is cast'?" Astle ignored Valerie's question and went on, "Valerie, we've a life to *share.* I am rich beyond your imaginings. We could be blissfully happy, away from this dreariness. Sunshine *every* day, not a one-off like today!"

176

Valerie was too weary to counter Astle's extraordinary requests. She couldn't begin to the think of the implications of what he was trying to say. She realised that Astle had done something dreadful but she was certain in her own mind that she wouldn't be any part of it. It was too preposterous for words. She fell into silence. Eventually she said: "What about the language, do they speak English in Argentina?" It was a banal riposte but the only thing she could think of.

"That doesn't matter, Valerie we can learn the language when we are there. Anyhow, everyone speaks English."

"Think about James and his schooling? It's too ridiculous to contemplate." Valerie put her head in her hands and began to weep silently. "I know you've done something awful on my account and you're not telling me," she sobbed.

Astle was aghast at this last remark. What he had ingeniously plotted he had done for *them all*. Not just him, but for *his* son and his mother. He suddenly realised the desperation of his situation, the place and the people. Valerie was right of course. He had been utterly stupid once again.

Now time was running out. Daphne could appear at any moment. People here knew him too well. They would be asking questions about this weeping woman in motorcycle leathers. And who was that delightful child that bore an uncanny resemblance to him. He had to try and salvage something before he left.

"Valerie my love, you've always had lots of common sense. Forgive me for being so stupid. It was seeing James, it's rather overwhelmed me." Astle turned his head away and blinked back some tears. He tried to summon up all his powers of persuasion. "Just promise to come and see me for a holiday with James? Use these tickets, they're first class, cost a fortune. Even in this desperate situation all Astle could think about was the amount of stolen money he paid for the tickets. Please say you'll come and at least see the country. It would be an awful waste of money if you didn't use them," he said pointing to the tickets lying at her side. Valerie had not dared to touch them since Astle had fished them from inside his jacket pocket.

177

The realisation dawned on Valerie that she really *didn't* want to know what monstrous act Astle had committed. Thinking back it all added up, the strange 'phone calls, his uncharacteristically odd behaviour and now seeing him in the flesh. He looks mad. He *is* having a mental breakdown. He is not safe to be near me or my son. I must get rid of him.

Astle seemed to have exhausted his verbal pleading. He looked to Valerie like a small child. His old dignity had evaporated, his authority gone. He had become so very fat, his red jowls hung from under his chin like a walrus, even his hands that were once slim and attractive had become bloated with fat.

"Gerald, whatever you are contemplating doing, *don't do it*. Go off and have a holiday on your own. You look as if you need a break. I don't think your fishing holiday has done you any good at all."

"I told you before, it's too late", said Astle miserably.

"What do you mean, too late?" asked Valerie dreading his answer. Astle didn't answer. After a long silence Astle whispered pathetically

"Done it."

"Done what?"

"Can't tell. You'll find out soon enough."

"WHAT?" Valerie shouted.

'Shhhhhh', Astle put a finger to his bubbling lips.

"Hello Mr Astle, lovely day for it," said Mrs Trubshaw as she walked past the recumbent girl and little boy.

Astle looks a bit peculiar and what *is* he wearing, she thought? That woman doesn't look like a Windelton customer, she seems a bit of a slut if you ask me, and I wonder where Daphne has got to?

"Are you completely MAD?" Valerie's voice was raised once again in alarm.

"You are leaving aren't you and not coming back? What about our allowance, how are we going to survive without it?"

"Shhh!"

"Don't shush me Gerald, what the hell are you thinking about?"

"It'll still be paid… until you come out to see me."

"Is that a threat Gerald? If you let me down I will spill the beans about you, everything will come out, you *bastard*."

James had never heard his mother use that word before and he sensed it was bad. He realised that something very serious was going on between his newly discovered uncle and his mother. He wished they had never come here.

"Can we go now Mummy, I don't like it here?" said James tearfully.

"In a minute darling, when Mummy feels better and your Uncle has gone."

"Is everything alright now?" enquired Mrs Hendry fiercely. She came striding over, brushing herself down. She was one of the women who tumbled to the ground in Valerie's fainting episode.

"I hope I'm going to get some sort of apology for knocking over my tea table and ruining my outfit?" she demanded menacingly. She was hoping to recover the cleaning costs of her tweed skirt that had collected a grass stain. "You really should be more careful where you faint young woman, only by the grace of God I wasn't hurt."

"I am so sorry," said Valerie faintly, "I had a bit of a shock."

"Just bugger off you interfering old busybody!" said Astle turning on one of the bank's oldest customers with an unsuppressed hatred that he had nurtured for the last eight years. Mrs Hendry was so stunned that she opened her mouth then closed it again as she took in what Astle had said.

"Did I misunderstand what you just said Mr. Astle?

"Are you deaf as well as stupid? I said bugger off and mind your own business."

"You can't speak to me like that I am a *customer!*"

"I can say what I like to you Mrs Hendry; I don't care if you are Lady Godiva, just GO away."

"You won't hear the last of this Mr Astle. Just wait until I find my husband. I shall be back and he'll tell you that we'll be closing our accounts forthwith. I have never been spoken to so rudely," she said turning on her heel and marching off in search of her spouse.

"Go and rot in hell!" retorted Astle with his final salvo of invective.

Astle's whole body wobbled with pleasure. He had wanted to do that for years.

Valerie sat gasping at Astle's unbelievable treatment of a bank customer. It confirmed to her that *he had gone mad*. The row with Mrs Hendry made Astle realise that it was imperative to get away from the festival before he caused any more trouble. Mrs Hendry was sure to return with her husband.

He bent down to kiss Valerie on the cheek, "You MUST come," he hissed in her ear. He fumbled inside his linen jacket and squeezed a thick bundle of five-pound notes into her hand. There must have been at least five hundred pounds in the wad.

"Gerald, I can't take this…"

"Goodbye James," and he leaned towards the boy but James's turned his head and shied away. Astle nearly over balanced in the effort to plant his farewell kiss but fortunately he recovered his upright position with some huffing and puffing. He waved a pathetic limp gesture of goodbye. Finally, he turned with head down and shuffled off behind the back of the main marquee. He narrowly missed an irate Mrs Hendry who had emerged from the refreshment tent dragging her reluctant husband by the arm to confront him.

"Where's Uncle going Mummy?" asked James, but his mother bit her bottom lip and looked away. She stared down at the crunched up bank notes and airline tickets.

- Chapter 22 -

The Call of the Argentine

Astle felt unimaginable sorrow as he slouched off leaving Valerie with his son in her arms. For the first time in his life, felt utterly defeated. He was shattered. He couldn't believe it had taken him eight years to realise what a beautiful son he possessed. Valerie had appeared worldly and different from how he remembered her. She was no longer the demure manager's secretary of the Hickleton branch. What was it that had changed her? She'd sounded no different on the telephone. And James had seemed perfectly normal, perfect in every way. Astle's emotions were in turmoil: elation at meeting his son and shame that he had never had the guts to take proper responsibility for him. He should have been involved in James's life from the start. Now it was all too late and he was running away again.

Yesterday James was no more than a standing order on a bank statement, just another transaction in Astle's banking career. Astle realised for the first time that James was Valerie's only priority, not him. He was merely a spectator. That was the role that he had chosen for himself eight years ago.

As he staggered towards his car he received some peculiar looks from other festival-goers. Only Astle's sense of self-preservation remained intact. His mind focused on reaching London and getting the morning flight to his new life. To do it he would have to concentrate and concentrate hard.

Then he spotted Sir Toby Inchdale striding towards him.

~

Astle had given scant regard to what he was going to do once in Argentina. He had booked himself into the best hotel available in Buenos Aires for a month and paid in advance from one of his newly opened bank accounts.

No Daphne, no bank, no Rotary, no Masonic Lodge, what would he do? He presumed they played golf. He would certainly have enough money, more than enough. He would wire more cash to Valerie and James through the Channel Islands account, lots more now he had seen James. They'd want for nothing. Then he would set about trying to persuade them to join him. But even Astle recognised that there were occasions when money alone couldn't solve every problem. He was going to have to consider other methods of enticement. The problem was money was the only currency of persuasion that Astle had ever understood. He resolved to write her a long letter. It would be okay once he got to Argentina when he could gather his thoughts. Yes, that's what he would do.

~

Getting a visa had been a tricky operation requiring a clandestine visit to London and the Argentine embassy. It had involved producing two forged character references. The Reverend Max Headcase had been more difficult than the eloquently 'dictated' version from Sir Toby Inchdale.

He had filing cabinets full of letters and half-baked promises from Inchdale for reference purposes. There were not quite as many from the vicar but enough for him to undertake some cunning patching and cutting of signatures using the latest new photocopying device that had been recently installed at the bank. Astle's own ingenuity surprised him. It had taken hours of painstaking photocopying and typing on old Miss Starkey's typewriter. She'd been intrigued by Astle's interest in how the new photocopying machinery functioned.

Astle had brushed his enquiries aside as routine: "It's important that I know how to work these new contraptions," he had said to the baffled Miss Starkey. "However mundane the machinery Miss Starkey, I need to be able to judge the effect on staff productivity." Miss Starkey took this to be a clear reference to her as the major user of the equipment and she'd trembled in alarm. Astle had gone on, warming to his own cunning. "Head office is always demanding to know how new equipment works in the branch Miss Starkey." Astle marvelled at his own complicity.

Laurence Payne, overhearing his remarks to Miss Starkey had looked skyward and wondered what was getting into Astle these days. He had never expressed an interest in anything remotely technical in the bank's workings. On the contrary, he was generally dismissive of new initiatives and ignored them for as long as possible until the bank inspection team were due a visit.

Astle passed off his London visa application trip to Daphne as a necessary visit to a customer down south. He had motored to York and caught the mainline express to King's Cross. Once at the Argentine embassy Astle experienced a nerve-wracking two hour wait in a queue of swarthy-looking foreign types. After endless form filling, finally his passport had been stamped with the necessary visitor entry visa, valid for one year. An oleaginous official had questioned him in a disinterested way about his visit. Astle explained that he was taking an extended holiday with a purpose. He hoped to trace a long lost relative who had moved to Buenos Aires just after the war. Why he made up this cock- and-bull story, Astle couldn't remember. The official started to take an interest in his story and quizzed him about his so-called relative. The official smiled slyly at Astle.

"There are many lost Europeans in Argentina Senor Astle," he had said expansively, "bad people escaping your stupid European wars. Be careful my friend, there are many 'banditos' in my country. Away from the cities they have little farms where they grow Alfalfa and hide away," he touched his nose in a confidential way, raising his eyebrows. "If you search for them you'd better talk to the British Foreign Office before you leave. Do you speak German? It could help you find your relative, no?"

Astle was initially horrified at the suggestion that he was in search of some long-lost Nazi relative, but he suddenly remembered why he was going there himself. He would be a fugitive too. "Yes, er, good idea, German you say, I think I had better swot up on the Kraut lingo, thanks," he replied playing along with the official's line of conversation.

"Watch out, Argentina is a big country and people can easily disappear," the Argentinian official threw up his hands in a gesture as if he was throwing sand into the air.

Bloody foreign dago thought Astle as he left, he couldn't imagine anyone at the British Embassy behaving like that. On the other hand there was something reassuringly dubious about the whole episode. It helped confirm that Argentina was the destination of choice for a man with plenty to hide.

~

Daphne Astle had been alarmed by her clairvoyant's reading. This week the green crystal ball which sat inertly on the cloth-covered table was delivering the goods. The clairvoyant had read Daphne's hand to seek confirmation of her predictions and she had finally resorted to her tarot cards for absolute proof. The results were unprecedented. The clairvoyant had started to swoon and moan rather unpleasantly. This was a new manifestation for Daphne.

The tarot cards always worried the clairvoyant for their uncanny accuracy. They were the most reliable in revealing brutal truths. So much so that she was sometimes reluctant to give absolute interpretations to avoid scaring her customers and herself. She refused to remove the death card; it had been her mentor's instructions to work in this way although she was aware that other mediums often removed the ace of spades from the pack. Crystal, tea leaves and tarot: to get a three-way confirmation was rare.

Last week the clairvoyant had been unnerved by losing a female customer who had been run over by a bus. Neither of them had seen it coming. The clairvoyant felt riddled with guilt and self-doubt. If she had foretold the misfortune the poor woman could have at least made some preparations. She feared that she might be losing her powers.

Today she felt rejuvenated. Daphne's was a clear reading. Her gifts were not failing her after all. She had become intoxicated with her clairvoyant's excitement. Sometimes she had been sceptical of the bland predictions, predictions that left so much to imagination that any result was feasible. But on this occasion a number of 'certainties' emerged. The clairvoyant was adamant. The strength of the signals received surprised and unsettled Daphne. Her emotions ranged from disbelief, to fright to outright joy and then finally, annoyance.

Daphne decided that she preferred doubts to certainties. The clairvoyant told her that she should do nothing but watch and wait for events to unfold. Now armed with this knowledge, Daphne wondered whether she could face Gerald again. Could she even face the great Windelton festival?

- Chapter 23 -

Delayed Departure

Senor Lopez, the assistant attaché at the Argentine embassy, was not a lazy man but he never undertook work that he regarded as unnecessary. He had been reviewing the references for Gerald Astle's visa application. Superficially it looked okay, if anything a bit too good for a man who was obviously on the run. Lopez was reluctant to check back over details once he'd followed correct procedures but on this occasion he decided he would. Just to be on the safe side.

He pondered the reference again from the Reverend Maxwell Headcase. Lopez never trusted anything to do with priests: they were always liars and fornicators; they gave the Holy Church a bad name. On the other hand English aristocrats were much more trustworthy and Sir Toby Inchdale was a proper baronet. He had looked him up in Burke's Peerage curious about the word 'Bart' after his name. His family was hundreds of years old. He must be 'a good sport' as the English were fond of saying.

But there was still something about Senor Astle that worried him. I will write to Bart Inchdale again just to double-check. Better to avoid any problems later with the Ambassador, he thought. He would get into trouble if Astle decided to rob a bank once he was in Buenos Aires. That was the sort of thing that could have him posted to some obscure little consular office in the back of beyond. He liked it here in England. Yes, the food was awful and it was always raining but the girls were friendly and let you have rumpy-pumpy.

The thought made him smile as he stroked his silky black moustache.

~

Sir Toby Inchdale had sold enough cattle over the years to spot a trade when he saw one. The letter from the Argentine embassy gave him that same feeling. He had nearly binned Lopez's missive but there was something curious and foreign about the flimsy tissue-paper envelope that caught Inchdale's attention. It would be too thin to fill cracks in the office walls so he fingered open the envelope until out slipped an official looking letter sporting a large embossed flag and the words: *'Embajada Argentine Londres'*. He didn't recognise its origin until he read that it was from The Office of His Excellency the Ambassador to Argentina. How on earth had they got his address let alone knew his name he thought? The use of the English language was equally bizarre.

Esteemed Inchdale Sir Bart

Further to your epistle concerning Mr. Gastley saying his good character thank you.

Before persons stay long in our wonderful country we make good look out to make certin only good chaps come. We like your first letter but can also you say Gastley has worked at Murchison's bank for 35 yers and wife is buried. Please confirm truth statement of truths.

Your obedient servant,

Senor H Lopez

Assistant Attaché, Embajada Argentine, Londres W1

Inchdale read and re-read this letter. He definitely smelt a rat. Why would Astle want to go to Argentina? What was this 'first letter' malarkey? He had never written to the Argie Embassy about Astle. He had penned a tastefully worded letter to Murchison's Regional Office recently complaining about Astle's habit of bouncing his cheques. Astle had never mentioned retirement to him. Inchdale knew there was still some years to go before his release date as he took a keen interest in Astle's career plans in case a new manager turned up with ideas above his station. Last time he had seen Astle was at the Inverhapless Hotel and he thought he looked fairly shot then. The business about his enormous fish had raised some eyebrows. Fish that size don't normally get caught on a fly. It would be typical of Astle to have cheated by rolling a worm or even worse, using a spinner. Not the behaviour of a gentleman!

Also there had been rumours about Astle being unstable. He never seemed to like anyone and his wife was obsessed with the occult. Rum pair when all told. Perhaps Astle was planning an extended holiday but clearly the Dago at the embassy was talking about 'stay long'. And where was his poor wife? According to Astle she was dead so he was not planning to take her too.

There was definitely some monkey-business afoot. Inchdale decided to keep the game going. He wouldn't tell Astle that he had been approached. He would save that for later.

He replied:

Dear Senor Lopez

I wish to confirm that Mr. Gerald Astle has worked at Murchison's Bank for thirty five years and that his wife is deceased.

Can you tell me when Mr. Astle is due to arrive in your magnificent country? I would like to be able to wish him well before his departure. I do hope you can furnish me with this information.

Yours sincerely

Inchdale (Bart)

A letter came by return.

Dear Bart Inchdale

Thank you for excellent informations. Herr Astle scheduled to come Buenos Aires on Monday June 1.

Your obedient friend

H. Lopez

Assistant Attaché, Embajada Argentine Londres

As soon as Inchdale received Lopez's second missive he realised that Astle was definitely up to no good. He had better move quickly. There was a smell of cash in the air.

~

For a moment Inchdale thought he had left it too late.

He'd been trying to get a meeting with Astle for the last seven days but his gnarled old secretary, Miss Starkey, had firmly informed him that he had no free days until Wednesday 3rd of June. Two days after he was due to arrive in Buenos Aires. The fact that old Miss Starkey knew nothing about his departure confirmed to Inchdale that Astle was about to do a runner. Inchdale had even considered marching into the branch and demanding to see him but he had ruled that out as being too melodramatic. With time running out he tried a visit to his miserable little house but there was no-one at home.

In desperation he headed for the festival in a final bid to track him down. The day after next was the first of June, the day he was due to arrive in Argentina. He searched the Red House garden and tents and was combing the car park when eventually he spied Astle's Morris parked in a side lane off the main car park.

Inchdale was about to go over to inspect the vehicle when suddenly Astle hove into view. He was threading his way uncertainly towards his vehicle wearing a large sombrero hat and sporting a garish shirt under a crumpled linen suit. He looked as if he had been weeping.

"What Ho! Heading for home?" said Inchdale in a jolly manner.

"What's it to you Inch, you stuck-up arse?"

Inchdale was somewhat taken aback by this uncharacteristic onslaught from Astle.

"I just need a little word in your ear, Astle," responded Inchdale more aggressively.

"Bugger off," said Astle grappling with the driver's door in an attempt to get into his car.

"I have been having some cosy fireside chats with your friends at the Argentine embassy," said Inchdale triumphantly.

"I don't know what you are talking about," replied Astle, still trying to unlock the Morris's door.

Inchdale went towards Astle and put his large paws on the fat man's shoulders.

"Get off me," cried Astle as Inchdale started to shake him. "I'll call the pol…" Then he thought better of that idea.

"*No*, you listen to me Astle. You are up to no bloody good and you know it. You should read the correspondence I've been having with the Argentine Embassy about *you*. If it wasn't for *me* you wouldn't have your ruddy visa. So just listen to what I have to say!"

"BUGGER OFF," said Astle shouting and trying to push Inchdale off.

Despite Inchdale's age he was a strong man, as Doreen, the Inchdale Hall cook, could testify when Inchdale pinned her to the larder wall demanding his monthly rights. He got Astle in a vice-like grip around the wrists and pushed his fat frame against the car to face him. "So it's Argentina on Monday eh?"

Astle looked about him wildly but there was no-one else in sight. He couldn't move. Astle could see all his plans unravelling.

"Don't shop me Inchdale!" Astle said in low voice. "What do you want? Money? You are always on your uppers. I can give you cash, untraceable notes, lots of it…"

"How come?" Inchdale demanded.

"Do *you* want it or not?

"Yes. How much?"

"Thousands but you'll have to keep your trap shut until I am in Buenos Aires," demanded Astle recognising the lure of money could get Inchdale off his back.

"Okay, where is it?" said Inchdale quietly.

What's a few thousand for old Inchdale thought Astle. I have got more money than I could ever spend. He would appreciate a bonus, the wily old bastard. "Just let go of me and I'll open the boot and I'll show you," said Astle regaining some calmness as Inchdale cautiously loosened his grip on Astle's pudgy wrists.

"No funny business Astle, I am not past clocking you one," said Inchdale.

Astle went to the boot and fiddled with his key. He was shaking so much it wouldn't go in.

"Get on with it man," said Inchdale losing his patience as Astle swayed around trying to insert the key in the lock.

Eventually, the boot lid lifted upwards and Inchdale spied Astle's suitcase. To the left of the travelling case were two black Homberg bags with brass clasps. Astle got out another small key from his trouser pocket and unlocked the one nearest to him. As soon as he opened it Inchdale saw the closely packed bundles of notes. Astle bent down and picked up two fat bundles of used five pound bank notes and waved them in Inchdale's face. They amounted to about a thousand pounds, perhaps more, Inchdale couldn't tell but there was a hell of a lot.

"What's in the other bag?" asked Inchdale, his mouth going dry at the sight of all this loot.

"Same again," said Astle with a pathetic grin.

"Where did you get all this?" enquired Inchdale nonchalantly, knowing full well where from.

"Where do you think?"

"I don't want to know," said Inchdale instinctively. Better not to be told.

"Here, have these," said Astle thrusting the packs at him.

Inchdale took the bundles and placed them back in the open Homberg.

"Don't you want them?" asked Astle incredulously.

"Yes, but I'll take the bag," he replied, leaning over the fat man and swiftly lifting the bag out of the car boot while at the same time pushing Astle out of the way.

191

"You BASTARD," cried Astle, recovering his balance he lunged towards Inchdale.

Inchdale quickly side-stepped Astle's charge and the fat man fell over onto the grass. Before Astle could scramble to his feet Inchdale was walking briskly off towards the festival crowds clutching his leather homburg under his arm.

Astle staggered to his feet and fell backwards into the car's open boot. Only his large case stopped him from falling inside. Cursing, he realised there was nothing he could do. Inchdale was nearly out of sight and he would never catch the old fox now. He couldn't call for help. The only thing to do was to get out as fast as possible.

Inchdale monitored Astle's disappearance from the safety of the gentlemen's latrine doorway on the car park field edge. Once the Morris vanished from sight he slipped back into the car park and placed the black bag under a tartan rug on the floor of the old Rolls.

As he sauntered jauntily back into the Red House garden he noticed a striking looking woman in leather motorcycle gear holding a young boy's hand. They were obviously leaving. The boy looked somehow familiar.

~

Astle noticed ominous black clouds gathering on the horizon. It looked like the beautiful afternoon's weather was going to change. The sun was still shining and the ballet dancers had started their first performance. Marjorie Nelson was seeing her ambitions realised.

The Morris moved cautiously through quiet roads towards the Great North Road on its southerly journey. Astle perspired at the wheel. He thought about blasted Inchdale. Maybe he had at least done someone a good turn. He knew Inchdale wouldn't blab. He needed the cash too much. Astle mopped his brow with a cake-soiled handkerchief. He leaned across the passenger seat and fished out a leather-bound hipflask from the car's glove compartment and took a long pull of whisky. The liquid burned his throat and he felt his chest warm.

The clouds ahead of him looked very dark.

PART 3

- Chapter 24 -

Disco Maniacs

It was raining hard by the time Jasper's E-Type Jaguar swept into the car park of the Heifer pub. As the car slewed sideways it showered the side window of the lounge bar with a pelting stream of gravel. Dawn and Ian were both staring out at the incessant rain when the unexpected shower of angry pebbles cracked on the panes. They both flinched instinctively. Ian narrowly avoided falling off his stool. The shared shock helped to dispel their separate, moody reveries.

Both had been wondering why they had agreed to this meeting. Dawn was feeling embarrassed and a little frightened about what she might be getting herself into. Ian recognised that Jasper was a predatory animal when it came to women and he had seen the way he had been looking at Dawn when they were at the Nags Head. He had not been so tight or as preoccupied with the lovely Rachel not to notice the warning signs. Perhaps, most worrying of all, was that Dawn had enjoyed the attention. It had made Ian feel jealous and aroused at the same time.

"What the hell was that?" said Ian

"Jasper," replied Dawn, seeing the athletic figure of Jasper charging toward the pub doorway. His arm was around Rachel's shoulders holding down a white mackintosh.

They burst through the pub door, clothes dripping and giggling like teenagers. Dawn's spirit lifted, Ian's sank. What was he so bloody happy about he thought? A fresh round of drinks soon appeared and the conversation picked up. Jasper and Rachel's energies lifted the gloom and doubt; such was the force of their collective personalities. New, more attractive horizons emerged, dull ones melted away as the evening unfolded and the banal chatter, alcohol and cigarettes took their narcotic grip.

Later, having left the cosy atmosphere of the pub and done battle with the festival's water-logged car park, they were dancing with drunken freedom in the steamy marquee. The discomfort of mud-spattered legs was soon forgotten as they danced in stocking feet to the pulsating rhythms of the high profile rock group so shrewdly booked by Marjorie Nelson.

The band worked hard to satisfy the cheering, chanting and swaying mass of dancers. The smell of hot bodies, stale beer charged with the hopeful expectation of sex, somewhere and somehow, gripped the youth of Windelton. Their hedonistic abandon had not escaped the thoughts of the not-so-young. Even those Windeltonians passed their first flush of youth, fuelled with drink and fortified with forgotten courage decided that tonight they too would not be left out of the fun. For once they ignored the excessive noise, deciding they would forfeit deafness for enjoyment and found their feet tapping to the pounding anthems. Soon they had broken free of any decorum and threw their arms about swinging creaky hips as they liberated their senses to experience their first swinging sixties night out. It certainly beat a game of dominos or a round of bridge.

As the evening got hotter and the drink took its toll, middle-aged ladies threw off their cardigans and danced in brassieres and slips as they forced their way into swathes of gyrating youngsters. Meanwhile, the Windelton husbands stood aghast, only capable of raising pint after pint of Bainbridge bitter to their gaping mouths. The town had never seen a party like this before. For those who could remember it made the VE day celebrations appear dull.

The arrival of the heavy rain had conveniently coincided with the finish of the festival's daytime programme of events. There was a three hour gap before the commencement of the evening's schedule. Most visitors had been prevented from venturing home because of the torrential rain and were imprisoned in the refreshment tent whiling away their time drinking. Their wait for a break in the weather to release them from self-imposed purgatory was going to be a long one.

The only beneficiary of the atrocious weather was Marjorie Nelson's swelled bar takings. Fortunately there were still ample supplies of alcohol. The cake stalls and tea tents had long since had their contents consumed.

196

The sound of falling water accelerated the thirsts of the festival goers as they sheltered under awnings and wondered if they would ever get home! Emergency supplies of beers and spirits had been hastily brought by tractor from Bainbridge's Brewery as the weather worsened.

A siege mentality set in amongst the drinkers. There was a resigned acknowledgement that they were all going to get completely plastered. It was becoming more like a wake than a festival of arts. Charabancs became stuck in the car park and the passengers disembarked and hurried back to the refreshment tent. The bar staff had to be relieved because of exhaustion, some members of the Women's Institute had already succumbed; Mrs Hendry had passed out inebriated onto the muddy ground at the edge of the bar. She lay immobilised where she had fallen, a glass of amontillado sherry still firmly gripped in her podgy hand, her breathing loud and elephantine. Mrs Hendry would not be the only Windelton woman to find herself awakened by bird song the following morning.

When Mrs Hendry did finally come to early the following Sunday morning she was lying amongst empty beer bottles and discarded articles of clothing. As she stared upwards under the white canvas roof she thought her world had come to an end. Her husband, Humphrey, the industrialist, was away visiting one of his overseas factories. Fortunately, he had been spared the sight of his wife as she staggered home in bare feet, gripping lamp posts and stopping only to vomit on the pavement outside Murchison's Bank. The normally hawk-eyed Mrs Hendry was so ill that she failed to notice PC Robson's bicycle and a black Wolseley police car pull up at the rear entrance to the bank. She also missed Laurence Payne nervously stepping out of the police car, cigarette in hand, accompanied by two detectives wearing dark suits and cheap trilby hats; they were followed by a tall, expensively dressed individual in a pin stripe suit.

~

197

When Jasper's party had arrived from the pub they had been surprised to find various men fighting in the rain outside the marquee. Once inside it was obvious to see why. The drunkenness was manifest; it looked as if the inhabitants of Windelton had gone mad.

Respectable Windelton ladies were dancing on tables while others were locked in passionate embraces with drunken young satyrs. The wooden floor of the marquee flexed under the pounding, foot-stomping weight of the dancers who flung their arms into the air, screaming in pure animal delight.

The tent was steaming hot. Normal codes of civilised behaviour were suspended. The alcohol gripped all but the Methodists. Marjorie Nelson was nowhere to be seen. Scuffles were taking place at the dance floor edge as brassiere-clad Windelton women fought off irate husbands; usurped girlfriends tried to win back their partners as middle age women, hormones reawakened from years of slumber and neglect, exercised their rights over Windelton's male youth.

With the cry, "He's mine!" Jasper was jumped on by Audrey Horsfall, the fishmonger's wife. Jasper took her fish-smelling hand as if to dance and engaged her in an exaggerated spinning movement that owed more to a rugby dummy pass as he deftly spun her off the dance floor where she rolled with some velocity onto the grass and skidded under the tent flaps landing outside in the mud.

Jasper and Ian fought their way into the centre of the thrashing mêlée, dragging their partners with them to create their own fortress-like dance circle. This protective shield helped ward off further attacks by marauding Windelton women. It was obvious they couldn't stay long. The atmosphere of abandonment had developed an edge of malevolence. Jasper's well-honed survival antennae recognised that the drunken ribaldry could soon go beyond joshing and swearing. Windelton under these circumstances could be as hazardous as a Harlem speakeasy.

The overthrow of the old order and a new irreverence towards the ruling classes were just part of the changes of the sixties sexual revolution. Pop stars were marrying daughters of peers of the realm but so far the Inchdales had

198

demonstrated no inclination to embrace these radical changes. In fact, far from it: the eviction of Walter from Gardener's Cottage had been the talk of the town and perpetuated the Inchdale family's robber-baron reputation.

The problem started with over-enthusiastic barging by some of the evening-widowed men at the bar. By now they were so drunk and incensed by being spurned by their normally passive wives that their reservoirs of resentment were fully primed.

Mr Hoskins, who was in the largest group of redundant husbands, finally turned his back to the dance floor in helpless disbelief. Sod it, he thought, let the town's lads get lucky with the wives. Hoskins' normal drink had moved up a gear from Bainbridge bitter to Scotch, the lubricant of choice for fighting. By now the men were on the cusp of venting their impotence on anyone who crossed their path.

Their ire would only be satisfied either by getting their drunken wives home for a good belting or if they couldn't wait that long the nearest target. That moment Jasper Inchdale was struggling to get to the bar.

"Planning on chucking out any more of your peasant workers?" shouted Percy Timson, the normally mild mannered, deputy postmaster. Jasper stood at the bar and ignored the remark. He ordered another round of drinks.

"Buying one for us? You can afford it with all that brass?" continued Percy.

Jasper could stand his own in a brawl but he was not going to take on this mob single handed.

"It's about time you sent that lardy sister-in-law of yours to the knacker's yard," chipped in Hoskins, the town clerk.

"You still think you can treat people like shite!" spat Reg Plummer, a farmer with a rattling cough, the result of over exposure to DDT powder. "Your time is coming to an end, lad," he paused for a moment. Then he shoved his ashen face right up to Jasper, their noses nearly touching, Jasper smelling Reg's hot beery breath. "Sooner than you bloody well think," he slurred. "The revolution is coming *your* way, mark my words, sonny!"

Jasper briefly contemplated head-butting this foul-breathed moon-faced farmer but thought better of it.

Suddenly there was a loud cry of: "Halleluiah, Halleluiah!" as the Reverend Max appeared. He barged between the startled men, pushing them aside with the end of his shepherds crook. He emitted a large burp like a car horn. "Get me the bloodiest bloody Mary, Mary," he called to the exhausted girl behind the bar.

"Yes, Reverend," said the bar-maid astonished at the clergyman's unexpected intervention.

"May the Lord have mercy upon my blasphemous tongue and evil ways," he continued to the astonished group pressed against the bar. Then Max addressed the drunken men, now subdued at his sudden manifestation. The Reverend Max smiled wanly at the swaying group of inebriates.

"Good evening, your worshipfulness," slurred Hoskins as he attempted to focus on the reverential presence.

"I thought you had burnt to death?"

"It's about bloody time," muttered Reg Plummer still fired-up after his delayed punch-up with Jasper. "You'd be right t'home in 'ell, eh Reverend," he said sarcastically.

"That's enough of your filthy lip Plummer. May the good Lord forgive your wicked sins and shameful husbandry!"

Reg Plummer's failure as farmer was legendary. He was known on some days not to bother milking his dairy herd. He would prefer to stay slumped in an armchair in the farmhouse parlour scanning the racing pages of the Yorkshire Post. While he inflicted distress on his animals he brought happiness to the bookies as his gambling selections were as poor as his farming practices.

As some form of redemption the Reverend Max gave Reg the holy sign of the cross. The unsteadying effort of this ecclesial gesture caused him to grip the bar. He tried to focus on the voluptuous figure of Mary and was about to order another very bloody Mary. It was clear to her that the Reverend Max was as drunk as the rest of Windelton. He should have been back at the vicarage hours ago penning his Sunday sermon (*What can we learn from Satan?*)

"Sins be damned, you blasphemous old goat," shouted Reg Plummer pointing his grubby bitten-down fore-finger at the Reverend Max. "If you expect me to believe all your mumbo-jumbo you must be out of your cassock. *Your* God can't even pick *me* a winning horse. What sacrifices are *you* making Reverend Max? You look prosperous enough with your vicarage, jewels and fancy get-up, where's *your bloody* donkey, Mr. Palmolive?"

"I am already doing my penance for being YOUR representative on earth, you useless wastrel," replied Max jabbing his finger in Reg's chest. "The Church of England is my asylum!"

"Where's your bloody God in Windelton, you tell me?" Reg shouted. "The wind never stops blowing, the people are knackered. Reg looked around with bleary, blood-shot eyes. He pointed vaguely in the direction of the assembled group but Jasper had surreptitiously made his escape.

"BUT GOD IS HERE!" bellowed the Reverend Max in a burst of uncontrolled rage. Then with two hands he lifted his scorched crook high above his head and brought it down it down across Reg's cranium with a fierce some blow.

"Never cease to marvel at His wonders," he cried as Reg crumpled to the floor, blood pouring from his left ear.

"This is the wrath of the Almighty," he said calmly, "God moves in mysterious ways and so do I," he pronounced. The stunned bystanders backed away out of range of his holy weapon. The Reverend Max then grasped his bloody Mary and downed it one snorting gulp.

"Hoskins is buying; let me have another of those Bloody Marys, Mary," cried the drunken Reverend. Then, turning to the astounded gathering, he commanded: "One of you unbelievers should make haste to the St John's Ambulance tent and tell them you have witnessed the retribution of God. Get them to come quickly if they want to avoid a funeral. I am busy enough as it is!"

Reg lay very still on the muddy ground. The blood ran down the side of his stubbly chin, the red flow contrasted with his deathly pale skin. The angry men dispersed, silently chastened as the Reverend Max downed another bloody Mary fearfully poured by the horrified bar maid.

Hoskins ran off into the rain in search of help leaving Reg quietly bleeding.

Max turned towards the dance floor and strode off in search of more heathens to convert, his crook suitably bloodied from another baptism of his bizarre ministry.

~

Dawn was pulled along by Jasper as they splashed out of the sweating tent into the cool rain, trying to distance themselves from the ugly violence of the bar. Ian was somewhere behind. He couldn't keep pace with the agile Rachel as she darted through the arboretum searching for the car park. Ian was truly drunk and it was not long before he tripped over an unseen tree root wrenching his ankle with a sharp twist. Rachel didn't hear Ian's cry of pain. She was hopelessly lost. She had left the shelter of the dark woods and reached the Japanese garden where she took refuge in a small mock wooden pagoda. She was puffed out but at least it was dry. Where the hell had Jasper gone? She had thought for a moment that Jasper was going to be lynched by that group of ugly, cursing men.

I bet Jasper is seducing the innocent Dawn, Rachel thought. Dawn was not such a goody-two-shoes as she likes to make out. A bit of danger makes Jasper as randy as hell. I suppose that's why he drives that car of his so bloody fast. He's just like a child! He is far too conventional for me. *I want someone really bad, someone like one of those wild looking, long haired boys in that pop group...!*

Rachel's prediction was accurate, Jasper and Dawn had reached the E-Type and they both piled in.

"Where on earth are the others?" said Dawn trying to re-arrange her sodden clothing.

"Don't fret, they'll be here in a minute, I told Rachel we'd meet up at the cottage. Ian will bring her along in your car."

Dawn couldn't remember any of this being discussed but wanted to believe that it was correct. It was difficult to think clearly after all that running and danger. It had been heady and frightening. Dawn could feel the hate emanating from the crowd towards Jasper. You could smell it, a horrible animal-pack stench.

"Let's get out of here, before they come and murder me," said Jasper, jokingly interrupting her thoughts. He laughed, leant across towards her and kissed her full on the lips. At first she just puckered her lips but Jasper's insistent tongue forced open her mouth. She replied with equal force, her hand clasping the hair on the back of his head, gripping the thick black curls. Jasper pulled himself away.

"Steady on, girl" he said a little breathlessly, taken aback by Dawn's unexpectedly direct response. He turned the key in the ignition and pressed the starter button to fire up the powerful engine.

With some prescience, Jasper had parked the Jaguar on the top of a grass mound. When he let off the hand brake the low car should freewheel down the muddy slope to the open gateway and onto the solid driveway. If he applied too much power the car would almost certainly slide out of control and they would never get out. With some skill Jasper manoeuvred the free-wheeling vehicle precariously past various abandoned cars and slid through the open gateway.

Now on terra firma, Jasper engaged first gear and pushed down the accelerator and the rear wheels spun ferociously, the tyres howling in protest as the car shot up the lane towards Gardener's Cottage. As the car roared along the road Dawn felt she had escaped from something dreadful, it was like being liberated from school at the end of term. She felt invisible and what the hell, this was fun!

She slid her hand across the transmission tunnel and pulled Jasper's shirt out of his trousers. She ran a warm hand over the top of his stomach, curling her fingers

203

into the top of his pubic hair. He groaned as she could see his swelling erection. He shifted slightly in his seat to get more comfortable, trying to ease the pressure of his cavalry twill trousers that was pinning down his straining cock. He slowed the car down and ran his left hand through Dawn's hair; his right hand gripped and twirled the wooden steering wheel.

He asked her to change the gears when he commanded; "third" he called as he accelerated out of a tight left hand bend, the rear of the car fish-tailing as the tyres fought to grip the slippery surface. The E-Type's three wipers flashed across the narrow windscreen, the gear lever was solid and reassuring and with each change she could feel the sensory power of the cogs meshing and the powerful engine responding. It didn't take long to get the hang of it and soon she was shifting the lever with ease. It was nearly as interesting as Jasper's flat hard stomach!

When the car had pulled into the cottage yard Jasper turned off the lights and he turned to kiss her again, harder this time. She unzipped his fly and wrested out his rock hard penis from the prison of his trousers. Leaning back her head she made a display of licking her fingers before grasping his dry cock head and firmly moved her hand up and down the shaft.

Jasper was gasping, "Let's go inside, this is too good for out here?"

"It's what you like isn't it Jasper?" Dawn teased, exercising the power she now had over him. Men are such simple creatures she thought, I could ask anything of him right now and he would agree to it as long as I keep holding his stupid cock!

"Yes, but….. I don't want a mess in the car!"

"Worried about your precious car eh?" She speeded up her hand movements.

But Jasper took her hand in his and removed it from his wilting organ, kissing her lightly, he whispered, "No, we *are* going in." He opened door and started to pull up his trousers.

"Spoilsport!" said Dawn, surprised at her own lascivious behaviour and disappointed that Jasper had to do everything, even sex, on his own terms.

The brightness of the electric light in the cottage kitchen brought Dawn sharply back into the real world. Gone was the cosy cockpit of the Jaguar, warm and womb like with its rich smell of leather and the dim lights of the dashboard. Here was domesticity in all its ugliness. Unwashed dishes in the sink, damp mould around the ceiling, filthy floors and empty bottles of wine stacked up on the window sills. How does Jasper live like this she thought? It's like a pig sty.

"Where the hell have Ian and Rachel got too?" Dawn asked, the magic spell of their brief sexual encounter broken.

"I told you, they are coming on later."

"Are you sure you told Rachel, I hope you haven't lured me here without telling anyone? Ian will have a panic attack; he is already scared of you! He thinks you are going to take advantage of me - *me* a married woman with two children! Can you believe it?" she said half mockingly and half serious.

"I think it's *you* who is taking the advantage."

I was a little drunk and I wanted to look at your cock. I am not entirely stupid you know. Jasper, I know your reputation. It would be fun, nice… but it wouldn't really be fair on Ian would it?"

"I wasn't thinking about Ian."

"That's your problem Jasper, I don't believe you ever think about anyone except yourself?"

"But Dawn darling, I really *do* fancy you."

"That's not enough in my book. You should have stayed in the car and let me make a mess of you. But you wouldn't let a nice thing like that happen would you, not without controlling everything yourself. You just couldn't let yourself go out there, could you? You silly boy!" Dawn laughed at his crestfallen face.

"You are just a terrible prick teaser Dawn!" he said, irritation entering his voice. "I just wanted to come in here so it would be more…"

"So you could seduce me more easily," she interrupted with a giggle, "and in a tip like this. That's no way to treat a lady. Surely you could do better than this? I am

205

sorry to let you down Jasper, but don't spoil things by getting huffy with me. Why don't you make a nice cup of coffee and light me a ciggie before the others turn up?"

"I thought you didn't smoke?"

"Only other people's!"

"Are you sure that's all *you* want?" said Jasper getting more irritated.

"I am just being Mrs Sensible like I normally am. It's very flattering to be chased around by a scoundrel like you but let's be realistic. You are on the make and I'm a happily married woman who is a bit tipsy. Anyway, my husband and your girlfriend are going to turn up here in a few minutes, which is providing you haven't been lying through your teeth to me all evening?"

Jasper couldn't argue with Dawn's unassailable logic but sex was never reasonable as far as Jasper was concerned. It was always at extremes. Being turned down for sex was not in his lexicon of experience, He *always* got his own way! He handed her a cigarette and lit it for her with a shaking hand.

"Calm down." She kissed him gently on the mouth. "There's plenty more fish in the sea, Jasper it's just that I suspect you are not often refused."

He tried to kiss her again and she gently pushed him away. "A coffee, I said."

"Don't you want something stronger?"

"No thanks."

"I am having a scotch."

"Where is your coffee? I will make one myself."

"In the cupboard on the left," he pointed.

Jasper flopped down into a moth eaten old armchair in front of a long dead open fire.

"What do you *really* want, Dawn?"

"Oh, I don't know, I am just a bit confused right now….I would like Ian to be happy again, like when we were first married. It's very nice to be wanted again as a *'woman'.* Being a mother makes you forget sometimes. Quite frankly you are a hopeless bet for most women."

"Why?"

"Do you want the full list or the abridged version?"

"The abridged one will do," he said with a weak grin.

"Why do you want the punishment, Jasper? You know the answers already, I am certain I am not the first woman to tell you. You must have heard it dozens of times before."

"I like to be reassured that I'm as bad as ever!"

"Jasper you are impossible!"

"Go on!"

"You're self-centred, spoilt, arrogant and too used to getting your own way".

"Anything else?"

Dawn pondered for a moment. "Yes, your cock is too small for my taste!"

"WHAAAAT?" That really did hit a nerve. He bounded to his feet.

"What do you mean? You've not tried it yet!"

"Well, I have had a jolly good feel," she giggled. "Compared to what I am used to… anyhow, it doesn't matter. I have decided. I won't say that I wasn't tempted. I was probably getting back at Ian for his failure to get on with his life!"

Dawn smiled at him sympathetically, "You beat him at golf isn't that enough? You don't have to seduce his wife as well."

Jasper laughed weakly, still feeling chastised over the size of his penis. "You are just using my cock as an excuse. It isn't the real reason, we both know that."

"Maybe it isn't but don't worry Jasper, you'll get over it. There are loads of girls out there," Dawn indicated with a toss of her head towards the doorway. "Why don't you marry Rachel, she's stunning, just your type? Or is it whatever you have, you'll always want something new after a few months?"

"Maybe you're right. I like the challenge. The relationship bit gets tedious. Girls always want to get engaged after three or four dates."

"Jasper, your problem is that you get bored too easily. You've got to learn to grow up. I think your mother must have neglected you as a child."

"God, you *sound* like my mother!"

Just then the lights of a car swung into the cottage yard. Rachel got out of the driver's seat and ran toward the back door. Jasper took a large slug of whisky as Dawn poured hot water on to the instant coffee powder. Her hand trembled slightly as she gripped the half-clean mug.

What have I been doing she thought to herself? Her cheeks coloured with embarrassment at the sight of Rachel's flushed and worried expression.

"I think Ian's broken his ankle. He's in the car, he is in agony, can't move. He needs to get to hospital quick."

"What?" cried Dawn in alarm?

"Dawn do you want me to drive him to hospital, I haven't had that much to drink. Why don't you just pile in the back?"

"Oh, the poor lamb." Dawn put down her cup in almost relief, "Yes please Rachel. Would you do that for me?"

"Of course, but I think we should get going. I quite fancy the drive, mercy dash and all that!"

"Well don't bloody kill us all', said Ian pathetically. His white face peered out of the half-open passenger door.

"Are you coming Jasper?" asked Rachel.

"No thanks, there's nothing I can do, anyway I feel a bit rough!"

"Bye Jasper, thanks for the coffee", said Dawn as she hastily scrambled into the back of the Mini, trying not to jolt Ian's ankle which he clasped painfully with both hands.

When they had gone Jasper poured another quadruple scotch, sat down in his battered armchair and swore very, very loudly.

"Bloody bitch!"

- Chapter 25 -

Getting Away From It All

The deluge started as the black Morris approached Grantham. Astle talked to himself to calm his nerves. He still couldn't quite believe what he had done; he felt as if he was in a nightmare from which he expected to awake to a normal world again. Calm and constancy: Sunday tomorrow, a drink in the pub, 'phone Valerie, home for one o'clock and a lovingly prepared roast dinner nervously presented by Daphne wearing one of her half-hopeful smiles.

There was no going back. He had become a fugitive. Astle instinctively looked behind him to check if he was being followed. He started to whimper pathetically. Tears rolled down his fat cheeks making his vision through the rain- soaked windscreen even more difficult. The windows were fogged up, aided by Astle's snuffling breath as he fought back hot, self-pitying tears. The wipers could barely drag themselves across the screen the rain was so heavy.

He frantically wiped the screen with a scrunched up silk handkerchief - a Christmas present from Daphne in 1959, neatly ironed by the home help. Daphne had been hopeless at ironing but she had been a good cook. Who would do his ironing in South America? What was the Spanish for ironing? He started to panic again until he realised he could afford to keep buying new clothes when the old ones became soiled. With the money he had taken from Marjorie Nelson he could employ dozens of maids, all of them good at some special domestic chore.

He cheered up a little at this thought then fell headlong back into a decline as he thought of how he would explain he didn't like cabbage and his beef well done? He decided to pull over at the next transport café and wait for the worst of the weather to pass. He'd have a nice cup of tea. Although he had been fretting about his schedule at the festival he had plenty of time to spare. His flight was not due to leave until two pm on the following day. He was leaving from the Oceanic Terminal at London Airport, now known for some reason as Heathrow. The thought of needless change made Astle think of his long dead parents. His father had raged against change. He had been a bank manager too.

Goodness knows what he would have thought of his only son's behaviour. He had been an absolute stickler for protocol, 'doing the right thing'. Now his son had got an unmarried woman pregnant, left his wife and robbed his employer – a fornicator *and* a bank robber! His moral depravity plumbed unimaginable depths; now they would *both* be looking at him from behind the net curtains of the afterlife at his shameful behaviour.

His father hadn't approved of Daphne, yet she had tried her best to please her future in-laws. "You could have done better for yourself than her," his father had said on learning of his impending engagement. The words still stung in his ears: "Not quite good enough, not quite the right drawer, Gerald."

Bloody snob, he thought. No wonder he hated the Inchdales and that bloody Nelson woman. They'd all looked down on him as some inferior species, just as his father had turned up his nose at Daphne. Poor Daphne, what had she had to put up with! No wonder she spent her time with that blasted clairvoyant.

Astle pulled the car off the road into a roadside café. As it was a Saturday there wasn't much heavy goods traffic about, just a couple of coal lorries and a petrol tanker, a removal van from Hitchin and a few cars parked in the muddy car park.

Inside the steamy warm shack a group of cigarette-smoking lorry drivers were congregated on the first two tables. They seemed to know one another. They looked up at the fat sweating man in the garish short sleeved shirt. Their curiosity was heightened when he produced a wad of large fivers from his back pocket. Astle stood out in this haunt of lorry drivers and motorcycle youths who liked to race along stretches of the Great North Road.

Armed with his mug of red coloured tea and two slabs of white bread, a splodge of margarine and some industrial looking jam that been extracted from a massive unhygienic looking tin, Astle made his way to a grubby, Formica-topped table by the window. The table's surface had not seen a clean cloth for days and the adjacent window streamed with condensation and mingled grime. Astle, despite his catalogue of vices, had never smoked. His parents had both strongly disapproved and claimed that the odour of cigarette smoke gave them stomach cramps. They were given to extreme opinions when they wanted to persuade their only son on some matter of upbringing.

In his teens Astle had harboured a desire to join the Royal Navy. His father had painted a horrifying picture of floggings, keel-hauling and hinted darkly at unsavoury practices that newly enlisted cadets had to endure. The dire warning of these imaginary evils never prevented his parents giving generously to lifeboat appeals or stopped his father puffing away on a foul pipe. After his Father had finished a pipe of his Balkan shag, his tobacco of choice, his eyes would glaze over and fall asleep, a seraphic smile playing about his lips. An exotic aroma would prevail in the house for hours afterwards. Astle had often suspected that his father's tobacco indulgence was more serious than he could fathom. Despite her in-laws' disapproval, Daphne had stood her ground and she had continued to puff away on her favourite Du Maurier tipped cigarettes. It was typical of Astle's parents to have double standards and it was not until adulthood that he recognised their duplicitous behaviour.

The tea fortified Astle and the stodgy bread and sweet-tasting jam proved to be very satisfactory. He ordered another round, but this time following the example of some of the truckers, he asked for his bread to be toasted. After devouring his round of toast and downing his tea he felt briefly energised. He wanted to get away from the fugged-up atmosphere and the alien, threatening atmosphere that haunts of the working classes always had on him. Astle was also worried about arriving at his hotel so late that they would lock the doors. He had a chosen a small, discreet place to stay, a haunt of commercial travellers. Astle had located the hotel in his RAC handbook. It had been awarded a one star rating – 'comfortable'. He had quite forgotten he could afford the very best, but old habits die hard.

As the rain slowed to drizzle he returned to the sanctuary of his Morris. Like an old and trusted companion, complicit yet un-judgemental in its relationship with the thieving owner. The car sat lightly on its springs, barely weighed down with the guilt of the boot's contents or the driver's foul deeds. Astle drove the car to a row of fuel pumps to top-up the tank prior to continuing his journey south.

A lank-haired youth loped out of a small hut, "Fill her up?" he asked insolently.

"Yep, to the top!"

Astle thought to himself that he wouldn't miss the surly indifference of Britain's youth. But as he stared out over the damp uneven tarmac towards a piece of woodland, it suddenly occurred to him that he would miss these wet English summer evenings. A time when the new leaves took on an iridescent shine and the air smelt sweet and freshly washed.

It had not crossed Astle's mind before that he might regret the loss of familiar surroundings or even English weather. He had only thought of the people and his singular distaste for most of them. This was a new unexpected pang. So crowded had his mind been with plans of the robbery, Valerie and the looming head office meeting, the reality of leaving everything behind had been blinded by his desire to flee. Suddenly a rush of nostalgia overcame him and he found himself blinking back tears as he pondered his old life that he had so single-mindedly and magnificently destroyed.

He thought of the unfulfilled promise of his career and marriage, his failure as a father and the pathetic and shabby way he had treated Valerie and his son. What had he been thinking of leaving her with the total responsibility of bringing up his son? What a waste, he thought as he saw the boy, *his* boy, and the smile James had given him as he handed over the extra piece of cake!

"That'll be ten and sixpence sir," the objectionable youth broke into his reverie. The 'Sir' was said with a menacing sarcasm. Astle struggled with his bulging wad of notes, eventually fishing out a ten shilling note with his fat fingers and fumbling in his trouser pockets counted out two three penny bits.

"Cor, you got a lot of dosh there Mister, have you bin robbin' a bank or summat?"

"How did you...?" Astle froze as his unguarded remark stopped mid-flow at the youth's innocently made question.

"A bit of luck on the horses," replied Astle hastily as he fumbled out the cash, avoiding looking the youth in the eye. Astle would normally have returned the money with a glare and a facetious remark but he couldn't summon the will power to take on the youngster. He just wanted to get away.

"You al'right mister, you look ill?" said the dangerous youth displaying an unexpected humanitarian tone.

"Fine, just a bit tired but thanks for asking," said Astle getting into his car.

He moved off jerkily, careering dangerously back onto the main road, crashing the Morris' gears. He had not been driving long before tiredness swept over him again. He felt he had to press on further before stopping for a nap. At least the rain had abated and a watery sun was emerging. On a straight piece of road just before Stamford he overtook the removal van he had seen at the transport café. There was a weasel-like, thin-faced looking man at the wheel and a young, fair haired apprentice at his side in the cab's passenger seat.

Astle struggled on for another forty five minutes but his eyes began to close and at one point he nearly lost control as the Morris's wheels started to throw up grit at the road edge and the car started to veer off the tarmac. Two more miles down the road Astle pulled the car into a lay-by that was partially obscured from the main road. It had once been part of the main carriageway before it was straightened out. Now this old stretch of tarmac served as a resting place and was conveniently screened by a thick hedge. This made it a popular stopping spot for long distance lorry drivers as it afforded some privacy from the main road traffic.

There wasn't much traffic about and as Astle brought the Morris to a halt a single lorry pulled away to re-join the Great North Road leaving the lay-by empty. He turned off the ignition, pulled hard on the heavy hand brake and swung open the front door. The air was fresh and he got out to give his legs a stretch. He walked about stiffly for a few minutes before unsteadily returning to the car. He opened the rear door and scrambled into the back. He tried to settle himself as best he could on the narrow bench seat. He put his legs up onto the burgundy leather and pulled a tartan travelling rug up under his chin and closed his eyes. His aim was to snatch half an hour's rest.

Astle's mind raced. It was filled with the extraordinary events of the day: collecting the cash from the bank safe had been easy. Now in the damp, cool evening he considered his actions with more circumspection. He whimpered at the thought of being caught. He ran over and over again in his mind the likelihood of this happening and reassured himself that no-one would ever suspect him. Inchdale would keep quiet but on Monday morning the balloon would go up. By the time Payne would have worked out in his feeble mind what had happened, Astle would be in Buenos Aires sipping an agreeable cup of tea. He hoped they *had* tea in Buenos Aires.

Astle smiled to himself when he considered Lawrence Payne's face when the pandemonium erupted at the bank. The visits from regional office, the fraud boys would be called in from Lombard Street. Heads would roll; someone would be to blame for the bank's sloppy security. Payne would take the brunt as deputy manager. Harry Webster at the Bugle would have a field day and the Yorkshire Post would lap it up.

Astle shifted in his cramped make-shift bed as he recalled his encounters with Valerie and James. That had not gone as planned. Valerie was no longer the demure bank manager's secretary that he had lodged in his memory. Only when she was lying in a dead faint had she regained the look of vulnerability that he remembered. That blasted Nelson man had nearly spoiled things getting in the way. It hadn't left him enough time to talk, to explain. James had had a mesmerising effect on him. He hadn't bargained for that. My God, he had a son!

214

Finally sleep overcame him and he drifted into fitful unconsciousness. He twisted his hand into the leather strap above the rear quarter light window to stop himself falling off the seat. The skies had cleared and as the evening lengthened some stars appeared in the inky darkness. Eventually, a removal van pulled into the lay-by and stopped quietly fifty yards behind the Morris. Its lights were extinguished and the driver and the apprentice boy looked at one another with knowing expectancy.

- Chapter 26 -

A Night Time Stroll

Walter liked to walk at night. The early summer months when the days were drawing longer were his favourite time.

Walter was one of the few Windelton inhabitants who avoided being sucked into the day's drunken festivities. Instead he had been hoeing in his allotment until the prospect of rain had driven him home. He had seen the weather building up in the west, high cumulus clouds had been forming and it had becoming menacingly dark. His years of outdoor working told him that there was going to be a few hours of very heavy rain and he needed to get home to avoid a soaking.

He had made himself some tea as his daughter and family had not yet returned from the festival. The rapid change in barometric pressure, an occurrence that often made him feel lethargic, combined with his hard labours at the allotment resulted in Walter dozing off in an armchair. He was suddenly awakened by the noise of his son-in-law, slightly tipsy daughter and tired grandchildren all bursting into the room.

They were all soaked to the skin and everyone was irritable, the children were worn out and ready for bed. Feeling in the way, Walter politely excused himself, telling his daughter that he was nipping out for a pint at the Nags Head.

The pub was nearly empty; Walter took off his wet raincoat and sat down by the open fire with his pint of best. The landlord was even more miserable than normal. He was still burning with resentment at having been fined for contempt of court by Sir Toby Inchdale. The lack of trade for a Saturday night, normally the best night of the week for takings, was not improving his humour.

Despite the early summer, the landlord had lit an open fire in the wishful hope that it might cheer himself and his few loyal customers. But this heart- warming idea had failed to raise his spirits and he was cussing and uttering threats of retribution to anyone who would listen. His rantings embraced the dreadful rain storm, the Inchdale family, the festival organisers, particularly Marjorie Nelson and the disloyalty of his customers.

"Serves 'em right if the bloody lot of 'em drown; how do they 'spect hard working people like me to survive when the bloody council hand out extended licensing laws to the likes of toffs like that Nelson woman and her bloody festival? You tell me!"

Warming to his subject he picked on another recurrent grouse: "Then when it comes to paying the rates they are soon on our backs. I might as well pack up and go home!"

"This is your home, isn't it?" said Walter enquiringly.

"You know what I bloody mean!" replied the landlord tersely.

Walter made his way to a seat by the fire. He had no desire to pursue this pointless conversation with the landlord; he had been bleating like a repetitive gramophone record about the injustice of the festival ever since his court case two months ago. Tonight, Walter had other things on his mind.

The quietness in the pub gave Walter time for reflection. His change of life still irked him. Tonight he had felt duty bound to get out from under his daughter's feet although nothing had actually been said. He didn't want to talk to them or probably them to him, though neither party would have owned up to such thoughts. Whatever, it was an unnecessary burden that they all had to bear because of that bastard Inchdale heaving him out of his rightful home.

Walter drank slowly and solemnly, savouring the hoppy taste of Bainbridge's Mild - creamy dark and smooth. Despite the catatonic ravings of the landlord at least he did know how to keep his ales. Good beer was a landlord's first responsibility, even if he failed in his second of being a welcoming host. Well at least he had lit a cheerful fire, he thought.

He had a second pint, then a third and was contemplating a fourth when the bell rang for last orders at twenty-five past ten. He decided on a half rather than having to gulp down a pint. Walter knew that with the mood of the landlord, he would be

217

clearing the few customers out as fast as he could after the ten minute drinking up time had elapsed.

Surprisingly, the warm fire and the beer had stimulated Walter's senses and his earlier tiredness had disappeared. The landlord's wife, a stocky, no-nonsense woman, emerged from a door behind the bar and started stacking chairs on top of tables with a lot of loud clattering and banging accompanied by heavy sighs. Walter got the hint and downed the remains of his beer.

Outside, the night was still warm and there was a sound of running water emptying from gutters. Storm drains gurgled as they fought to clear away the excess of the earlier deluge. It had stopped raining and the wind had died down. There was a sweet smell of ripening vegetation, Walter imagined he could hear the trees organising their branches, leaves turning outwards, preparing themselves to receive the life-giving synthesis from the sun when morning finally arrived.

At the festival ground dozens of Windeltonians were searching for discarded clothing they had removed during the course of the evening. They arose as if from a terrible battle, stumbling out of the battered marquees, emerging from wet nettle patches and unsteadily mounting bicycles. Many were nursing aching limbs as they made their best attempts to reach the sanctuary of their homes. And still some slept on.

Walter, still refreshed from his earlier sleep, decided to take off on one of his late night rambles. He had a key for his daughter's house and she was accustomed to his late night roving around the Windelton countryside. His perambulations generally followed a familiar tread; tonight he skirted the Inchdale Home Farm, not too close to wake the dogs or Courcey's braying wife. He had been known to encounter her as she was another nocturnal predator, often roaming the stables on the pretext of keeping her eye on her beloved hunters. Griselda had startled him on a number of occasions and she had once propositioned him with the invitation to come into a loose box for, 'a bit of breeding!' He had fled in terror.

218

Leaving Home Farm he went into Badger Wood and followed an ancient woodsman's path that eventually led into One Hundred Acre Pasture. Here the river meandered across low-lying meadows before he climbed upwards to Rigg Wood that had been planted as game cover one hundred years ago. Now it was an excellent holding place for pheasant, partridge and woodcock.

The skies had cleared and moon was up providing a good light in which to walk. Walter's eyes had long grown accustomed to the dark and he edged around the southern perimeter of the wood and then cut through a copse of self-seeding birch that was in need of thinning. Typical Courcey, he thought, too mean or lazy to tend it properly!

As the land fell away Walter carefully trod the soft earth of the copse. Just before the scattered trees gave way to open land again he caught the rank smell of a fox that had marked the bark of a tree. Later he heard a vixen's strangled scream. He looked at his watch, it was approaching one o'clock. He should be getting back home soon. By now he was close to the back garden of his old cottage. At this point he had two options: he could either follow the fence around the perimeter of the rear garden that would eventually lead to a track that would take him to the metalled driveway and the Windelton road.

Alternatively, he could save time by clambering the wooden fence and nip past the kitchen-cum-sitting room. He would have to cross the small patch of lawn and pass his old tool shed and join another pathway that led back toward Home Farm – his normal way to work in times past.

He decided on the shorter route.

As he crossed the grass Walter could see a light coming from the sitting room. He ducked down to avoid being seen. He was nearly past the window but at the last moment he couldn't resist the temptation to peek into the room. He crouched down under the window sill and slowly lifted his head above the sill edge. There were no curtains and the window was dirty. He caught a glimpse of a figure asleep in his old armchair in front of the fire. By the time he had registered there was a person in the room he had made off towards his old tool shed for fear of being detected.

Bugger it, he thought, his curiosity having got the better of him he'd have another look so he crept back. On closer inspection, he recognised Jasper Inchdale. He was prostrate in the armchair, his head thrown back and his mouth open, his hands resting on the arms of the chair. There was an empty bottle of what looked like scotch lying on its side with a smouldering butt-filled ashtray accompanying it by the chair. Young Inchdale looked out for the count.

As Walter surveyed the dirty cottage and the empty bottles he suddenly felt a surge of anger for the place that had been his home for so many happy years. Jasper's disrespect for the property and his careless disregard for himself - his clothes strewn over the floor, shoes tossed off, his tie hanging loosely from his neck. It all added insult to Walter's sense of outrage at his eviction. Thrown out after all those years of labour and loyalty to *that man's* family! For what? So that scoundrel could have a cheap place to sleep off his excesses. His cottage stolen from him and now it was being disabused for the benefit of a selfish prig and his self-serving family.

Nobody had thought how *he* might feel. Just because he was old they thought he only qualified for the knacker's yard. As he stared through the grubby window pane into the heart of his old home Walter blinked back tears of righteous anger. Then an idea suddenly came into his mind.

- Chapter 27 -

Inspector Payne

Laurence Payne had a feeling. He had had it for some time but now two and half weeks before the Windelton festival, a Wednesday to be precise, matters came to a head.

Astle had become more and more officious over the last few weeks. His mood swings had got more extreme. He had taken to locking himself away in his office, reticent to discuss any customer issues.

For Payne, years of working alongside Astle had inured him to his superior's erratic behaviour and quick temper, but recently he had appeared forlorn and distracted. Payne put it down to his impending retirement or the strange relationship that Astle had with his wife.

It was always in Payne's best interests to keep in Astle's good books. It would be Astle's recommendation that would finally determine whether Payne would get his own branch. Payne's own retirement date was looming, he had only three years to go before he would hit the buffers.

Over the years Astle had ceased to be the collaborative colleague of old and had grown remote and dismissive towards him; in fact, on occasions Payne thought that Astle despised him. This had made Payne more nervous and as a consequence he had become abrupt with his own staff creating a downward spiral of unhappiness throughout the office.

Murchison's Windelton was no longer a happy bank. Payne was smoking more and more Senior Service cigarettes and Ernie Trott's panic attacks had become all too frequent. Ian Henderson appeared defeated and only the oleaginous Seedman remained smug. Dear old Miss Starkey seemed close to a nervous breakdown and only Peter Firth remained his dream-like, distant self.

Payne had always kept a close eye on Marjorie Nelson's various accounts and investments, although as the largest customer, this was strictly the manager's responsibility. He had noticed in recent weeks that a considerable number of her blue chip investments had been sold for cash. The bank acted as her discretionary adviser across her investment portfolio. This meant the bank could buy and sell stocks and shares on her behalf, merely informing her of the bank's actions at quarterly meetings. If an especially large buy or sell transaction was planned the protocol was that a phone call would be placed by Astle or Payne, informing Marjorie of the proposed course of action. However, these calls were not obligatory.

In recent weeks the UK stock market had been meandering in a downward trajectory. Superficially, it did not appear to be a propitious time to be dumping large quantities of shares. Payne also noted that the cash proceeds from these sales were being transferred to bank accounts in Buenos Aires and Zurich. On the Wednesday in question Payne saw that £175,000 was transferred to Argentina and the following Monday £84,000 had gone to Credit Suisse in Zurich and more had followed to both banks as the broker's settlement days had become due. The sale proceeds arrived in one day and went out again the next. Payne had commented to Astle about these large movements of cash.

Astle had been dismissive as always: "The Nelson woman's lost confidence in the stock market and is liquidating a lot of her funds. She'll reinvest when things pick up."

"But why offshore?" Payne had enquired.

"Tax shelter, I would guess, I am just following instructions. Who am I to reason with Marjorie Nelson?" Astle smiled thinly. That should put Payne off the scent he had thought. "By the way, I would rather you didn't mention it if you have any dealings with her. She was most reticent when she instructed me and wanted absolute discretion. You *know* what she's like. Mum's the word eh!" Astle touched his nose and gave Payne a conspiratorial wink. As an afterthought, Astle remarked, "I have kept regional office in the picture. We don't want the bank inspector's paying us a surprise visit do we?"

222

Payne raised his eyebrows, half quizzically, half as if he understood this unnecessary remark.

Payne returned to his mahogany cubicle and took off his half-moon spectacles and rubbed his eyes, trying to fathom the meaning of Astle's remarks. He put his glasses back on and pulled out the last Senior Service from the packet, he tapped the end of the cigarette on his desk top to secure any flaking pieces of tobacco. He placed the cigarette precisely in the centre of his mouth, pursed his lips to push the fag forward toward his treasured gold Dunhill lighter. His fingers spun the wheel on the side of the lighter and ignited the gas in a gentle 'whumpth' of flame. Payne inhaled with a rasp of pleasure as his lungs sucked down another killer-cloud of smoke that he exhaled seconds later through nose and mouth in a thin stream of blue oxygen enriched vapour. His head felt slightly fuzzy as the narcotic hit his blood stream. The cigarette glowed red and his hacking cough could be heard throughout the banking hall.

He reached into his top right hand draw of the mahogany desk, it slid open silently and he pulled out a new white and blue packet of Senior Service, removing the cellophane wrapping with accomplished ease he pulled out the silver foil from the right hand side half to reveal ten untouched, inviting virgin cigarettes. Payne gazed at the cigarettes in pleasurable anticipation. He left the open pack on his desk and crushed the silver foil between his forefinger and thumb, rolling it back and forth in a comforting exchange as he thought about Marjorie Nelson and the extraordinary cash transfers.

A feeling inside was telling him something was wrong; Astle was being very arch but still as cool as a cucumber. The remark about the regional office was unnecessary. That was information that Payne didn't need to know.

Why was Astle justifying his actions, he normally never did that? All this sudden 'mateyness' was not natural. Funny, he'd not seen any paperwork to support these transactions and not a dickie bird from Marjorie Nelson. It *could* have been done over the telephone but that was highly irregular considering the sums of cash involved.

He knew that Astle was a bit of a maverick but he didn't have him down as a fraudster. But if he challenged Astle or went behind his back and everything turned out to be above board Payne realised he was finished. His career was over with a capital 'O'. Astle would destroy any smouldering hopes he held for his own branch. He stamped out his cigarette and pulled out another from the new packet as he continued to wrestle with possible courses of action. Every alternative seemed to spell danger or at worst doom.

Three more transactions took place over the following ten days leading up to the festival. Then on the Friday before the great festival weekend, Payne noticed that just before the close of business at three o'clock, Astle had personally authorised the transfer of Marjorie's two deposit savings accounts, one valued at £56,000 and the other longer term account of £110,000. They had both been transferred: one to Zurich the other to Buenos Aires, both to numbered accounts. And there had been NO previous indication that this transfer was to be made by either Marjorie or Astle. Because there was no advanced warning the transaction would have incurred a hefty penalty charge from the bank, reducing the interest due on the account.

This broke all Astle's personal rules and those of Marjorie Nelson too! Payne's reaction was real shock. He checked the ledger of the current account, there was still a healthy £8,756 credit balance. But still £166,000 being transferred in one day from a personal account at Murchison's Windelton - this was a major movement of cash. It would be seen as a blow to the internal prestige of the branch within the bank as a whole.

Payne decided to tackle Astle about it immediately. He had not seen his boss for half an hour and Astle always informed him if he was not going to be available for till balancing and the usual close of business matters.

"Mr Astle has left to see a customer and will be out for the remainder of the afternoon," said Miss Starkey officiously in answer to Payne's worried enquiry. "I'm surprised *you* didn't know," she went on as if it was Payne's fault that his boss had scarpered without a word. "And this Saturday is his morning off so he won't be back until Monday," she continued triumphantly. "Ian Henderson and you are doing the safe today and tomorrow."

Payne hadn't been told this either. Very odd!

Payne returned to his cubicle. He was much shaken. It was all highly irregular. He thought he might telephone Astle this evening out of hours but what good would that do?

Alternatively, he could make some gentle enquiries at regional office to see if they were aware of these massive transfers. But that would mean going behind Astle's back and burning his bridges. This was the worst moment of his career. The potential for disaster was palpable.

The implications looked even worse than when he discovered that well-dressed clerk had been stealing till proceedings to pay his tailoring bills.

Payne made up his mind. He had chain-smoked three Senior Service cigarettes. The cashiers were about to balance their tills for the day, soon there would be a rush to get the money into the safe and go home. Payne drew a deep breath and with trembling fingers dialled the regional office number in Leeds.

"Headrow Fisheries?"

"It's Murchison's bank here, can I speak to…Who did you say that was?"

"Headrow Fisheries! We are not open for business until five pm on Friday's luv."

"Sorry, I think I have got the wrong number, what number are you?"

"Leeds 682868"

"Sorry, I wanted 682886"

"Prat!" Click brrrrrrrrrrr

He tried again and was finally connected to the Regional Office receptionist.

"Mr Haymarket, regional control please, Laurence Payne, Windelton branch."

"What was your name again?"

"L A U R E N C E P A Y N E." He spelt out the letters one by one.

"Which branch?" Payne went through the same rigmarole again.

"I'll just check if he is still in, he normally leaves about now, especially on Fridays. He likes to get home and be with his family……."

"PLEASE put me through this an emergency."

"Keep your hair on, why didn't you say so."

Payne could hear the dim-witted receptionist speak to someone on the other end of the line.

"There's a Larry Crayon on the phone from Widcup, says it's an emergency…… there must be a branch there….okay I'll check."

"WINDELTON, you stupid girl, WINDELTON!"

"If you speak like that to me again, I will report you, I know where you come from. Widcup isn't it?"

"WINDELTON," Payne shouted.

Suddenly there was a long silence followed by a click and the merest hint of an exasperated sigh from the other end of the phone. Alexander Haymarket didn't need this phone call. In fact he hated phone calls. They generally meant extra work. He disliked them even more when they occurred at 4.35 on a Friday afternoon and emanated from some obscure country branch in the deepest northern regions of the county – all sheep and farmers' bad debts.

"Yerrs, Haymarket here, what is it?" The laconic voice drifted down the wires to the panic stricken Payne.

"Payne, deputy manager, Windelton branch", his voice reverberated like a bleating sheep. "Something….something… is… a…bit …odd… here,"

"Sounds like it to me. Can you speak clearly, I hope the oddity is more than your diction," said the urbanely sarcastic Haymarket. "I am afraid I can't help in that quarter but I would suggest you consult the Murchison's doct….."

"£166,000 transferred today, no records," Payne blurted.

"What did you say?"

Payne repeated the figure, stammered out the relevant account numbers and the destinations of the cash transfers. There was a moment's silence.

"Good God," said Haymarket, now suddenly interested.

"Are you sure… these *are* substantial sums, £166,000 you say. Windlelton… Windelton? Ah yes." said Haymarket suddenly remembering the name. "Oh yes, I think head office was planning to feature your branch in a TV advertisement. Cosy, little country place, very reassuring… Isn't Gerald Astle your manager, I worked with him once many years ago. A bit of an oddball if I recall. Where's he today?"

"With a customer, I can't reach him, that's why I am calling."

"Have you asked him about this… don't you trust the man?"

Payne wasn't expecting this, he stumbled on. "Well… he can be a bit strange… and there is more, this lady's account appears to have been nearly cleaned out over the last four weeks. Over half a million has gone!"

"What, no notifications from the customer?"

"Nothing I have seen in writing."

"Have you called the account holder?"

"No, it's a discretionary account."

"But nonetheless, amounts like this in a private account would really require the customer's say so. I'll have to call you back. Give me fifteen minutes. Don't go home until I've called back. And phone Mrs. whatever she is called straightaway. Try and be discreet, don't set any alarm bells ringing for God's sake. Goodbye."

Christ! He thought, well what's done is done. No turning back now. He lit another Senior Service and pondered his fate.

He dialled Marjorie Nelson's number and got hold of a domestic servant who informed him brusquely that Mrs Nelson was unavailable all day unless it was on festival matters. Payne explained it was an important and delicate matter concerning banking issues. The domestic was having none of it and told him in the firmest possible tones that it would be Tuesday before she was available to any trade or commercial callers. For the second time in minutes Payne stared back at a mute black telephone receiver.

Bugger, he thought and lit another cigarette. Just as he was wondering how he could survive the next ten minutes without having a heart attack, Ernie Trottman appeared around the edge of his cubicle to inform him that they were ready to load the cash back into the safe in the bank's vaults.

"It will have to wait ten minutes Trottman, I'm busy," Payne croaked. "Just get the coin onto the trolley and down in the lift ready for me to unlock the safe and don't disturb me again."

"Very well Mr Payne."

At that moment Miss Starkey gravely informed him that a Mr. Haymarket was on the line from regional office and needed to speak to him urgently.

Payne told her that he would take the call in the manager's office. Miss Starkey looked perturbed. Mr Astle wouldn't like this one bit when she told him on Monday morning. She reluctantly acquiesced; she could tell from the expression on Mr Payne's grey face that he was not going to be thwarted. Oh no, not another bossy man in the office, thought Miss Starkey.

He closed the door behind him and locked it.

"Payne?"

"Yes, Mr Haymarket."

"Are you in private?" Payne's heart raced.

"Yesss," stuttered Payne. He drew heavily on his cigarette. A large piece of ash fell onto Astle's desk and for a brief moment the marquetry smouldered. He pressed his thumb on it in desperation and squeaked in pain as it burnt his thumb.

"Are you alright Payne, you sound like a mouse?" He went on: "We have found no notification of these transactions. It's highly irregular but I suspect there will be some simple answer for Astle's actions. All the same, damn peculiar method in his madness. Where did you say Astle was?"

"Out with a customer and not expected back in today."

"I see. Is he in tomorrow?"

"No, it's his Saturday off, there's a big festival going on in the town, I suspect he'll be involved in that in some way or another. I never know, he doesn't tell me much these days."

"Strange, you *are* the deputy manager aren't you?"

"Of course, I am."

"Have you got Astle's home telephone number?"

"No, he's never let me have it. He won't take bank calls at home."

"Isn't he in the telephone directory?"

"He's ex-directory."

"All very odd, oh, well, we'll have it in our personnel records here somewhere. What's his address, I presume that's not a secret as well?"

Payne spelled out the address, feeling ashamed and embarrassed about being unable to furnish regional office with this basic information.

"What's your number in case I can't get hold of him over the weekend? I might need you to pay him a personal visit."

Payne froze at the prospect of turning up on Astle's doorstep to tell him regional office wanted to speak to him about some 'irregularities' with the bank's largest customer!

"He won't like that!"

"Damn, he won't like it, we're talking over half a million pounds here," said Haymarket angrily. "Did you get hold of the account holder by any chance, it's a Mrs Nelson isn't it?"

"I am afraid no luck, according to her staff she's incommunicado until next Tuesday. I explained it was urgent but got given short shrift."

"Hell, that's inconvenient. Oh well, thanks for calling me Payne", said Haymarket more affably, "Well done. As I said before, I am sure there will be some explanation but better say nothing to anyone about this until I've got hold of Astle. I'll be in touch. Bye for now."

"Goodbye."

Laurence Payne breathed a massive sigh of relief. His rash actions had been vindicated and acknowledged. He was in the clear with Regional Office but certainly not with Astle. The idea of a visit to Astle's house over the weekend was a nightmare Payne dared not contemplate. He lit yet another cigarette.

~

Eventually Haymarket managed to obtain Astle's home number after corralling some Regional Office staff to comb through staff records.

The staff phoned Haymarket at his golf club at twelve-thirty on Saturday morning. Haymarket scribbled the number down on the back of his score card in the Captain's office. He immediately tried Astle's number but there was no reply.

Damn, where is the bloody man, he thought? He tried again at two-thirty, a little worse for wear after having downed two large gin and Italians and a bottle of mediocre claret over lunch with his golfing partner. Still no reply.

He retired to the lounge and fell asleep overlooking the eighteenth green. He stirred around three-thirty and went to drive a few balls on the practice ground to freshen up. At just after four-thirty he called again, this time from the public phone in the club lobby to avoid offending the Club Captain. Again no answer. There was no other option. He would have to ask that little busy-body of a man Payne to pay his boss a visit.

The phone rang in Payne's hallway at home.

"Haymarket here, I can't get hold of your manager. I am sorry to inconvenience you Payne but you will need to pay him a call this evening."

"But... the whole town is at this festival thing," Payne stuttered and stammered, coughed and wheezed. "There's terrible storm going on... it's raining cats and dogs here. Can I go on Sunday morning?"

"*You will go this afternoon and that's that*", said Haymarket emphatically. "What's the matter with you man, he won't eat you?" Just be normal and try not to scare him off just in case he *has* done something stupid. Ask him to call me on my home number, Leeds 586334. Got that? Good. Ring me as soon as you get back whatever the outcome. There may be some other things I'll need your help with."

Payne breathed deeply, he realised that there was no way out of this nightmare. But he recognised being Haymarket's stooge wouldn't harm his own career prospects. That was providing Astle *had* committed some fraud. If he *hadn't* it would be curtains for him. He regretted his earlier attempts to wriggle out of the Astle home visit.

"Got that Payne?"

"Absolutely, Sir," croaked Payne obsequiously.

- Chapter 28 -

Half Vision

Daphne's clairvoyant had seen it all with perfect clarity. It was there in the tea leaves, in her faithful crystal orb and finally the Tarot cards had provided the seal of certainty.

It was so clear that she had frightened herself with her own powers. She could barely wait to tell Daphne. The clairvoyant had decided that she wouldn't hold back, this was a time when veiled hints wouldn't do. Her professional code of ethics advised against imparting either dreadful or portentous news. But somehow she felt compelled to spill out what the tools of her bizarre trade had revealed.

Daphne would need to make plans. She was not yet aware of the maelstrom that was about to embroil her, she *must* be prepared!

Daphne left the house just after midday to watch the festival opening parade, do a little shopping and then catch a bus for her scheduled two-thirty 'reading'.

The clairvoyant had been most enigmatic over the telephone.

"The Forces are strong," she had said dramatically, "There is much to reveal, much to take heed, come with all speed."

Daphne couldn't understand why the clairvoyant always spoke in this rather quaint late nineteenth century English patois, perhaps it was to give her customers more confidence in her far-seeing abilities, but it didn't wash with Daphne. Did she speak in this yesteryear language to her butcher while ordering the copious quantities of offal required to sustain her menagerie of cats, bats and other assorted creatures that slunk, swam or hopped about her tiny house?

Daphne arrived slightly late and out of breath. The bus had been running behind time because of Windelton's festival traffic. The clairvoyant was rather agitated and brusquely asked Daphne to sit down at a small round table opposite her. She was dressed in a bizarre dirndl. She placed a grubby, multi-coloured silk

232

scarf over her head and shoulders which looked as if one of her many cats had been sleeping on it.

The clairvoyant began to hum some tuneless dirge while holding her hands over a large green crystal ball. Daphne was familiar with this routine; it had alarmed her when she had first visited. The clairvoyant rarely spoke until after ten minutes of this astral warm-up, then her voice would come out as either far away or in some high pitched squeak.

Today it was the far-away voice.

"Many years ago your betrothed was tempted by a lascivious woman, a woman...' she hesitated as if daring to say the words, *'...a woman of the night! Your husband wants to ravish her once again in a bestial, loathsome manner and then take her away with him to a far-off land."* The clairvoyant spat out the last few words of this statement as if she had found a maggot crawling in her lettuce.

"I see another person with the evil pair. He's a man of medicine, very good looking and so... so very attractive ... I can see him clearly, he cares a lot about the human soul and he has the most beautiful hands, I can see they have a faint covering of red hair on the wrists... I would like to meet this man!"

This was indeed strong meat for the clairvoyant who was not normally given to so much detail. She couldn't believe that Gerald would ever contemplate an affair with another woman. She knew he was a misogynist and the idea that he might be about to 'ravish' someone was completely preposterous.

The clairvoyant continued: *"The temptation is very strong now, I feel the vibrations."*

Her hands started to stroke the surface of the crystal ball and Daphne half imagined she could see the green orb throb at her touch, a greenish light passed through the gaps in her fingers, giving her tapered digits a translucent, magical hue. *"But he will not succumb. He is ashamed of his actions and wishes to make amends but it is too late... I see fire... and a great heat... you will never hear his confession, he'll be engulfed in the conflagration..."*

233

Her voice faded away into muttering. Daphne couldn't decipher her mumblings. The clairvoyant went silent for a moment and then resumed her humming. Daphne shifted uneasily in her chair.

Suddenly the clairvoyant was off again:

"I see an ale house in the countryside. There is a telephone box nearby and a village green." The clairvoyant frowned as if she was straining to understand some message that was coming to her from some long distance away.

"Does your husband have a motorcycle?"

Daphne looked up, startled to be asked a direct question. Knowing that she was forbidden to speak in the sessions, she said nothing. The clairvoyant asked the question again, loudly and more firmly. The clairvoyant's turned up face peeking out of her shawl demanded an answer.

"Er... motorcycle? Good heavens, no! He can barely walk upright, let alone mount a motorcycle."

"I *can hear the motorcycle, it is very powerful,"* said the clairvoyant, reverting to her far-away, ethereal voice.

"I see someone riding over lonely moor-tops in darkness. The road is black and wet, and now... the moon, oh yes, the moon... the rider is wearing a black leather tunic..." her voice faded again.

"Where are you, show yourself to me... please show yourself. My communicant is anxious to know who you are. Gerald Astle is that you?"

The clairvoyant rose silently from her seat. She slipped the grubby silk shawl from her matted hair and it fell from her shoulders into a little heap on the floor. Almost immediately a large moth-eaten tabby sprang from nowhere and sat on top of the shiny pile, it purred with pleasure as it worked its furry body amongst the folds.

As the clairvoyant moved away from the crystal communicator, Daphne sensed that it ceased to radiate its 'Power'. The sheen became dull as it returned to a tasteless lump of glass. The mystic telephone connection to the other side had been unplugged.

The clairvoyant crossed the small room and slumped onto a battered chaise longue.

"I am exhausted," she said, adopting a language and tone that Daphne could identify as being nearly normal. "I can see no more, my channels have been clogged up. The Fates have determined; I do not have the Power or the Authority to progress further. Others may see what I cannot. It is beyond my gifts," she said dreamily. "You have to prepare for the worst. Yesterday my vision was clear, the pathways were open to me but now there is conflict. Everything is fading. This can happen when there are traumatic celestial occurrences in the making. My mystic messengers are telling me the sequence is nearly over Mrs Astle. I am sorry... prepare yourself for bad news, very bad news," she swooned. But she soon recovered. "That'll be two pounds ten shillings as usual," she said returning to her normal voice.

"Bad news for whom?" choked Daphne ignoring the clairvoyant's matter of fact demand for her cash.

"Your useless husband, of course," snapped the clairvoyant, forgetting the normal social niceties. "Who else do we ever discuss?"

"Did *I say* he was useless?" said Daphne rather annoyed at the clairvoyant's tactless remarks and springing to the defence of her useless husband.

"I am sorry Mrs Astle, I am very tired. I always am after Great Insights have taken place. Just pay up and go now." She got up from the chaise longue with her hand out towards a bewildered Daphne. "Come on pay up," she said as she manoeuvred Daphne towards the cat-scratched front door. Her hand remained insistently outstretched, her lined palms now only capable of summoning up cash.

But Daphne was having none of this. She was not content with these lucid predictions of her husband's imminent demise. "I need vague predictions, hints, doubts - not facts! You can't expect me to go home and wait for my husband to be consumed by fire, fall off a motor cycle or ravage my next door neighbour," she said angrily to the surprised clairvoyant. "This was not why I have been paying you for the last three years. I want uncertainties, tasty morsels of self-doubt that I can spin my own fantasies around. Lucidity from your planet messengers was not the bargain I struck with you. I want open ended suggestions that I can run through my mind. "You have spoiled everything with FACTS. I work out the predictions for myself from your ludicrous hints."

"How dare you tell me that my predictions are ludicrous? I'm sorry if I have told you what I saw and you don't like it. Why come here in the first place?" said the clairvoyant getting angry. "I know *something* is happening or going to happen to your husband. Now just pay up and get out of here. I am *so* tired."

Daphne was fully aware her clairvoyant's predictions normally lacked much conviction but this vagueness had satisfied her. Over the years it had been pleasant to discuss her worries with this bizarre woman and unburden her fears in this dingy room. Now she could never come here again. Her trust in the clairvoyant's dishonesty had been broken. She had breached all the rules by trying to tell Daphne the truth.

"I'll accept a couple of quid to be going on with!" said the clairvoyant gamely as she feebly tried to open the front door.

"Fiddlesticks to your money, you are not getting a penny more out of me you old fraudster. I have a good mind to report you to the police!" Daphne grabbed the door, threw it open and stormed out at a near run while the clairvoyant stood aghast clutching the door frame for support. Exhausted, the clairvoyant turned back into her dirty house and stumbled back to the chaise longue and immediately fell into a deep sleep. A toad jumped onto her reclining figure and nestled under her armpit.

~

Daphne returned home a little after four-thirty. Black clouds loomed ominously over the town. She rarely got angry. The wind rose to rattle the hydrangea bushes in the garden and she furiously mulled over the veracity of her clairvoyant's predictions. She must have gone mad thought Daphne as she gazed at the first few drops of rain as they splashed onto the crazy-paving terrace. She was shaking slightly; she needed a strong cup of tea. It was a three- teaspoons-of-sugar moment.

Overdraft, Astle's poodle, whined pathetically and disappeared into his dog basket. He sensed bad things; would the mistress forget to feed him tonight? She occasionally did when she became distracted. Daphne pondered the imminent departing of her husband. Who would she invite to the funeral? She sat down in her favourite chair in the morning room and stared out through the leaded-light windows at the neatly trimmed lawn and carefully maintained shrubs. The small herbaceous border appeared as if it had sprung into life with the help of the afternoon's warm sunshine. It was too late to go to the festival, a pity she thought. She would have liked to have seen the ballet and listened to some of the concerts. She hoped Gerald had seen something of them although he had always been a bit of a Philistine when it came to matters musical. A Strauss waltz was about as far as his classical music repertoire ever stretched.

She dipped her hand into the tartan-lidded biscuit tin and took a bite into a sugar-dusted shortbread, Daphne's favourite, always a comfort particularly when accompanied by a nice cup of china tea. The tin had originally been a gift from an old school friend who had married a Scot and now resided in Peebles. Over the years they had kept in touch although they had not met since before the war. Their relationship had become more like pen pals but for Daphne, her Scottish companion was one of the few people she could truly call a friend. Right now, she had an urge to 'phone her dear old confidant but she was afraid that Gerald might arrive home unexpectedly and quarrel with her about the unnecessary expense.

She reluctantly decided against making the call but she started thinking about Gerald and the happier times that they had spent together. She had already started to think about him in the past tense. She became wistful and filled with nostalgia as she thought of when they first met. She recalled the happiness of their honeymoon and the contented early days of their marriage when they had played cards in the evenings, gossiped, led normal lives. She leant back in her chair and listened to the rain start in earnest. She took off her glasses, setting them down on the table next to her chair and closed her eyes. As the rain thudded onto the window panes she squirmed deeper into her chair; she felt safe in her little morning room away from the cares of the world, the unpredictability of Gerald and the strange predictions of the clairvoyant.

The ding dong of the front door awoke Daphne from her slumber. Overdraft raised his head, sniffed and then thought better of it and went back to sleep. It was followed by a loud knocking, Good Lord, she thought, and who could that be?

It was still pouring with rain and the wind had got up, she could hear it gusting and whistling in the eaves. Daphne tried to focus on her watch, it was just after six and she had been asleep for a good hour. She went to the front door where she sensed the smell of cigarette smoke and heard a wheezing cough from outside. Through the frosted glazing of the front door she could make out the distorted figure of someone small.

Daphne struggled with the sliding barrel bolts at the top and bottom of the door. Gerald was always a stickler for security and insisted these were secure as well as having a Yale lock. Eventually she eased the door gingerly open and cautiously peered around the door edge; the dishevelled and soaking sight that greeted her was a surprise.

Laurence Payne was wet through and he looked half petrified with fear. His bicycle was propped up against the garden fence, water dripped from its handlebars, seat and wheels.

"Oh, it's you Laurence, why didn't you say something? Come on in quickly, you are wringing wet, you poor man, you'll catch your death."

"Is Mr Astle at home?"

238

"No, I believe he is still at the festival. To tell the truth, I have got a bit behind myself. This blasted festival has made everything so topsy-turvy hasn't it?"

Payne stepped across the threshold like a terrified animal heading for the slaughter house. He looked around half expecting Astle to appear from some room of the house and strike him down with a powerful blow. He had only once before been inside the Astle citadel when he and his wife Gloria had been invited to dinner shortly after Astle had taken up his position. It had been a rather stiff and embarrassing evening; it was meant to be a pleasant get-to-know-you evening but it had failed on nearly every count.

Payne had been so nervous that he had dropped a cigarette on the new Wilton carpet burning a neat round hole; Gloria had swilled down too many glasses of sherry before the meal, had got the giggles and was eventually sick in the Astle's newly installed avocado coloured lavatory. Daphne had served the dinner from a new Hostess Trolley, an item considered nearly as advanced as a sputnik in domestic gadgetry circles. Unfortunately she had managed to get the device wedged in the dining room doorway and in so doing had ruined the dramatic effect of her entry. This had infuriated Astle and Payne and Gloria had to stifle their laughter.

"You look as if you have seen a ghost!" said Daphne as he stood in their hallway dripping water onto the carpet. As she said this Daphne suddenly remembered her clairvoyant and the thought flashed through her mind that Gerald *was* already in the spirit world!

"You didn't see any fire engines on the way here did you?" enquired Daphne in a worried voice.

"Fire engines.........er, let me think. As a matter of fact I did, yes one passed me on High Street. I expect it was because of the flooding. Any reason why you ask?" said Payne puzzled.

"Why do you want to see Gerald on a Saturday? Is it about one of his secret Masonic meetings?" Daphne said, ignoring Payne's question about fire engines.

Payne looked even more horrified.

"No, no, erghhh," Payne coughed bronchially. "It's a b.b.bank matter. I take it that Mr Astle is not in?" he said, clarifying matters and already preparing in his mind his report back to Haymarket.

"Well, I'd better be off if he's not here," he repeated again confirming that he could justify making a run for it before Astle *did* turn up.

"Won't you wait a little while? I am sure Gerald will be back soon. Stay until half past six and give yourself a little time to dry off. Look, it's still pelting down with rain. I would welcome your company. Let's have a nice cup of tea, or maybe something stronger? You look quite done in Laurence?"

"Oh no, I couldn't possible impose on you anymore," said Payne defensively. Then he remembered something: "There's one thing you could help me with Mrs Astle. Could you let me have your phone number here at The Limes? It's extraordinary but I don't have the number and I may have to 'phone Mr Astle later on once he's back from the festival."

"Do you really need it? Gerald doesn't normally allow anyone to have the number. It is something that he is *very* particular about. He only likes to make outgoing calls, not receive any!"

"Well, I am not a customer am I Mrs Astle? As Deputy Manager I should be able to contact him on occasions out of office hours. I could have called him today only if I had the number. Instead, I have had to cycle here in the pouring rain and bother you. And back again," he said glancing out of the window at the sheeting rain. "Surely you understand….?" Payne gave Daphne a pleading look as he straightened himself up to his full five foot six inches tall. "It is important that I am able call him, this is a serious bank matter," he continued.

"Can I get him to give you a ring just as soon as he returns? You could stay and wait for him if you would prefer?" replied Daphne, standing her ground despite Payne's whingeing insistence. It was more than her life was worth to give anyone the 'phone number, even a bank employee.

240

Payne's resolve crumpled at the thought of Astle's imminent return and the fireworks that would undoubtedly erupt when he found his deputy manager hob-knobbing with his wife on a Saturday afternoon. Any communication with Astle he'd prefer to do over the 'phone but he couldn't order Mrs Astle to give him the phone number against Astle's wishes. Payne realised the trouble Daphne would get into if she agreed. He had done his best!

"Oh, very well then," said Payne reluctantly. "But please *do* tell him it is very urgent." Payne gave Daphne his own number and then dashed out of the front door and grabbed his bicycle.

Daphne watched the diminutive figure in the grey mackintosh scoot his way down the garden path wheeling his bicycle for all it was worth. Once at the garden gate he looked furtively to left and right before bolting out into the road and hurriedly pedalling off up Lime Tree Road.

Daphne hurried back to her kitchen to start preparing Gerald's Saturday sausage, mash and onion gravy supper. Until she heard to the contrary she would continue as normal, but in her heart she believed that Gerald was already 'elsewhere'. This made her feel a little wobbly with excitement, tinged with annoyance as she didn't know for sure.

One moment she had remorseful misgivings about the inevitability of the fates, on the other hand practical matters came to the forefront. When could she get her hands on Gerald's pension and start her new life?

However, if the clairvoyant had got her timings wrong and Gerald arrived back and the supper wasn't on the table, there would be all hell to pay. He would be furious about Laurence Payne turning up on their doorstep too. She would have to pass on Payne's plaintive messages but she knew that Gerald would never lift the receiver to call. Heaven would have to be falling in before he'd make a call on bank matters over a weekend.

~

When Payne eventually reached the sanctuary of his home he was soaked to the skin. A rime of rain water clung to his ashen-lined face, the cracks of his skin acting like drainage channels funnelling water down his face and neck creating a reservoir of soaked fabric on his shirt collar. He staggered wordlessly to the bathroom of his bungalow to dry off and change. He had to prepare himself before phoning Haymarket with the bad tidings.

Payne rarely drank, cigarettes were his vice. But tonight he required fortification. He dug out a bottle of whisky that normally only saw the light of day at funerals. He poured a modest, restorative measure. He added some ginger wine that Gloria liked to drink on Saturday evenings while she gawped at the TV. He turned the gas fire up to two bars to warm his numb legs, downed his tipple in two swigs and lay back in his armchair. The soothing effects of the whisky and ginger wine seeped down his chest and into his legs before rising like a swirling wraith to infuse his tired brain.

He became good humoured. He lit a cigarette and the nicotine added to his heightened sense of wellbeing. He then picked up the phone and dialled Haymarket.

The phone was answered by a lady with a clipped southern accent. In Yorkshire it would have been called 'educated' but Rosemary Haymarket's only education had come from reading 'Tatler' magazine. Haymarket came to the phone quickly.

Payne sounded rather jocular. "Hello Haymarket. I am sorry but that blighter Astle was not at home…"

"Mr. Haymarket, please, Payne. Have you got his number?"

"Er… I am afraid not. Mrs Astle refused to give me it."

"Are you taking this seriously Payne? If any of this is true it will not look good for your own position. This situation would have never occurred in the first place if the proper protocols had been followed."

"But you don't know Mr Astle… he's so *secretive*, he tells me nothing. It's not *my* fault. The account is discretionary. Astle behaves as he pleases."

"Quite obviously," said Haymarket sarcastically.

To Payne Haymarket was the personification of the Bank writ large. Haymarket's remarks shook him to the core. In his mild alcoholic stupor he had misguidedly believed that his prompt actions in alerting Regional Office would be the passport to his branch manager position. An endorsement from Haymarket could be the deciding factor and now he had jeopardised his earlier good work by being over familiar… and now he had hinted that *he was implicated!*

He snapped back into action and thought how he could retrieve the situation with Haymarket. He suddenly remembered Daphne Astle's question about fire engines. "In our conversation Mrs Astle asked me whether I had seen any fire engines on my journey to the house. She's always been a touch eccentric. Do you think this could have any bearing on Astle's absence?" intoned Payne in his most business-like manner attempting to wrest back the initiative of the conversation.

"I can't see what bearing Mr Astle's bonkers wife could possibly have on stealing hundreds of thousands of pounds from one of the Bank's most esteemed customers!" said Haymarket, irritated by Payne's banal and irrelevant remarks.

Payne fell into a shocked silence. First his dreadful rebuff from Haymarket but equally shocking, Haymarket had voiced his thoughts that Astle *had stolen* the money and *his* slack procedures were the reason he had got away with it.

"If I don't hear from him tonight, I'll call you back," Haymarket went on brusquely, "We'll have to do an immediate spot check at the branch tomorrow, so don't go too far away from your telephone. And Payne, for God's sake get a grip, I am going to need your co-operation to get to the bottom of all this."

Payne stretched back in his armchair and wiggled his legs up and down like an excited child. Haymarket still needed his help. It was Astle who was in for the chop for sure. Even Haymarket sounded rattled. He poured himself another whisky and ginger and took a gulp. It really was a rather pleasant tipple.

~

It was so obvious Walter did not know why he hadn't thought of it before. He ducked down from his view of Jasper's sleeping figure in the armchair and made his way stealthily back to the tool shed.

He pushed the latch up and the dry smell of creosote and old wood reminded him again of the happy hours he had spent potting up seeds, keeping out of his wife's way and having a good read of the Windelton Bugle. Although his eyes were accustomed to the dark he could have found his way around the shed blindfolded.

Predictably no one had set foot in the place since he'd left. He knew there would be some old rags he used for cleaning the mower under the work bench. He got out his pocket knife, an item he never went anywhere without, and started to cut some strips of oily rag which he stuffed into his trouser pocket. On a brass hook attached to the back of the shed door he picked up his bee keeping mask and his white overalls that hung untouched where he had left them. Finally, reaching up to a shelf at the far end of the shed his hand located a small bottle of chloroform.

Making his way quietly, he closed the door on the latch and crept around to the front of the cottage. Using his fingers he pushed up the poorly fitting parlour sash window that was located to the left of the front door. The window catch had been broken for years and he knew Inchdale wouldn't have bothered to get it fixed. Stepping carefully from the path and avoiding leaving a boot print in the garden soil, he clambered through the raised sash.

Once in the room he gathered his thoughts and regulated his quickened breathing. Walter gently opened the parlour door into the hallway. The light from the kitchen shone from under the door casting a narrow shadow on the stone flagged hall. He could hear Jasper's rasping breathing and the smell of alcohol and cigarettes secreting out of his inert body. Walter had to be careful not to awaken Jasper otherwise there would be some difficult questions to answer; questions for which he didn't have any plausible answers.

In the hallway Walter had donned his bee keeping mask, coat and thick gloves that made his disguise. He removed the longer strip of rag from his pocket and

244

doused it generously with chloroform. He then gingerly opened the kitchen door before moving toward the back of the armchair in which the recumbent figure of Jasper snored gently. Walter placed the rag over his nostrils. Jasper gasped a little and appeared to slump deeper into his chair. Walter tilted back Jasper's head, opened his slack jaw and inserted the strip of oily rag into his mouth. The anaesthetic had worked perfectly. Just the way Walter used to knock out unwanted litters of kittens before drowning them.

The final piece of the jigsaw was simply undertaken. Walter opened the back door from the inside using the key in the lock and returned to the garden shed. He picked up a can of two-stroke motor mower fuel. There wasn't much fuel in it but enough for what Walter had in mind. He returned to the kitchen and spread the fuel on the carpet around Jasper's chair and onto the sides and the back of his armchair. Walter thought that Jasper would wake up once the flames started to burn his clothing and he would escape with a few burns and one hell of a fright. The cottage would be a goner though.

Jasper didn't stir; the chloroform was working its anaesthetic magic. Finally, Walter picked up a box of matches from the fireplace mantle, walked behind the chair and struck a match. With a 'crump' the ragged carpet ignited and leapt up the back of the armchair, catching Jasper's black curls of hair alight. Walter didn't wait any longer. He locked the back door and left the way he arrived via the front parlour window. Walter returned the sash to its closed position. He quickly slipped around to the shed and removed his bee keeping outfit and placed them back on the hook behind the door, he returned the empty fuel can and chloroform to their rightful places and dropped the latch on the shed door.

As he came out he could see no outward signs of distress from the cottage, he slipped across the lawn to peer in through the kitchen window. The room was filled with smoke but there was a burning glow from the where the armchair had been located and he could hear muffled cries. Good, thought Walter, he must be realising what's happening to him. That'll wake him up.

As Walter hurriedly returned on his familiar path to Home Farm it felt like the old days; he was setting out with anticipation and expectancy of completing a good day's labour, milking the dairy herd, mending fences, coppicing hedges, comfortable with himself, confident of his capabilities and value, a worthwhile member of the human race. Strange that he should have that feeling once again tonight. He felt no remorse; it was typical of Walter, a good job done to the best of his abilities. The way he tackled every task.

- Chapter 29 -

Fading Daylight Robbery

The occupation of a removal man didn't pay that well and it also played hell with your vertebrae. Joe Laycock supplemented his meagre wages by nicking the odd piece of furniture, nothing too big mind, objets d'art, a piece of tasty china or some other trinket that was easy to miss but fetched a few bob on the open market. Joe had a good eye for items that got forgotten during a house move; his theory was by the time the owners found out something had gone missing they couldn't remember when they last saw it.

Over a career of successful thieving Joe had built up a solid network of dodgy antique dealers and fences that were more than willing to move Joe's 'stock' of collectables, no questions asked. Joe had a knack of identifying saleable items and it ensured that his network of business associates could quickly move on the spoils of his hard labour. Not only did Joe have a good eye he often knew a lot more about the items he filched than their owners and he had an uncanny intuition of whether they appreciated their true value. If he had an inkling that they understood an item's true value he would show due restraint, such was his professionalism, a master of his trade. No point in having his boss breathing down his neck when an irate customer suddenly discovers that a nice antique Crown Derby plate has gone absent without leave!

Joe had accumulated substantial savings from his hobby. He planned to buy a cottage on the Norfolk coast when he retired where he would indulge in his other great pastime, sea angling.

Mick, Joe's apprentice, was a different kettle of fish – young, hot-headed and the nephew of the boss. Joe had made it clear that he would retire when he reached his sixtieth birthday and would not be waiting for the state pension to support him. As a precaution his boss had installed Mick as Joe's apprentice to be trained up. If all went to plan, Mick would eventually take over from Joe as main driver and supervisor. Joe's boss harboured a desire for his nephew to run the whole business in due course, as his own children had shown no interest entering the family concern.

Mick's mother was the boss's younger sister. He had been pleased to help her after her husband had died prematurely. Mick had been a wayward teenager and had managed to dodge his National Service by claiming he had flat feet. Mick needed a father figure in his life and his Uncle fulfilled this role.

Joe's boss also had an ulterior motive to helping out his sister. He had long suspected that Joe had been stealing items off the van but had never managed to unearth any cast-iron proof. Casual workers weren't interested in 'shopping' their boss, especially as Joe was the one who hired them.

On the other hand, Joe was a solid worker and was always happy to do long hauls, the more lucrative overnight stay jobs as he had no wife or family of his own. Joe was essentially a loner, his own man.

Mick was an unexpected and unwelcome addition for Joe. His previous mate was an old codger who had shown no interest in Joe's habit. He would occasionally growl at Joe and tell him that one day he would get nicked. But with Mick's arrival Joe had to adapt his ways; he became extra vigilant and trod warily. He reduced his stealing to the occasional item and made sure he was not spotted.

But Mick, like many 'difficult boys' of his age, was sharp and quick witted. After just a couple of months of working with Joe their relationship had moved from mute to a plateau of guarded friendliness.

One day on a removal from a 'quality home' in Northamptonshire, Joe had espied a very good eighteenth century snuff box. He had concealed this worthwhile item, estimated value fifty pounds, by wrapping it in a soft cloth in the van's tool box. After loading up the van they were heading with the contents to the occupants' new home in North London when Mick suddenly piped up:

"What do you reckon you'll get for the snuff box Joe?"

"I dunno what you're on about?"

"You know, the one wrapped up in the tool box under your seat."

Joe was astonished that he had been discovered. It was clear from Mick's question and matter of fact delivery that he had been caught bang to rights.

"So Joe what's my percentage going to be or do you want me to shop you to my Uncle?"

"Twenty percent's the norm, Mick", he replied as casually as he could.

"I think thirty is nearer the going rate, don't you?"

It could have been a discussion in a boardroom it all sounded so measured. Joe realised that the undercurrents for him could be fatal if he couldn't strike a deal with Mick. He was 'family,' for crying out loud, he thought; he would just have to work something out with him later but he had better settle this issue now and quick before it blew up in his face!

"Twenty-five", said Joe and turned to the tousled-haired boy and held out his hand. From that moment on they had been partners in petty crime. Joe never asked Mick the question why he was stealing from his Uncle or what motivated him to risk his job and a possible future inheritance.

Mick turned out to be like Joe, naturally gifted at thieving. He was subtle in lifting items and he often spotted pieces that Joe had overlooked. Mick being family made it less likely that customer complaints were taken seriously by the boss.

~

Joe and Mick had both noticed the fat, sweaty man in the transport café, his wallet bulging with fivers. It was so stuffed he could barely fold it shut; he looked an obvious target. But they didn't do daylight robbery and what could they do in a steamy café on wet summer's evening on the Great North Road?

Joe and Mick discussed it briefly back in the cab. Opportunity missed perhaps, but better sticking to what they knew best, always safer in the long run! 'Know your territory', as Joe would say.

The fat man with the wad had been forgotten until about fifteen minutes later the black Morris car wobbled past the van accelerating into the distance. "There goes the fat bundle," said Mick with a laugh. "I wonder where he's off in his fancy shirt and carrying a wad like that?"

"Probably got some fancy piece somewhere mores like?" growled Joe.

"She'll get rid of his cash faster than we can," laughed Mick.

"He needs to be more careful, someone will take it off him sooner or later," said Joe portentously.

"He didn't look the Casanova type to me," replied Mick and they fell silent wondering where the fat wad was going.

It was Mick who first saw the black roof of the Morris parked in a lay-by. They had been going about an hour since leaving the café and were a few miles outside Baldock. On an impulse, Joe suddenly brought the van to a halt about half a mile down the road at a filling station. "I think we'll just go back and have a quick shufftie at our fat friend! See what he's up to?" said Joe spinning the heavy steering wheel and manoeuvring the vehicle back onto the road in a northerly direction.

Mick grinned with excitement, wondering what lark old Joe was up to this time? In a few minutes the van slipped into the parking area, freewheeling the heavy vehicle in neutral gear past the Morris and easing it quietly to a halt forty yards beyond the black car. There was no-one else parked up. Joe signalled to Mick to go and have a look at the car.

He got out of the cab silently and casually walked past the vehicle. Astle was asleep on the back seat. He gestured to Joe who dropped down from his cab carrying a small metal gemmy in his hand. They had to act quickly while the lay-by remained empty.

Mick took the gemmy from Joe and gently tried the rear door; it was unlocked. Before Astle could stir Mick struck him a single blow to his head. Astle grunted and rolled off the bench seat onto the car floor. His body became wedged between the squab of the seat and the back of the front seat. He was out cold.

Mick dropped the heavy metal bar and dived on top of the fat sprawling figure. He quickly pulled out his wallet from Astle's trouser pockets. An airline ticket fell out of the car and onto the tarmac. Joe opened the other rear door and with Mick at the other side tried to manhandle Astle back onto the rear seat but he was too heavy to move. Astle's breathing had become laboured and blood was flowing from the top of his head where the gemmy had struck his cranium.

"He looks knackered!" said Mick anxiously, suddenly realising what he had done.

"Leave him," said Joe urgently.

"Give us the gemmy, quick! I'll have a butchers in the boot." Joe used the gemmy to wrench the flimsy lock and the boot quickly sprung open. There was a suitcase and a leather Gladstone bag with a brass handle that looked vaguely interesting. It had an 'official look' about it. Joe ignored the suitcase but grabbed the Gladstone bag and ran to the van and threw it up into the cab.

Meanwhile Mick was trying to shut the Morris' back door but Astle's head was sticking out dripping blood onto the road. Joe jogged back to the car and opened the other side rear door and gave Astle's legs a final heave bringing his head nearly back into the car. Mick slammed the door shut on his side giving Astle's head another hefty bang.

They ran back to the van, started up the engine with a spluttering cough and headed out of the lay-by. On reaching the road, Joe turned the heavy vehicle through one hundred and eighty degrees to point them southward. Fortunately, the traffic was light and they were soon trundling down the main road at a good forty-five miles per hour. The whole robbery had taken a little more than three minutes.

As Joe drove Mick counted out two hundred and eighty-five pounds in cash.

"Not a bad haul for a few minutes work. Bloody stupid bugger carrying all that cash with him, I told you he ought to be more careful!" laughed Joe.

"I hope I haven't killed the bugger" said Mick.

"Nah! He looked alright to me; he'll just have one hell of a headache tomorrow," said Joe reassuringly.

"Now let's have a look-see in that bag."

"Let me get cleaned up a bit," said Mick as he busied himself wiping the blood off his hands and trousers with a rag from under the seat.

"We'll need to get washed up properly when we get back. You'd better come back to my place for a good scrub and divvy up the loot before you goes home to your Mum. You don't want your darling ol' girl asking any questions do we?" said Joe with a grin.

"Have you got your knife?" asked Mick still breathless with excitement. He couldn't believe how easy it had been. Joe leaned forward and put his hand under the seat and fished out a thick bladed hunting knife which he handed to Mick.

"Be careful with that young Mick, its bleedin' sharp!"

Mick stabbed the leather near the brass clasp on the top of the bag and slit the leather in a diagonal. Despite the sharpness of the blade it took some sawing to create a hole large enough for Mick to get his thick fingers inside. Finally he forced an aperture big enough to get in two fingers and he started to probe and push around inside the bag. What he touched felt like paper.

He picked up the knife once again and widened the hole. This time he could get his complete hand inside, he grabbed a bundle wrapped in paper and managed to extract his hand. The bundle fell on the cab floor. Mick picked it up and ripped the cover off and out spilled used brown ten shilling notes that fell into his lap. He grabbed another from the bag, ripping the paper wrapper, this one contained green one pound notes.

Joe's eyes had been staring so intently at the ripped Gladstone bag and the notes cascading out that he had to pull the wheel of the van sharply to the right to avoid it running off the road.

"Bloody hell!" he exclaimed, "its A BLOODY POOLS WIN!"

- Chapter 30 -

Party Over

The terrible fire at Gardener's Cottage was not discovered until late Sunday morning. Under normal circumstances the milkman would have delivered to Gardener's Cottage at around seven-thirty in the morning but the festival's ugly grip of excess had left few Windeltonians untouched. It had been a supreme effort of will to reach the milk delivery depot by ten am to pick up his daily round.

It had a taken a little time for the milkman to register what had occurred at Gardener's Cottage. He had been concentrating hard on manoeuvring the small milk van over the jarring pot holes in the lane to the cottage. Each hole sent shock waves of pain across the milkman's forehead. The sound of the rattling glass milk bottles was making him feel nauseous. He had got out of the float not noticing the building. It was not until he was about to place the bottle on the door step he realised the cottage had no door or roof. Suddenly, through his alcoholic haze he smelt charred, burnt wood.

He stepped back to take in the scene. Gardener's Cottage was no more. He gingerly peered inside what was left of the window apertures but he could see nothing except burnt pieces of furniture and fallen roof timbers. There were still a few wisps of smouldering smoke drifting upwards.

Then he heard a low moaning coming from the cottage garden. He went over to investigate the source of the noise. The sight that greeted him was one of a naked 'thing'. It looked like a human piece of burnt toast. The 'thing's' legs were an awful bright red colour and there was some tufts of black hair sticking out of the head area and a pink hole making a noise like a snuffling hedgehog.

For reasons he couldn't explain he left the bottle on the step next to the remains of the back door before he ran back to his float and headed of at maximum power (7 mph) to the nearest phone box to call an ambulance and the fire brigade. It was another forty-five minutes before the ambulance and the volunteer fire brigade could be raised.

Jasper's crisp body was carefully wrapped in foil and gently carried to the ambulance and taken to hospital. He was not expected to survive the journey. There was little for the fire fighters to do except call the police and douse the smouldering remains with some water extracted from a nearby beck. The police were indifferent; they would have to interview the victim if he survived and follow up his whereabouts on the previous evening. There wouldn't be much doubt that he was another casualty of the Great Drunken Festival as Marjorie's cultural triumph had already been dubbed. The heat from the fire had gutted the majority of the property; the stone walls were the only part of the structure that had survived in any recognisable form.

Rachel and Dawn were traced by the police and confirmed that they had left Jasper in an inebriated state, smoking a cigarette, sitting in his moth-eaten armchair. The cottage had an ancient oak cruck frame with timber panelling and doors. The beams were tinder dry and once the fire had taken hold it had fed on itself to create a raging inferno.

Ironically, the fire had started after the rain had stopped and any chance of the deluge dampening the flames had passed. It was speculated that perhaps the flames had been fanned by one of Windelton's famous winds that had so aided Jasper's golfing victory. However, nobody could be certain as those that could remember anything on that fateful night had few memories of any clarity or coherence.

Later, Dawn and Rachel were interviewed more closely by the police who had been puzzled by some material that the hospital had found wedged in the back of Jasper's mouth.

There was much show of public sympathy for the plight of the Squire's second son, none more so than on the front page of the Windelton Bugle. Harry Webster's journalistic integrity had been compromised once again. This time by Sir Toby Inchdale who personally delivered an envelope containing a closely typed sheet of script from a Leeds advertising and PR company. It was accompanied by a large wad of used fivers.

Amazed Bugle readers were enthralled with Jasper's philanthropic past and his remarkable career in advertising which seemed at odds with all normal Inchdale family virtues. This was in contrast to the few cursory lines of copy about the massive Murchison's Bank robbery and their absconding manager for whom there had been a nationwide search. It was only later in the week when Harry Webster decided to throw caution to the winds and risked all to blow the combined bank heist and drunken festival story in full. Harry never disclosed his source who leaked everything about Gerald Astle and his strange ways at the bank but it finally gave Harry the scoop of his life.

- Chapter 31 -

Changed Lives

The efforts of the Murchison's Bank staff department had at last unearthed Astle's home telephone number. At just before nine o'clock that evening Haymarket dialled the Astle residence. He was greeted by a tearful Daphne Astle. Her clairvoyant's definitive predictions were indicating possible signs of accuracy. Astle had not returned home

Daphne had lifted the telephone receiver within two rings of calling. She was hoping that it was Astle 'phoning from the golf club with some silly excuse to say that he'd had 'a couple too many' and was getting a lift home. Daphne had started to feel guilty about speculating on the rosy prospect of life unimpeded by her angry spouse. Over the years there had been many occasions when secretly she had wished him out of the way. But now, facing the reality that he might have gone up in flames, Daphne was beginning to have doubts.

There would be some pitfalls to a life without Astle. Who would cut the hedges, mow lawns and weed borders? She positively hated weeding! How she would carry in the coal for the fire with her bad legs? She couldn't even drive a car... the list seemed to get longer the more she thought about it. She didn't even have a bank account of her own! Astle gave her the house-keeping money in cash every week and she submitted the bills for checking. Every Saturday morning she was made 'to reconcile the expenditure' as he called it before he would give her the following week's cash. Well that tyranny wouldn't be missed!

Daphne had a small clothing allowance that could only be spent with Astle's authority. He had to approve colour, style, materials, and of course, the cost. He relented when it came to choosing undergarments and stockings. She always bought the most expensive lingerie she could find.

Daphne had no access to liquid funds, no idea how much money they even had. She wondered if she *couldn't* get any money, would she starve to death. Suddenly the phone rang.

"Good evening Mrs Astle…" Haymarket was immediately interrupted by the near hysterical voice of Daphne.

"Where's my Gerald? Is he with you? Are you both tight?"

"I am so sorry to trouble you at this late hour," purred Haymarket, "I need to talk to your husband Gerald. Are you sure he is not in, Mrs Astle?"

"Who are you?" said a tremulous voiced Daphne, "You are not from the fire brigade are you?"

"No, no, no, oh I am so sorry Mrs Astle. Let me introduce myself, I am Alexander Haymarket from Murchison's Bank Regional Office. Perhaps Laurence Payne has mentioned my name to you. I *really* would like a word with Gerald if he is available?"

"Oh yes, Mr. Payne from the bank… he came earlier, everyone seems to want to see my Gerald today. He is *not* here. It's all very odd, highly unusual… Gerald's a… man… a man of routine… oh."

Daphne started to sob quietly.

"I am certain there is a simple explanation to his whereabouts. No need to worry. When were you expecting him?"

"Well er… he should have been here *three hours ago*. I think something dreadful may have happened to him. Please help me, I'm all alone?" She started to sob again.

"I will do everything in my power to assist you."

"Oh thank you Alexander," Daphne said with relief, "Please call me Daphne."

"Daphne it is then. Daphne, have you any ideas where Gerald might be? Do you think he might be at his golf club? He enjoys a drink on Saturdays, I understand. Don't we all," he purred.

"I have a feeling he may have passed away in a fire, but I can't be sure."

"Passed away… do you mean died, Daphne? Surely not."

"I've received predictions from my clairvoyant..." Daphne couldn't bring herself to say an empathetic 'Yes'.

"You can't be serious? You mustn't believe such nonsense," Haymarket crooned incredulously. Payne had mentioned she was a bit peculiar. She was obviously obsessed with fire. Haymarket was now beginning to believe that things really were seriously amiss. He hadn't dared admit it to himself before.

God he thought if these amounts *have* gone astray there will be absolute hell to pay. It could be the biggest fraud in Murchison's Bank's two hundred and twenty year history and he, Alexander Haymarket, had presided over this Titanic of a banking disaster! His unblemished career suddenly irreparably blighted by some madman in an obscure country branch of the bank.

Haymarket wouldn't be able to immunise himself from this scandal. Blast and bugger he thought! He tried not to think of the consequences but the sooner he got to the bottom of this farrago the better.

"The clairvoyant told me everything this afternoon."

"Everything?" enquired Haymarket with incredulity. "Can you elucidate further on the '*everything*?'"

Daphne wailed down the telephone: "I want him back, find him for me, I beg you..."

Suddenly the 'phone went dead in Haymarket's hand. He tried telephoning back but there was just an engaged signal. She *is* out of her mind. That old fool Payne was right about something, he thought to himself, "Stark staring bonkers," he muttered under his breath. He was going to have act and act quickly. Haymarket called Payne, who sounded drunk. He told him to meet him at the Windelton branch at seven thirty am the following morning. Sunday or no Sunday he would take a snap inspection of the safe before a thorough investigation of the books by the inspection team.

"Do you have the code for the safe?

258

Payne's heart raced when he remembered that Astle had mistakenly had sight of next week's code. He decided to say nothing about this until events unfolded further. He was already in enough of a mire with Astle if this turned out to be a storm in a tea cup.

"I'll get the over-ride codes because we'll need Astle's numbers to get in," continued Haymarket not waiting for a reply from Payne who could only be heard wheezing on the other end of the phone. "I don't think Astle is going to be around judging by what I have heard from his wife. She *is* mad, you were right on that score!"

"Have you discovered where he is?" Payne mumbled desperately trying to regain some sort of composure.

"No, I haven't the foggiest. He has vanished. I tried his golf club but they haven't seen him all day. Daphne Astle is convinced he is dead, burnt to a cinder according to some clairvoyant she sees. Can't put too much store by that story, but you never know. There's something fishy going on and we are going to have to get to the bottom of it damn quick," continued Haymarket briskly.

Payne had another intake of breath. Astle dead, embezzling bank funds, good God, it was like an amateur dramatic society rendition of an Agatha Christie novel!

"See you tomorrow Payne, seven-thirty sharp, at the branch, not a word to anyone. "By the way where *is* Windelton?" he asked as an afterthought.

~

By eleven am on Sunday morning the police had put out a nationwide alert for Gerald Astle. The number of the black Morris Oxford was circulated to all forces throughout the country. Immigration officials were informed at ports and airports. New passport applications were scrutinised and embassies were circulated asking for details of visa applications, particular notice was being taken of South American countries. Interest was centred on flights bound for Zurich and Argentina as were ferry terminals to European destinations.

It didn't take long to find out that a passenger booked under the name, 'G. Astle,' had failed to connect with the 10.30 BOAC flight to Buenos Aires via Madrid. The police's attention switched to the United Kingdom and at seven-thirty that evening a call from Luton General Infirmary confirmed that they had admitted a patient who had been bludgeoned over the head. He had been found in a parked Morris Oxford car with a matching license plate. He was alive but his injuries were severe. He was in a coma. No money had been found at the scene but there was a passport and a one way airline ticket to Buenos Aires.

~

All Astle could remember was the sensation of being pulled from the car and his foot getting painfully wedged somewhere; it was a bad dream from which he would have liked to have awoken but somehow unknown forces kept holding him back. However hard he struggled he was incapable of returning to consciousness. There was intermittent blackness, interrupted by noises, faces, pain and an inability to move. He felt as if he was frozen. When he eventually did open his eyes, he saw a nurse with a kindly face peering down at him.

"Can you hear me?" she asked. Astle was confused, he tried to speak but nothing came out. He managed to raise his eyebrows but this hurt.

"You've had a bit of a knock on your head and you are in hospital."

The voice seemed to be coming from a long, long way away. Out of the corner of his eye he could fathom the blue-blackness of someone. It was a policeman but Astle couldn't appreciate such subtleties. Not after having his head cracked open with a gemmy wrench. Once he saw a white coat and the coat was talking to another nurse. He couldn't quite hear what was being said but the coat got hold of his arm and wriggled it about, pulling it this way and that.

Strange, Astle thought as he could feel nothing. He had enough reasoning to ask himself if he was in another world. Astle pondered if this was heaven, perhaps it was...? He felt very tired and his eyes closed... lovely, lovely sleep. The next encryption on his memory was a tear-stained woman whose face was very close to his own. If he had been capable he'd have recoiled in horror. She seemed vaguely familiar. The face was speaking to him angrily. She did not use the gentle, concerned tones he had heard when other people had been close to him.

"This wasn't meant to happen like this! Where are your burns? Show them to me, you are hiding your burns, I know you have got them." Then someone appeared to be lifting up his bedcovers and the face repeated the question over and over again as the tears streamed down her wrinkly powdered cheeks. Then the nurse appeared again and pulled her away.

"Mrs Astle *please!* Stop interfering with the patient, you are upsetting him. He's had a severe blow to his head. He can't understand you."

If Astle had been able to articulate any words he would certainly have agreed with the kindly nurse. The powdered woman was a frightening and unwelcome intrusion into his dream-like state. Her voice faded away as she continued to remonstrate with the nurse.

~

Haymarket's prediction of a hell of a row was accurate. The extent of Astle's fraud was breath taking in its scale and audaciousness. Coupled with the mysterious fire at the Gardeners Cottage and the drunken conclusion of the Festival of Arts, the Windelton district was catapulted into the national media spotlight. Sunday newspaper journalists cruised the local pubs. They interviewed anyone with a vivid imagination, a loud mouth and empty pockets. There was no shortage of candidates. The local economy received a much needed boost. The ill winds that continually blew in Windelton had finally brought home its own bounty.

Marjorie Nelson was regarded as the root of the evil as it was claimed by witnesses that she had schemed from the start to intoxicate the whole town to boost brewery profits. Her egotistical desire to have a hospital named after her was commented upon widely. The crazy orgy of bestial debauchery that had ensued was only to be expected when unsophisticated hard-working northern folk were exposed (and without warning) to decadent music, exotic dancing and Byronesque arts 'performances' live on stage.

National newspaper headlines opined:

'Town Drunk While Bank Robber Strikes.'

Another read: **'Festival Heiress Robbed of Her Fortune during Sex Romp.'**

More outrageously: **'Drink Crazed Heiress Torches Lover's Cottage.'**

The stories became more lurid and far-fetched as journalists shovelled cash into anyone's pocket who could come up with an even more outrageous storyline. Even the Tatler ran an eight page feature entitled:

'Brewery Magnate's Frothy Ball at Agreeable Lutyens Home.' And UFO Monthly claimed: **'Mystery Indoctrination as Aliens Take over Sleepy Town.'**

Television documentaries were produced by European and US networks. A BBC Panorama special asked why a meteorologically challenged Yorkshire town's festival of arts (now dubbed the Great Windelton Festival of Tarts by the media) should suddenly erupt into a Bacchanalian orgy.

The Archbishop of Canterbury spoke out on the evils of mammon and strong drink in a special address to the Synod. Questions were asked in the House of Commons and it was agreed that an all-party select committee would investigate the effects of windy weather on rural communities. The committee, which would take three years to reach an inconclusive result, cost three hundred and fifty thousand pounds, not quite as much as that stolen by Gerald Astle.

262

Marjorie Nelson pilloried by the local community and the national media, was having battles of her own in recovering her lost money. So ingeniously had Astle woven the various accounts and trusts around the globe it was taking a team of international bankers' months to unravel.

The only person who could quickly recover the funds was Astle. Unfortunately, he continued to drift in and out of consciousness either induced by a blow to his head or sheer laziness. The doctors were unable to ascertain for certain what had caused his soporific state.

Laurence Payne managed to retain his job. He was swiftly moved to a sub-branch in a mining village in South Yorkshire to keep him away from unwanted publicity. His demotion to Branch Accountant was a cruel reversal.

The clairvoyant's television series was a big hit with viewers as was her daily column in a national newspaper. She was in demand to attend strategy 'think tank' meetings at the highest levels of government circles throughout the developed world. Her long term prognoses were as ridiculous as her fees were predictably large.

Joe Snipe's 'cottage' turned out to be larger than originally planned and gave him more room for his fishing tackle. The adjacent harbour mooring offered speedy access for his live-in fully equipped fishing boat. Florida was also a warmer location for his old age and the Marlin more plentiful than off the Norfolk coast.

Valerie and James slipped out of sight. They returned quietly to the Whiteley house. The Triumph motorcycle remained impotent, lying low in its hut, waiting its night time rider.

Jasper commenced a long, slow period of painful recovery and rehabilitation. After his release from the hospital burns unit he was rumoured to being looked after by an attractive nurse at Inchdale Hall. Sir Toby appeared to be back in funds as he was spotted wearing some new cavalry twill trousers and an outrageously yellow cravat. It was said that a large win on the horses had been responsible for his reversal of fortunes.

~

For Rachel, Jasper's horrible accident was a watershed. She had tried to visit him in hospital but had been refused admittance. Only close family were being allowed near the intensive care ward. Two weeks after the fire, bluffing her way back stage at the Rolling Stones' concert, she joined the band's retinue of hangers-on a European tour, undertaking secretarial and any jobs going. Her father had her checked into a fashionable Surrey drugs and alcohol rehabilitation clinic when the tour came to an end many months later.

Dawn was traumatised at the suddenness and proximity of Jasper's horrible accident. However much a scoundrel he was she felt that his life had been cruelly stopped in its tracks. The nature of his misfortune was characteristic of his attitude to the world, yet it was also so random and shocking. Dawn still couldn't get over the thought that if she had submitted to his demands he might not have suffered his fiery fate.

Dawn visited Rachel in a confessional moment of grief before Rachel had run away with the band. She told her about Jasper's well-rehearsed seduction attempt and her rejection of his advances.

"Darling, this was how Jasper always behaved as soon as any good looking girl crossed his path," said Rachel in a matter-of-fact voice.

Dawn was rather shocked at Rachel's candid assessment of Jasper. No wonder Ian had been so taken with her. He liked females that were clear headed and determined. Dawn had thought up until then that Rachel was just a 'nice' spoiled girl with not much between her perfectly shaped ears.

"He was a hopeless, serial womaniser," Rachel had summed up. "Anybody who went out with him knew this from day one. It was the rules of the relationship. If you understood it you didn't get hurt. Too many girls fell in love with his charm and good looks and thought they could change him. It didn't take them long to find out

264

that they were being used. He never really cared. It wouldn't have surprised me if some jilted lover hadn't sought a fitting revenge? God knows he would have deserved it but you shouldn't worry about having turned him down. "It's life, it was Jasper's destiny. For God's sake don't fret about it. It's Ian you should be worrying about. He *is* a nice man. Look after him. *He* needs your help!"

Epilogue

The wind blew down the high street and under the door of the Nag's Head pub. Harry Webster was asleep on a bar stool, quite drunk. He was still celebrating his finest hour. The Windelton Bugle had won the coveted Press Council's Regional Newspaper of the Year Award for its 'fearless and pioneering journalism for his story: '24 hours that Shook Britain'.

Although it was only October, the wind was coming from the east and with it a refreshing Siberian bite. The pub trade had been good in recent months the landlord reflected as he cleaned a pint glass with a grubby tea towel, rubbing the rim until it shone dully with germs. The journalists and TV crews had vanished as quickly as they arrived and finally Windelton life was settling back into more familiar patterns.

The cafés had begun to fill up once again with gossiping housewives. There was a collective amnesia surrounding the events of the Great Festival of Arts. Some coffee regulars were absent and never mentioned. Marjorie Nelson, now greatly reduced, was barricaded up at the Red House. The garden had been become rather shabby and neglected as the retinue of garden staff had been laid off. Rose Bainbridge was enjoying a quieter life with her daughter who had become rather subdued. This muteness afforded Rose more opportunities to make conversation of her own. Neither the festival nor the hospital was ever mentioned.

The scandalised Mrs Hendry was rumoured to be moving abroad, meanwhile others re-appeared from their press interviews, 'Woman's Hour' appearances and book signing tours to return to their normal domestic routines.

A beverage company offered to sponsor a drinks calendar featuring scantily clad Windelton ladies enjoying various tipples but it was ruled out as being 'a bit too close to the knuckle'.

It was noted in more than just golfing circles that the new shop in the market place, 'First on the Tee', run by Ian Henderson, appeared to be thriving.

Also by D. A. Adamson

Windelton & The Bavarian Incident

Printed in Great Britain
by Amazon